"Do I know you?"

He took a cautious step forward.

"You did once," she whispered past the lump in her throat. "Better than anyone else I've ever known. It's me, John. Anne."

A muscle twitched along the uncompromising line of his jaw. "What is this, some kind of sick joke? Who the hell are you and what do you want?"

"I'm Anne," she insisted. "And I want to see our daughters."

"Knock it off, lady. Whatever you're trying to prove—"

She cut him off. "When Rachel was four, her imaginary friend's name was Jessica. Holly has a heart-shaped birthmark on her bottom. You scored 1550 on your SATs. And there was a part of your anatomy I called BD, for Big Dude."

His green eyes widened even as the color drained from his face. "My God," he murmured, his voice hoarse with strain. "My God . . . Annie?"

Dear Reader:

Romance readers have been enthusiastic about the Silhouette Special Editions for years. And that's not by accident: Special Editions were the first of their kind and continue to feature realistic stories with heightened romantic tension.

The longer stories, sophisticated style, greater sensual detail and variety that made Special Editions popular are the same elements that will make you want to read book after book.

We hope that you enjoy this Special Edition today, and will enjoy many more.

Please write to us:

Jane Nicholls
Silhouette Books
PO Box 236
Thornton Road
Croydon
Surrey
CR9 3RU

MYRNA TEMTE

Room for Annie

Silhouette Special Edition

Originally Published by Silhouette Books
a division of
Harlequin Enterprises Ltd.

*First published in Great Britain in 1994
by Silhouette Books, Eton House, 18-24 Paradise Road,
Richmond, Surrey TW9 1SR*

© Myrna Temte 1994

*Silhouette, Silhouette Special Edition and Colophon are
Trade Marks of Harlequin Enterprises B.V.*

ISBN 0 373 59241 8

23-9406

Made and printed in Great Britain

Dedicated to the Class of 1970,
Bozeman Senior High School, Bozeman, Montana.
Here's one for the old hometown. See you in 2000.

My thanks to Gordon Gum and Judy Waughtal
for timely and helpful information.
And to Vickie Freeland Lutz,
the woman who knows Bozeman.

MYRNA TEMTE

grew up in Montana and attended college in Wyoming, where she met and married her husband. Marriage didn't necessarily mean settling down for the Temtes—they have lived in six different states, including Washington, where they currently reside. Moving so much is difficult, the author says, but it is also wonderful stimulation for a writer.

Though always a "readaholic," Myrna Temte never dreamed of becoming an author. But while spending time at home to care for her first child, she began to seek an outlet from the never-ending duties of house-keeping and child-rearing. She started reading romances and soon became hooked, both as a reader and a writer.

Now Myrna Temte appreciates the best of all possible worlds—a loving family and a challenging career that lets her set her own hours and turn her imagination loose.

Other Silhouette Books by Myrna Temte

Silhouette Special Edition

Wendy Wyoming
Powder River Reunion
The Last Good Man Alive
*For Pete's Sake

*Silent Sam's Salvation
*Heartbreak Hank
*The Forever Night

*Dawson Series

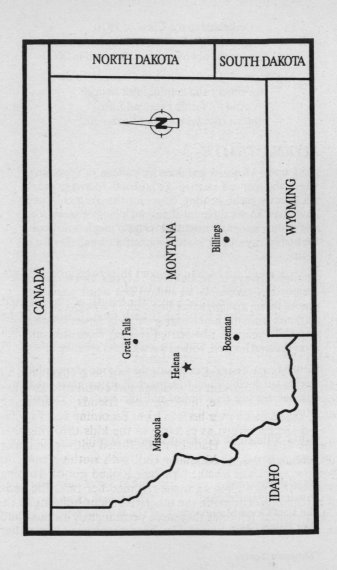

CANADA

NORTH DAKOTA

SOUTH DAKOTA

MONTANA

WYOMING

Billings

Great Falls

Helena

Bozeman

Missoula

IDAHO

Chapter One

"If he doesn't get here in the next thirty seconds, I'm going to vomit," Anne Martin muttered.

Checking her watch, she paced the length of the deserted corridor for what had to be the fiftieth time. Halfway to the end, she paused at the window and looked out at Montana State University's campus, picking out the buildings in which she had once attended classes.

The years she'd spent in Bozeman had been filled with all the fun and excitement any college girl could ask for—living away from home, making new friends, challenging ideas, falling head over heels in love. Becoming John's wife.

Had she ever been as carefree as the kids throwing that Frisbee down there? Had she really flirted with John under the tree in front of Montana Hall with nothing more to worry about than whether her hair looked good? Turning away with a nostalgic sigh, she resumed her trek, the heels of her pumps echoing in the otherwise silent building.

Her insides felt as if they were permanently twisted into an aching mass of knots. Her head throbbed. No matter how many times she wiped her palms on the sides of the cranberry-colored skirt she'd bought for the occasion, they remained cold and clammy.

Desperately needing to bolster her flagging courage, she whispered, "What's the worst thing he could do to me?"

John's always had a temper. He might strangle you on the spot, a helpful little voice inside her head suggested.

"Come on, he's never been violent," Anne protested.

Well, whatever he does, he's going to be livid, the voice insisted. *Absolutely livid.*

"Thanks so much for reminding me," Anne grumbled.

Her stomach went into a slow, nauseating barrel roll. Panic welled up inside her, but she gritted her teeth and fought it down. Scared as she was, she couldn't turn back. Not without seeing her daughters. The last time she'd seen Holly and Rachel, they'd been four and eight. Holly was ten now, and Rachel almost fifteen.

Would they be glad to see her? Would John? If only she hadn't divorced him. If only they'd had time to finish reconciling. If only—

"Stop that," she whispered, digging her fingernails into her palms. "'If onlys' won't help. He's probably got a new wife and two more kids by now."

The thought was enough to curdle her blood, but she couldn't ignore it. During the past six and a half years, she'd become an expert at facing harsh realities. She would face whatever situation lay ahead of her now, and she would cope. Somehow, some way, she would cope.

The heavy fire door at the end of the hallway banged open. Her heart lurched. Her lungs froze. The fine hair on her forearms and the back of her neck prickled with a primitive fight-or-flight response.

And suddenly, there he was, all six feet two inches of him. Professor John Miller. The only man she had ever really loved.

He walked toward her with a confident stride, one hand tugging at the knot of his tie, the other gripping the handle of a black briefcase. She caught a glimpse of silvery strands in his hair, a suggestion of deep lines carved at the outer corners of his eyes and at the sides of his mouth. He shot her a preoccupied glance, nodded politely and hurried past her to the door of his office.

The scrape of his key in the lock made her realize she was still standing in the middle of the hallway, staring at him as if he were the first member of an alien species to arrive on the planet.

Go after him! the helpful little voice shrieked. *What the heck are you waiting for? Christmas?*

By the time Anne could convince her feet to budge, however, John had entered his office, flipped on the lights and carried his briefcase to the other side of a battered wooden desk that looked as if it had been around longer than the university. Hardly daring to breathe, she approached the doorway on tiptoe.

He shrugged off his suit jacket and hung it on a coat tree standing in the corner to the right of a laser printer. Her heart lurched again as she watched clearly defined muscles rippling beneath the cotton of his crisp white shirt. Her fingertips tingled with memories of all the times she'd touched those broad shoulders, traced the knobs of his spine, caressed the thick dark hair brushing the edge of his collar.

A giddy, almost hysterical sense of unreality swamped her as he turned back toward his desk. God help her, what could she possibly say to him after all this time? She doubted he would see the humor in an opening line such as "Hi, honey, I'm home."

He looked up at her, and for a sickening moment, she feared she'd actually said those words aloud. His eyes were still that fascinating smoky shade of green. And...oh, his face. That wonderful, ruggedly handsome face. The crooked little scar on his chin. The straight, prominent nose. The dark shadow of beard that lingered no matter how many times he shaved. It looked exactly the same as she remembered, but different somehow. Sadder. More mature, like his father's. Yet so very much like—

"May I help you?" he asked, a dark eyebrow raised in query.

The sound of his deep, gravelly voice, the voice that had tormented her dreams for six and a half endless years, the voice she had lost all hope of ever hearing again, nearly undid what little composure she had left. An uncontrollable shudder rippled through her, and the pleasant, if somewhat impersonal expression on his face became concerned. He stepped out from behind his desk.

"Is something wrong, miss?"

His reassuring smile almost made her weep. Dear, dear, wonderful John. How she had missed him.

He was a brilliant, complicated man who could almost make computers sing and tap-dance on command. A sexy, passionate man who had given her incredibly beautiful children. A strong, proud, infuriatingly obstinate man with a ton of integrity and the heart of a Montana cowboy bred into him through four generations of ranchers.

A man who would undoubtedly want to wring her neck the second he figured out who she was.

Calling on every shred of courage she'd developed, Anne pulled herself as tall as her five-foot-four-inch height would allow. He stopped three feet away, eyeing her with a quizzical expression, as if he was beginning to sense something unusual in the atmosphere.

She cleared her throat and plastered on what was, no doubt, a shaky smile. "Hi, John. It's been a long time."

He tilted his head slightly to the right, a frown creasing his forehead. She could almost hear the clicks and whirs of his computerlike brain as he tried to place her. His frown deepening, he propped his hands on his hips.

So. He didn't recognize her. Why that surprised her, she couldn't say. She still felt too vulnerable to go out without her disguise. Everything had changed so fast, she hadn't had time to think about returning to her former appearance. Besides, she was thinner now, and he'd rarely seen her without glasses. The curly auburn hair and brown contacts had fooled a lot of people over the years. Why shouldn't they fool John, who wasn't expecting to see her?

He took a cautious step closer. "Do I know you?"

Her nerve endings vibrated with excruciating tension. She wanted to touch him so badly she had to gouge her fingernails into her palms again to keep her hands at her sides. She gulped, then finally nodded.

"You did once," she whispered, forcing each word past the jagged lump in her throat. "You knew me better than anyone else I've ever known. It's me, John. Anne."

His dark eyebrows shot up and he studied her face so intently she felt as if he was delving into the darkest secrets in her soul. Then he closed his eyes, shook his head violently and looked at her again.

"No." A muscle twitched along the uncompromising line of his jaw. "I don't know who you are, but you're not Annie. What is this? Some kind of a sick joke?"

Anne squared her shoulders and returned his glare without flinching. "It's no joke. I know this must be a terrible shock for you, but—"

"Knock it off, lady." He crammed his hands into his trouser pockets, as if he feared he might deck her otherwise. "Who the hell are you and what do you want?"

"I'm *Anne,*" she insisted, raising her chin another notch. "I want to see Rachel and Holly."

Nostrils flaring, he grabbed the edge of the door and started to push it shut. "I've had enough of this. I'm not interested in whatever you're trying to prove, so—"

She cut him off with an exasperated snort. "The only thing I'm trying to prove, you hardheaded, unreasonable jerk, is that I'm Anne Huston Miller."

He hesitated when she used that old, familiar insult. Sensing what might be her only opportunity to get through to him before he slammed the door in her face, Anne rushed on.

"When Rachel was four, her imaginary friend's name was Jessica. Holly has a heart-shaped birthmark on her bottom. You scored 1,550 on your SATs. And there was a part of your anatomy I called BD for Big Dude.''

His eyes widened a little more with each item she ticked off, their rich green becoming even more pronounced as the color drained from his skin. His lips released a hiss of air, as if he'd been punched in the solar plexus.

Deciding to settle the issue once and for all, Anne cupped her hand under her eyes and popped out her contacts. Without corrective lenses, he wasn't much more than a big blur, but his harsh gasp told her he was finally convinced. Honestly, you'd think the man was from Missouri, not Montana. But if he'd ever learned to listen to her, she never would have divorced him in the first place and they wouldn't be having this conversation.

She tucked her contacts into her skirt pocket, then fumbled her glasses out of her purse, stuck them on her face and looked up in time to see him staring at her in stupefaction and swaying like a drunk at the end of a three-day toot. He braced one hand on the desk behind him and steadied himself. His lips moved, obviously trying to form words, but no sound came out.

"It's all right, John," she said, cursing herself for not finding a gentler way to reappear in his life, instinctively reaching for him. "I'm not a ghost."

He jerked back as if he feared her touch would shatter him. The action cost him his balance and his knees buckled, his butt awkwardly plunking onto the desk. He gripped the wood on either side of him until his knuckles whitened and his shoulder muscles strained the cloth of his shirt.

"My God," he murmured, his voice hoarse with strain. "My God . . . Annie?"

Anne nodded, though it had been so long since anyone had called her Annie she felt as if the name belonged to someone else. In a sense, it did. The Annie Huston Miller John had known and loved was only a fond memory now.

Still gaping at her, he inhaled a ragged breath. His color improved as he inhaled another and another, and then a hot, dark flush slowly suffused his face all the way to his hairline. Though she had expected an angry reaction, Anne stiffened, watching with a kind of horrified fascination as his eyebrows swooped into a scowling V, transforming his shocked expression into one of fierce, masculine outrage.

He rose to his feet and came toward her with such a murderous look in his eyes she backed up, matching him step for step until she found herself in the middle of the hallway, her palms held in front of her chest.

"Now, John, I know you're upset—"

His answering roar probably rattled the windows, but she couldn't hear anything except the fury in his voice.

"Up*set?*" Grabbing her right elbow, he yanked her back into the office, then slammed the door and held his arms rigidly at his sides, his hands bunched into fists. "Honey, up*set* doesn't even come close. You wanted out of my life? Fine. Why didn't you just *stay* out?"

"I can explain—"

"There's nothing to explain. I don't care where you've been, what you've been up to or who you've been with. But you'd better get one thing straight. The girls and I have worked damned hard to build a new life, and you're sure as hell *not* going to waltz back in and mess it up."

"I have no intention of messing anything up," Anne retorted. "I just want to see my daughters."

"Stay away from them. You've hurt them enough. If you think I'll let you set them up to be abandoned again—"

"I didn't abandon anyone—"

"Bull."

Clutching her purse tightly against her side, Anne stared him down. She suddenly felt claustrophobic with him towering in front of the door like an enraged warrior. A vein throbbed in the center of his forehead. He flexed his hands once, twice, and for a moment she feared he really might strangle her. It hurt. God, how it hurt to know he'd chosen to think the absolute worst of her.

Well, she'd be damned if she'd let him see that. She wasn't about to give up, either. As painful as dealing with John was going to be, she had to see her children. There was such a thing as strategic retreat, however, and this didn't seem like a good time to reason with him.

"All right," she said. "Have it your way, John. But you're wrong about me. There's a reasonable explanation for where I've been, and I've got the evidence to prove it. If you're ready to listen, meet me for coffee at the 4B's tomorrow. Ten o'clock."

"Don't hold your breath." He stepped aside and opened the door for her. "I'm not interested."

She paused in the doorway and looked up at him, bleeding inside at the bitter fury she saw in his eyes. "*Get* interested. I have a legal right to see the girls, and I won't hesitate to exercise it."

"Is that supposed to be a threat?" he demanded.

"If it has to be."

"Give me a break. There's not a judge in this country who'd give a woman like you the time of day."

"Don't be too sure about that, John. And let's get one thing straight. You're not dealing with Annie anymore. She died six and a half years ago. My name is Anne Martin."

"I don't give a damn *what* your name is. Stay away from the kids or you'll answer to me."

Anne gazed sadly at him for another long moment. "Make it easier on all of us and hear me out. Tomorrow morning. Ten o'clock. If you're right, what have you got to lose?"

What *did* he have to lose? John asked himself as he watched her sashay to the exit, her head held high, her stride confident and unhurried. Only his sanity. His self-respect. His hard-won peace of mind after years of wondering what he could possibly have done to drive Annie away from him when he'd been so positive they were well on the road to a reconciliation.

He'd never harmed a woman in his life. Never intended to in the future. But for a moment there, he'd wanted to wrap his hands around Annie's throat and choke the life out of her. For God's sake, what kind of a fool did she think he was? Considering how smoothly she'd executed her escape six and a half years ago, probably a pretty damn big one.

He walked back into his office, shut the door and shoved his hands deep into his pockets. Parking his rump on the edge of the desk, he stretched his legs out in front of him, the heels of his wing tips braced on the floor. Remembering that time was enough to make him want to puke.

They'd been living in Chicago then. He'd never believed Annie had really wanted the divorce, so he hadn't tried to fight it. He'd been unpleasantly surprised when she'd gone ahead, moved herself and the girls into an apartment and let the papers go through. Shaking his head, John snorted in disgust.

Man, he'd come around in a hurry when he'd received the final decree. Idiot that he'd been, he'd sent her flowers and candy, helium balloons and singing telegrams. Though he wouldn't admit it under torture, he'd actually stooped to reading women's magazines and romance novels, hoping to figure out what it was that Annie had wanted from him. For a while, he'd thought he was making progress.

Annie had started dating him. Hell, she'd even slept with him the night before he'd left to bring the girls out to Bozeman to spend the month with his folks before school started. He'd gone back to Chicago, planning to woo that woman until she begged to marry him again. He'd had love in his heart and lust on his mind.

But Annie had been gone. Her car was gone, her bank accounts cleaned out. Her apartment had been stripped to the walls, and the only thing her landlady had been able to tell him was that three men had moved Annie's things for her. One of them had been a big handsome blond guy who claimed to be a "close friend" of Annie's.

He hadn't been able to believe it at first. Hadn't wanted to believe it. She'd always been such a devoted mother it had been especially hard for him to believe she would abandon Rachel and Holly. For a while, he'd even feared she might be dead.

But the cops found no evidence of foul play. Nothing to suggest that she hadn't just decided to rid herself of all responsibilities and start a new life. With the big handsome blond guy.

Hurt and confusion had consumed him for months. A dark, simmering rage followed. He quit the job Annie had resented so much and moved in with his folks at the Flying M, the family ranch twelve miles west of Bozeman. They'd all wept together. Had some counseling. And slowly started picking up the pieces of their lives.

The girls were doing pretty well now. They were both bright and pretty, and he was damn proud of the close relationship he'd built with them. He would burn in hell before he'd ever let Annie get near enough to hurt either one of those kids again.

Her remark about having a legal right to see Holly and Rachel bothered him, though. Granted, she'd been given custody of the kids in the divorce decree, but surely that wouldn't stand up in court after the way she'd abandoned them. Would it?

What *reasonable* explanation could she possibly give for a six-and-a-half-year absence, without a single phone call, without a birthday or Christmas card for the kids, not even a lousy note to let him know she was all right?

Shoving himself off the desk, he rushed around to the other side, plunked himself into the swivel chair and reached for the phone book. The only lawyer he knew was the guy who handled the ranch paperwork. If he didn't know anything about family law, maybe he could recommend someone.

Punching the numbers into the telephone, he muttered, "Dammit, Annie, why the hell did you have to come back?"

Anne made it as far as the downstairs lobby before she had to find a rest room. She quietly lost her lunch, then stood at the sink, cupped some water in her hands and rinsed out her mouth. The haggard, haunted face staring back at her from the mirror made her cringe.

Lord, no wonder it had been so hard for John to believe she was Annie. Maybe she should have waited longer to make absolutely certain she was finally safe, taken a more indirect approach to contacting him, allowed someone to pave the way for her.

She'd refused any such offer, of course. Partly because she desperately wanted her freedom. Partly because she couldn't stand to wait one second longer to see John and the girls. And partly because of a ridiculous, romantic hope that John would be so glad to see her after all this time that he would sweep her into his arms, kiss her senseless and welcome her home. No questions asked.

"Do the words 'fat chance' mean anything to you?" she asked her reflection.

Shaking her head in disgust, she splashed cold water on her cheeks and repaired her makeup. She might have lost this battle, but she would do whatever it took to win the war. She'd already paid a horrendous price for doing what had been necessary. She wasn't going to pay any more.

Dammit, she wanted her life back! She wanted her daughters back. She even wanted her pigheaded, angry husband back.

The latter might not be possible. John hadn't been wearing a wedding ring, but that didn't mean he was unattached. In fact, she'd be awfully surprised if he was. Still, she had to try. If not for her own sake, then for Chad's.

Her son needed his daddy. End of discussion.

The only question was, how on earth was she going to tell John he'd fathered another child the night before he'd left for Montana all those years ago?

She gulped. Took a deep breath. Squared her shoulders.

"One step at a time, Anne," she told her reflection. "Take it one step at a time."

Chapter Two

After supper that night, John Miller propped one forearm on the top rail of the corral fence, fished a cigarette out of the crumpled pack in his shirt pocket and held it between his teeth while he dug a book of matches out of his jeans pocket. He lit up, then took a deep drag, welcoming the biting taste of tobacco. After years of struggling to kick the habit, he'd finally decided that one smoke a day wouldn't shorten his life enough to sweat it.

He might go hog-wild tonight and have two. Hearing the crunch of a boot sole pressing a rock into the hard-packed dirt behind him, he sighed with resignation. He'd come out here to smoke in peace, but he should have known that was too much to hope for. Sure enough, his father appeared at his side a second later, scowling at the cigarette.

"When are you gonna get smart and give those damn things up for good?" Mike Miller asked.

"Probably about the same time you stop nagging me to quit," John replied.

"Yeah, yeah, I hear you." Mike tipped his head back and casually studied the glittering stars. "Nice night."

"Not bad for May," John agreed. "What can I do for you, Dad?"

"Nothin' much." Mike poked the tips of his fingers into his pockets, turned around and leaned against the fence. "You were such a grouch at supper I just wondered if something had happened I should know about."

So much for my poker face, John thought. Squinting against the smoke, he took a long pull on his cigarette. "Yeah, you might say something happened."

"Want to talk about it?"

"Not really," John muttered. Then he took another drag. "But I guess you'd better hear about it from me. I don't want you to have a stroke if she shows up here unannounced."

"If who shows up here?"

"Annie."

Mike's eyes bugged out. "*Your* Annie?"

"You know any other Annies?"

"You've *seen* her?"

"At my office today. Just showed up out of the blue."

"Well, I'll be . . . She say where she's been?"

"I didn't give her the chance," John admitted. He quickly recounted what had happened that afternoon.

"Dammit, boy, one of these days that temper of yours is gonna get you in one hell of a fix," Mike chided him. "Why didn't you listen to what she had to say?"

"I don't *care* where she's been, Dad."

"Did it ever occur to you that maybe the girls and I *do?*" Mike ran a hand over his salt-and-pepper crew cut, then hooked the heel of his boot over the bottom rail of the fence. "You're not the only one involved here, you know."

"I never said I was. But she nearly destroyed those kids once. I'm not gonna give her a chance to finish the job. If she shows up, send her packing, Dad. I mean it."

"Not until I've heard that reasonable explanation she told you about," Mike insisted. "I've never believed she just up and abandoned Rachel and Holly. She loved 'em too much. Your mother agreed with me before she died.''

"It's none of your business," John snapped.

"The hell it's not. Annie was a good wife to you for ten years and a damn good mother to those children. In my book, she's earned the right to tell her side of the story. Now, either you go talk to her tomorrow morning or I *will.*''

"Dammit, she's not the same woman. She doesn't call herself Annie anymore. She doesn't even *look* like Annie. She's skinny and tense, and her hair's real short. Kind of an ugly reddish-brown color.''

"What difference does *that* make? She's still Annie.''

John waved one hand, as if groping for the words that would make his father understand. "I'm not sure she *is,* Dad. She didn't even cry today. Ever see Annie get through an emotional event without shedding a few tears?''

Mike's eyebrows shot up in surprise. "Hell, she used to blubber at Hallmark commercials.''

"Exactly. The Annie I knew would've bawled all over me. She would've been hugging me and talking ninety miles an hour. But this gal was so cool and dignified...well, she didn't act like Annie at all. That's why I didn't recognize her.''

Mike thought about that for a moment, then slowly shook his head. "Something awful must have happened to change her that much. You'd better find out what it was.''

Sighing, John flicked his cigarette butt into the dirt and ground it out. "Yeah, maybe you're right.''

"You'll go talk to her then?''

John nodded reluctantly. "But don't say anything to the girls, Dad. There's no sense getting them all stirred up until we know more about her.''

"I won't. But this time, get your damned ego out of the way and listen to her, willya? It'd do both of those kids a world of good to find out their mother didn't just walk off and leave 'em behind.''

"They don't need her anymore," John said. "They've got Paula now.''

Mike shot him a pitying look, then straightened away from the fence and propped his hands on his hips. "You can lie to me all you want, son, but don't lie to yourself. Paula's a fine young woman, but you don't love her. Not like you loved Annie."

"Love's a highly overrated emotion," John said, uttering a bitter laugh.

"Not when you give it the attention it deserves."

"Dad, *please*. You don't have to tell me again. I've already admitted the divorce was my fault. I did everything I could to get Annie to come back to me, but she chose somebody else."

"Dammit, John, you don't *know* that. Don't get an idea like that lodged in your head until you hear what Annie has to say. She coulda had amnesia or something."

John laughed, but there was no humor in it. "Right. Then why was her apartment cleaned out before I got home? Why was her car gone? How did she manage that kind of stuff if she couldn't remember who she was?"

"I didn't say she *had* amnesia. I said she coulda had something like it. All I want you to do is listen to her with an open mind. Think you can manage that?"

Sincerely wishing his dad wouldn't look at him with those mournful basset-hound eyes that always made him feel inadequate, John shrugged. "I'll try."

Mike eyed him skeptically for a moment. "You'll have to do better than try. If Annie *does* have a legitimate excuse for being gone all this time, she's gonna be in your life to some extent because of the kids. At least be smart enough not to go out of your way to antagonize her."

"All right, so I didn't handle her very well today," John admitted. "It was a helluva shock."

"Yeah, I suppose it was." Mike clapped him on the shoulder and gave him a lopsided smile. "I didn't mean to sound so critical."

"Go on in and hit the sack, Dad. I've got some more thinking to do."

"Don't stay out here too long. It'll all look better in the morning if you get some sleep."

When he heard the screen door on the back porch bang shut, John rolled his head back and forth to get the kinks out of his neck and fished another cigarette out of his pocket. He studied the white cylinder for a moment before putting it back. If he started using tobacco as a crutch again, he'd be smoking a pack a day within a week.

He shut his eyes, and his thoughts automatically returned to that scene in his office. Frustration filled his chest and a lump formed in his throat. Damn. He really hadn't handled seeing Annie at all well today, and he wasn't too sure he could handle seeing her tomorrow any better.

Her eyes still haunted him. He'd always thought Annie had the most expressive, most honest eyes he'd ever seen. There was something about that soft hazel color that made a man think of a forest glade dappled with sunshine. And made him want to trust that a woman who possessed eyes that pretty could never tell anything but the truth.

After the way she'd betrayed him and the girls, he'd be a fool to risk believing anything she said. If he could only figure out what she was up to, what she wanted from him, maybe he could save himself and the kids a ton of grief. Dammit, he *had* to do that before he saw her again.

The logical place to start was to put his feelings toward her into some kind of rational perspective. Unfortunately his response to Annie had never been rational. Realizing that it still wasn't, that she could still twist his guts into knots, even after a divorce and more than six years of separation... well, as his dad would say, it put one helluva nasty wrinkle in his shorts.

A cloud drifted in front of the moon and a cool breeze kicked up from out of the west, ruffling his hair. A horse whinnied in the pasture beyond the corral. Swollen with the spring runoff, the Gallatin River maintained a muted roar on the other side of the gravel road that ran in front of the house. The crickets tuned up for their nightly serenade. Annie had always loved to listen to the crickets.

His throat ached and his eyes burned. He felt as if his life was starting to come apart at the seams, and he didn't even know what to hope for. Did Annie care about him, or had she come back only to see the kids? Was she still involved with the blond guy? Or with someone else? The divorce he hadn't bothered to fight gave her that right.

His back teeth ground together at the thought. His gut clenched and his knuckles hurt from gripping the fence rail.

"Dammit, Annie," he muttered, glaring up at the full moon hanging over the jagged peaks of the Gallatin Range to the southeast. "I was finally doing okay without you. Why didn't you just stay gone?"

Anne arrived at the 4B's restaurant ten minutes early the next morning and requested a booth next to the windows. She ordered coffee, sipped the steaming brew and watched the morning traffic on Main Street zipping past, trying to figure out her next step if John didn't show up.

A dusty red Suburban pulled into the parking lot and stopped two spaces to the left of her rental car. The driver stepped out a moment later wearing boots, jeans and a denim jacket. Though a pair of mirrored sunglasses covered his eyes and he had a Stetson pulled low on his forehead, Anne would have recognized that rangy build and loose-jointed walk anywhere.

She'd always thought John was the most handsome man she'd ever seen in a suit, the epitome of the hard-charging executive who knew what he wanted and how to get it. But heaven help her, the sight of him in his cowboy duds reminded her of the earthier side of his nature, the side that had made her pulse race and her insides quiver. He must be helping Mike on a regular basis. A man who spent all his time teaching and working with computers didn't have shoulders as broad and muscular as his.

Sitting up straight, she took a deep breath, silently scolding herself for her lusty reaction to his looks. She couldn't allow anything as inconsequential as sex to distract her. She should be worrying about whether or not John would listen to her this time. The rigid set to his jaw and that stern slash of a mouth didn't look promising.

He removed his sunglasses as he entered the restaurant, pausing just inside the glass doors. His gaze swept the room in search of her, his posture stiffening at the instant of recognition. Anne winced inwardly at that small but telling movement.

There had been a time when John's automatic reaction to seeing her had been a warm, intimate smile, the kind exchanged by soul mates and lovers. Where had they gone wrong? How had they allowed the love they had shared during their early years of marriage to slip through their fingers, even before their lives had been ripped apart?

The restaurant's hostess approached him. John nodded, then headed toward Anne's table with long, determined strides. He looked powerful and sexy and, she gulped, downright dangerous. She couldn't help noticing that nearly every female head in the place turned to follow his progress. A waitress bustled after him, a coffeepot in hand and a come-hither smile ready and waiting while he slid onto the bench seat on the other side of the table.

After the young woman filled his cup, he sent her on her way with no more encouragement than a distracted smile. Tossing his hat onto the seat beside him, he raked one hand through his hair and muttered, "Morning," at Anne. Then he sipped his coffee and drilled her with a piercing, unrelenting stare.

Why, the big jerk was deliberately trying to intimidate her, she thought, noting a challenging gleam in those green eyes of his. Well, he was in for a disappointment. She'd learned to face down men who were colder, meaner and more brutal than John could ever hope to be on his worst day.

"Good morning, John." She casually traced the rim of her cup. "I'm glad you could make it."

Leaning forward, he jabbed the table with his index finger. "Look, I haven't got all day, so let's hear this story of yours. Where have you been?"

She gave him a wry smile and shifted to imitate his posture. "Lots of places. I've been living in Denver for the past two years. Would you like to know why?"

"Don't get cute with me," he said. "I already know that a big blond guy moved everything out of your apartment. I've always wondered what made him so special you'd abandon your kids for him, though. Tell me, was he filthy rich or just damn good in bed?"

Anne sat back and, lowering her hands to her lap where he couldn't see them tremble, reminded herself that she'd expected him to come out swinging. "You're going to feel awfully foolish when you meet that big blond guy."

John's eyes narrowed and his tone sharpened. "You're still *with* him?"

"He's in Denver, but I was never *with* him. Not the way you mean, anyway." Anne sadly shook her head at him. "And, for the record, I didn't abandon anyone. I had no choice but to leave the way I did."

"I suppose somebody stuck a gun to your head?"

"In a manner of speaking, that's exactly what happened."

He stared at her for a moment, then snorted in disbelief. "Right. And this...this somebody kept the gun to your head for over six years."

Determined not to let him goad her into losing her temper, Anne forced herself to answer in a calm, even tone. "That's right. In a manner of speaking."

"What the hell is that supposed to mean? Cut to the chase, will you? I want details. *Now.*"

"What's the point in giving you details if you're not going to believe anything I say?"

His nostrils flared and the glare he gave her could have fried raw meat. Though caffeine was the last thing she needed at the moment, Anne picked up her coffee cup and took a sip, feigning indifference to his anger. Three heartbeats passed before he gulped from his own cup, then rubbed the back of his neck and sighed with what sounded like resignation.

"All right," he said. "I'm listening."

Carefully setting down her cup, she clasped her hands in front of her. "Three days before you were due back in Chicago, I went shopping at Fox Valley Mall. When I returned to my car, I witnessed a drug-related murder. I've been in the Witness Security Program ever since because the two men I helped to convict swore they'd get revenge."

John gave her a measuring look. Then he let out a harsh bark of laughter. "Nice try, but it won't wash. If you were in that kind of danger, the kids and I were, too. The government would have put all of us into the program."

"We were already divorced, John," Anne replied. "My car, driver's license, lease, social security number—I'd put everything in my maiden name. Other than the divorce decree, Rachel's school records and our medical records, there wasn't anything that tied me to you or to the girls. The FBI took care of those."

"And the guy who cleaned out your apartment?"

"Is Steve Anderson, the deputy U.S. marshal who's saved my life more than once. I'm going to miss him a lot now that I'm leaving the program."

"Isn't it dangerous for you to do that?" John asked, his tone still heavily laced with skepticism.

Anne shook her head. "The men I testified against died in prison. I'll always keep a low profile, but as far as the government agents have been able to tell, there aren't any more contracts out on me."

Another long, tense silence followed. Anne held her breath while John studied her face, no doubt sifting through what she'd said, looking for a hole in her story.

Finally he spoke. "What are you doing for a living now, Annie? Writing fiction?"

The waitress chose that moment to top off their cups. Grateful for the interruption, Anne took a deep breath. Trying to convince John of anything when he'd already made up his mind was like trying to wear down a rock with dripping water. She dug Ben Thorn's business card out of her purse and shoved it across the table.

"Call this man," she said. "He's the director of the U.S. Marshals Service. He'll confirm my story."

"Aw, come *on,* Annie." John picked up the card, glanced at it, then laughed and tossed it back onto the table. "You don't really expect me to believe—"

"No. I expect you to check it out."

"Hey, the card's a nice prop, but anybody can have anything printed on a business card."

Anne slid out of the booth and stood beside the table. "Call directory assistance and verify the number. Go to the library and look at the March sixteenth issue of *Newsweek.* On page forty, there's an article about the WITSEC program, and Ben is quoted. Do whatever you have to do to convince yourself that I'm not lying, but do it fast."

"And if I don't?" John asked.

"You've got twenty-four hours before I file for a court order that will force you to allow me to see the girls. When you're done talking to Ben, call me here." She gave him the name of a nearby motel. "Ask for *Anne* Martin. Room 205."

Taking a five-dollar bill out of her purse, she tossed it onto the table and marched out of the restaurant.

Seething at her ultimatum and her snotty parting gesture, John shoved the card into his pocket and headed for the university. He'd check out her story, all right. Damned if he wouldn't.

He glanced at his jeans and grimaced. He hadn't planned on going into the office today because he didn't have any classes on Fridays. He liked to present a professional appearance for his students when he was on campus, but...aw, the hell with it.

Heads turned as he raced up the stairs to his office. Ignoring them, he unlocked his door, shut it behind him and shrugged out of his jacket. Then he grabbed the phone and dialed the library's reference desk.

A librarian listened to his requests, asked him to hold the line and came back on a few moments later. John thanked her for the information and hung up, then leaned back in his chair and linked his hands behind his head. Okay, so the *Newsweek* article and the phone number were real. Big deal.

Annie—no, make that *Anne*—wasn't stupid. But maybe she'd figured he'd go this far and accept the rest on faith. Muttering, "When pigs fly," John took the card out of his pocket and dialed again. A feminine voice answered.

"U.S. Marshals Service. How may I help you?"

John gave his name and asked to speak to Ben Thorn, drumming his fingers on the desk until a male voice came on the line.

"Ben Thorn here. What can I do for you, Professor Miller?"

"I didn't give your secretary my title," John said.

"You didn't have to," the man replied with a chuckle. "Anne's told me a lot about you. I assume you're calling to verify her participation in the Witness Security Program?"

"That's right."

"Let me assure you, she's not making up a fairy tale. Knowing Anne, she's probably downplayed the entire situation. You should be extremely proud of her, Professor. She's the most courageous woman I've ever met."

John cleared his throat and repressed an urge to squirm in his chair. "She hasn't told me much. Would you mind filling in a few details?"

"What would you like to know?"

"Was she really in danger?"

"Of course. We wouldn't have made her a protected witness otherwise. Thanks to her testimony, two of the most vicious criminals in the country went to prison."

"Well, uh, was there any reason she had to go alone?" John asked. "Don't you take whole families sometimes?"

"When it's necessary, but Anne's case was special."

"In what way?"

"For one thing, she wasn't a criminal herself. Many of our witnesses are, or they wouldn't have the kind of information our prosecutors need. Anne simply happened to be in the wrong place at the wrong time."

"What's that got to do with anything?"

"I'm coming to that. She was horribly frightened by the whole experience, and she was willing to pay any price to protect her family. She didn't want any of you exposed to the danger she was facing."

"Wait a minute," John said. "Are you telling me it was *her* choice to keep the rest of us out of the program?"

"Well, yes, but we supported her decision. It's easier to hide one woman than a family with young children. The more people involved, the greater the chance that someone will accidentally blow everyone's cover."

"Okay, maybe I can see your point," John admitted grudgingly. "But surely you have to notify the person's family, don't you? I mean, at least let them know the person's alive and well?"

Thorn hesitated before answering. "Normally, yes."

"Then why the hell wasn't *I* notified?"

Another hesitation. "I think you'd better get Anne to answer that question."

"Dammit, man, do you have any idea what my kids and I have gone through since she disappeared?"

"I'm afraid I do. But if I may offer you a piece of advice, Professor, it's forget about the things no one can change and get on with the business of living your lives. Whatever you and your children have suffered, believe me, Anne has suffered more."

"How can you say that?" John demanded.

"Ask the lady what happened to her. I doubt she'll tell you much, especially if you've already questioned her honesty. But if you ever succeed in getting her to tell you everything, I think you'll understand. And then maybe you'll deserve to have a magnificent woman like Anne Martin in your life again."

Feeling chastised, John terminated the conversation. He leaned back in his chair and propped his feet on the corner of his desk. From the beginning of that phone call, he'd sensed that Ben Thorn didn't like him much. What the heck had Annie told the guy about him?

That he was a hardheaded, unreasonable jerk? A dolt who would probably blow her cover? A coward who couldn't protect his own wife and children?

And just what *had* happened to her? Had it really been that bad? Or had Thorn laid it on thick because he liked Annie so much?

The more John thought about the conversation, the more uncomfortable he felt. He was already carrying a heavy burden of guilt for his past failures as a husband and a father. Knowing he'd misjudged Annie all these years added at least another ton to the load.

In addition, since she hadn't been lying, he had to admit that she probably did have a legal right to see the kids. She also had a right to expect an apology from him. As nasty as he'd been this morning, it was a wonder she hadn't slapped his face.

So, maybe he *was* a hardheaded, unreasonable jerk.

He'd been shocked and confused, but Annie had deserved more consideration than he'd shown her. And wasn't that the way it had always been between them? When he looked back over their marriage, it seemed that Annie had always needed more from him than he'd been willing or able to give.

His chest tightened with the familiar ache of regret. No doubt about it, he'd do a lot of things differently if he could go back to the beginning of their marriage. While he'd been off flying around the world, playing the hotshot computer genius, he hadn't understood the burden of responsibility Annie had carried. Not until she'd disappeared and he'd had to shoulder it alone.

Remembering how completely overwhelmed he'd felt, trying to take care of the kids and the house and maintain his career at the same time, he sighed and shook his head. Annie had made it all look easy, but if it hadn't been for the help both sets of grandparents had given him, he would have lost his mind during that first year without her.

Shoot, the only blame for the divorce he could lay at Annie's feet was that she hadn't complained often enough or loudly enough. It had seemed to him as if everything had been fine one day and he'd been served with divorce papers the next. She'd interpreted his failure to see that she needed his help as a lack of love, when the truth was that he simply hadn't been able to read her mind.

Well, he'd loved her plenty. Despite his anger at what he'd thought she had done to him and the girls, he'd never forgotten her. Never stopped wondering where she was. Never stopped worrying about her.

Dammit, why hadn't she let him and the girls go into the program with her? And why wouldn't Ben Thorn tell him why he hadn't been notified that Annie had entered it? A sick feeling in his gut told him he already knew the answers, but he wanted to hear them from Annie.

Grabbing his jacket, he rushed down to the parking lot and took off for her motel. It was time to try a more rational approach to Annie's return. He'd start with an abject apology. If she hadn't changed *too* much, she might even accept it. He glanced at himself in the rearview mirror, grimaced and shook his head. Talk about wishful thinking.

She'd probably hand him a fork and serve him a crow the size of an elephant.

Chapter Three

John bought a couple of sodas and a packet of cookies from the vending machines in the hallway off the motel lobby. His peace offering tucked under one arm, he climbed the stairs to the second floor, found room 205, took a deep breath and knocked on the door. A moment later, Annie's voice came from the other side of the wooden panel.

"Who is it?"

"It's me. John."

He heard a chain rattling, then the click of a dead bolt and finally a thump that sounded like a chair being pulled from under the doorknob. The door opened just enough to let him see that the chain was still attached. Annie peeked out, shut the door again, and he heard the chain slide along its track. For broad daylight in Bozeman, Montana, she was being awfully cautious about security.

Then the door swung fully open and there stood Annie, barefoot, wearing jeans and a Denver Broncos sweatshirt, eyeing him with a wary expression that dropped another five pounds of guilt onto his head. He took off his Stetson and shifted his weight to the other foot, hoping she'd let him in or say something. She didn't.

"Hi," he said. "Could I, uh, come in and talk to you for a few minutes?"

Without saying a word, she stepped back and allowed him to enter. He walked into the main living area while she reset the dead bolt and refastened the chain. They turned to face each other, and a chill shivered up his spine when he noticed the small automatic pistol in her right hand. She came toward him, carrying that gun as naturally as if it were a calculator.

"I'll admit you've got a right to be mad at me, but I hope you're not planning to use that," he said, gesturing at her weapon with his hat. "Is it loaded?"

"Wouldn't do me much good if it wasn't."

"I thought you said you were safe now."

"It's going to take me a while to get used to the idea," she said, shrugging one shoulder. "This is the first time I've traveled without an escort."

"Do you know what you're doing with that thing?"

"Yes."

She said it with such conviction he didn't doubt her for a second. Nor did he know what to say. She clicked on the safety, set the pistol on the desk and gestured toward the round table and chairs by the window.

"I talked to Ben Thorn."

He set the cookies, sodas and his hat on the table before removing his jacket. Annie took it from him, laid it on the bed and sat in the chair opposite his. Crossing her arms over her breasts, she gazed at him expectantly. He pushed one can of soda onto her side of the table, then the cookies. No reaction. Not even a hint of a smile. Damn. Here came the crow.

"I'm, uh . . ." He had to stop and clear his throat. "I'm sorry I didn't believe you this morning."

"Or yesterday," she pointed out.

"Or yesterday. I apologize, Annie."

Her solemn eyes continued to search his face, as if testing the depth of his sincerity. He returned her scrutiny, his heart aching at the wall of misunderstanding and mistrust that yawning gap of years and traumatic events had erected.

"All right," she said. "I apologize for showing up so unexpectedly. Steve wanted me to wait until he could contact you first, but I was too impatient."

"When did you find out those guys were dead?"

"Wednesday afternoon."

And she'd shown up at his office on Thursday, John thought. She sure hadn't wasted any time in coming home. "I guess you're pretty anxious to see the kids, huh?"

A spark of hope lighted up her eyes and she reached for her soda, her fingers closing around the can with enough force to leave dents. "God, yes. I've already missed so much I can hardly stand to think about it. Please, tell me about them. Everything you can think of."

"Well, they're kids," he said with a what-can-I-say? shrug. "Sometimes they're great. Sometimes they're brats. But mostly, they're just . . . kids."

Her eyes sparkling with eagerness, Annie leaned closer. "Does Holly still have ear infections?"

"No, she grew out of that about four years ago. Rachel has a little touch of asthma, but other than that, they're both pretty healthy."

"How tall are they?"

"Rachel's really shot up since she hit puberty. I'd guess she's almost as tall as you are," John answered. "Holly's still kind of a runt."

Chuckling, Annie shook her head at him. "That doesn't tell me much. Don't you have any pictures in your wallet?"

Now, *this* was the Annie he remembered. Bubbly. Animated. Bemused by the sudden change, John couldn't take his eyes off her, not even while he dug his wallet out of his hip pocket, flipped it open and fished out the most recent photograph he had of the girls.

Annie snatched it from his hand, then gulped in a deep breath as if she was bracing herself to look at it. When she finally did, the air whooshed out of her lungs and he saw her shoulders tremble.

"Oh, God," she whispered, staring at the photo as if looking away for a second would kill her. "They're so big and Rachel's got breasts.... Oh, they're both *gorgeous*."

John agreed with her assessment. This particular photograph was his all-time favorite of both girls. Shamelessly mugging for the camera, they were standing in front of the barn, wearing paint-splotched jeans and T-shirts. Rachel had her arm around Holly's shoulders.

Holly's dark hair was pulled back into a ponytail. Rachel's equally dark hair hung straight to her shoulders, her bangs teased and sprayed into a fluffy mass the way all the junior-high girls seemed to wear them lately.

"And Rachel's got braces," Annie murmured, her voice thick with emotion. Shaking her head, she bit her lower lip and finally raised her eyes to meet John's.

If there'd ever been any doubt in his mind about her love for their children, that one tortured look erased it. Permanently. Annie had always been a sentimental softie, and though he'd teased her about it, it was one of the things he'd liked best about her.

Figuring a flood of tears was imminent, John dug his handkerchief out of his other hip pocket. To his surprise, however, Annie simply sniffled a little, gulped, then squared her shoulders and held the photograph out to him.

"Keep it," he said. "I've still got the negative."

"Thanks." After clearing her throat, she glanced at the picture again. "Those Miller genes are doozies. You couldn't deny either one of them if you wanted to, John."

He chuckled. "Yeah, Dad always says they look just like me. Only on them, it's cute."

"Do they fight much?"

"Only when they're awake." John rolled his eyes in fond exasperation and smiled when Annie laughed. "Rachel tries to act like she's all grown-up and tells Holly she's *so-o-o-o* immature."

"How does Holly retaliate?"

"She quotes Rachel's diary at the dinner table and eavesdrops on her phone calls. That kind of stuff."

"I can't wait to see them," Annie said softly, her eyes openly begging for his consent.

"I know. But you can't just pop in on them like a ghost. You're going to have to give me a little time to prepare them."

"What did you tell them about me?" she asked in a choked whisper.

Unable to bear watching while he inflicted more pain, John clasped his hands between his knees and studied the scuffed toes of his boots. "I didn't know what to tell them at first. It was a bad time, Annie. Try to remember that."

"What did you *tell* them, John?"

He looked up at her. She had one hand clutched tightly against her sternum. Her other arm curved across her midriff, the hand curled into a fist, supporting her bent elbow. The picture she made was of a tormented woman at the end of her strength, physically holding herself together.

"I told them the truth," he said. "That you'd gone away and I didn't know where you were or when you were coming back. They think the same thing I did. That you abandoned them."

An anguished cry escaped her lips. She shot out of the chair and paced across the room, her hand still clutching her chest as if she was trying to staunch the flow of blood from a mortal wound. Keeping her back to him, she stopped at the wall dividing the bedroom from the bathroom and bowed her head. He heard her taking quick, ragged breaths and wondered what it was costing her to maintain such fierce control over the violent emotions she must be feeling.

He considered going to her, holding her in these moments of grief. If she had turned toward him, made the slightest sign that she would welcome his comfort, he would have done it without hesitation. But she didn't. All he could do was sit there and watch. And wait.

After endless moments of agonizing tension, she turned around and came back to the table, her steps as slow and measured as an octogenarian's. Her head was up and her eyes were dry, however, surprising him once again. He had obviously misjudged the extent of her strength, he thought. She looked about as fragile as a damned tank.

"I'm sorry, Annie," he said quietly.

"Did you tell them your suspicions?" she asked. "About the big blond guy?"

"No. But Rachel overheard me telling Mom and Dad."

Her face became a rigid mask. Her eyes flashed with fury. She muttered a word that shocked him and turned her head away as if the sight of him disgusted her. Then she let out a bitter laugh and shook her head.

"Dopey me. I was afraid you'd think I was dead."

"I did for a while," John said. "I didn't want to believe you'd run off with a lover."

"Then why *did* you? For God's sake, John, I'd never been unfaithful to you. Didn't that last night we spent together tell you *any*thing about what I felt for you?"

Though she still wasn't looking at him, John shrugged helplessly. "That's what made it all so impossible to understand. But you'd just divorced me, and the only evidence I could find pointed in that direction, Annie. At the time, it seemed like the only rational explanation."

She looked over her shoulder at him, blistering accusations in her eyes. "I don't care how rational your explanation was, you should have *known* I would never desert my babies. Dammit, you should have trusted me more—"

"Trusted *you*?" John snapped, surging to his feet. "Oh, that's rich, Annie. How much did you trust *me*?"

Turning to face him, she propped her fists on her hips. "What are you talking about?"

"Your pal Thorn said *you* were the one who decided to leave the girls and me behind. I want to know why."

"Those men were killers, dammit. It wasn't safe."

"It wasn't your decision to make. By leaving me out of it, you *did* abandon us, Annie, and you'll never know how much that hurt. I'm not sure I'll ever be able to forgive you for that."

"I did exactly what you would have done in the same position," she argued. "I protected my family the best way I could, and I won't apologize for that."

"I didn't ask for your protection. Just because you saw some guy get killed—"

"It wasn't just some guy, John. I saw five people cut down like steers at a slaughterhouse. I wasn't about to let you or my children anywhere *near* the creeps who did it."

"Dammit, Annie, will you listen to me? It doesn't matter what you saw or how scared you were. Our place was with you. Your leaving without one damn word of explanation did more to destroy our home and family than anything anyone else ever could have done to us."

"You're wrong. At least you had each other. You could stay in one place and use your own names. The girls had their grandparents and their friends, and a chance to go to school without looking over their shoulders in fear every time they left the house. If you'd come with me, you would have lost all of that, and you might even have lost your lives. Think about that before you condemn me, John."

"That still doesn't explain why you didn't let them notify me. That was your decision, too, Annie, wasn't it?"

Her eyes widened, telling him she recognized the soft, deadly tone he'd used. It should have intimidated the hell out of her, but she raised her chin in defiance. Though it irritated the hell out of him, he had to admire her grit.

"The men who were after me don't leave witnesses alive if they can help it. They would have killed me whether I testified or not, so my life was already shot to hell. But you and the kids had a choice."

"Then why didn't you let me make it? For God's sake, if I'd known what you were going through—"

"You would have reacted exactly the way you're reacting now," she shouted. "I *knew* that no matter how the situation was presented to you, you'd do everything in your power to ride to my rescue like a damned cowboy before you realized you even had a choice to make!"

"That's not fair, Annie."

"Baloney. I can count the times I ever won an argument with you on the fingers of one hand. There wasn't much time to make the decision and I was afraid you'd raise such a stink you'd drag yourself and the kids into the program before I could make you understand what it would mean for all of you."

"Oh, I get it. Since I was too stupid to figure the situation out, you decided to be a martyr. Well, if you expect me to thank you, don't hold your breath."

"I never expected to be able to see you again, so I was hardly expecting your thanks. I already had a whole horde of federal agents to protect me. It wasn't necessary to risk any of your lives."

"Come on, Annie. Aren't you being just a little melodramatic here? If those agents could protect you, why couldn't they protect the rest of us?"

A piercing sadness entered her eyes as she studied him. Her shoulders sagged slightly and she exhaled a sigh reeking of resignation. "Believe what you want," she said, turning away to gaze out the window. "You always do."

Damn, he thought, shaking his head in confusion. A second ago, she'd been filled with fire, taking him on without giving an inch. Now she looked so drained he felt as if he'd been hammering away at an invalid.

"It's not that I don't believe it was bad for you, Annie," he said.

"I don't want to talk about this anymore."

"Do you want me to go?"

"Not until you tell me when I can see the girls."

"Okay. Let's sit down and have some pop and cookies, and maybe we can figure something out."

She looked over her shoulder and gave him a crooked smile, as if his suggestion had amused her. Then she gazed out the window for another moment before joining him at the table. He opened both soda cans and the packet of chocolate-chip cookies. She nibbled at one without any real appetite. Leaving it half-eaten, she propped her feet on the side of the bed and laced her fingers together behind her head.

Craving a cigarette in the worst way, John wolfed down three cookies and gulped half of his soda. Searching for a safer topic, he asked, "What are your plans now that you're leaving the program, Annie? Will you stay in Colorado?"

"No," she said without hesitation. "I'll have to tie up some loose ends, but I want to be close to the girls."

"Does that mean you'll be moving to Bozeman?"

"As soon as I can find a place to live and a job and track down my parents. I tried to call them, but I guess they've left Billings. Dad always said he wanted to retire to Arizona." She looked at John, chuckled and smacked her forehead with the heel of her hand. "Well, for pity's sake, you must know where they are. They wouldn't lose touch with Rachel and Holly."

John's heart skipped a beat, then took a quick, sickening plunge to the pit of his stomach. Oh, God, she didn't *know.* But surely the government would have known. Would have *told* her.

"Annie..."

Ignoring his halfhearted attempt to stop her, she hurried over to the desk and grabbed a pen and one of the motel's notepads. "Let me write their phone number down and I'll call them as soon as I can."

Damn. An only child, Annie had always been extremely close to her folks. No matter what she'd done, he didn't want to be the one to tell her. How *could* he tell her? On the other hand, how could he *not?*

"Okay, I'm ready." She looked up at him, pen poised over the paper. "What's the number?"

"I, uh, I don't have a number. You see—"

"You don't know it by heart? Well, find it when you get home and call me. I can't wait to catch up with them."

"Annie, please, sit down for a minute," John suggested quietly and, he hoped, calmly.

Whether some hint of anguish sneaked out in his voice or in his expression, he didn't know, but something alerted her. Her spine stiffened. Her eyes narrowed. Her chin lifted, suddenly making her look very brave. And frighteningly vulnerable.

"What's wrong, John?" she demanded.

Standing, he grasped her shoulders and pushed her down onto the chair, overcoming her automatic resistance as gently as he could. Then he lowered himself to one knee in front of her and took her right hand between his palms, wincing inwardly at the icy feel of her skin. Her gaze never left his face for an instant.

"It's been so long," he said. "I thought...well, they must have told you."

"What is it?" She clutched at the front of his shirt. "Dammit, John, tell me!"

"I don't know how to tell you, Annie," he said softly. "Your folks are...I'm sorry, honey, but they're gone."

"No," Anne whispered, violently shaking her head. "Not both of them, John. Not *both* of them."

"I'm afraid so."

Unable to bear the pity in John's gaze, she closed her eyes and gritted her teeth against the pain crushing her chest at his confirmation. She heard him murmuring comforting sounds, but she couldn't understand the words. She felt him stroking her hands, but the chill racing from the center of her body outward made it impossible to absorb any of his warmth.

"When?" she asked, her voice a hoarse croak.

"Your, uh, mom passed away about eighteen months after you disappeared. She had a brain tumor. Your dad had a massive coronary a year later."

Anne couldn't stop shivering. The chill inside her kept growing and growing, no doubt trying to cushion the shock. But even this god-awful numbness could only cushion so much. Her vision blurred, then started to grow dim. Though passing out held a certain appeal at the moment, she *had* to know the rest.

Taking a deep breath, she pulled her hands away from John's. He got to his feet, watched her anxiously for a moment before going back to his chair.

"Did Mama suffer a lot?"

John shook his head. "It was pretty advanced by the time the doctors found it, and she went really fast."

"Did she ask for me?"

"Right up to the end. Your dad and I were with her."

"What about Daddy? Did he die . . . alone?"

"No. He'd come up here for a visit. He and my dad had taken the girls riding. Mike did everything he could, but your dad was gone in a matter of minutes."

"Did, uh, did they think I ran off with a lover, too?"

"No. They were worried sick about you, but they never stopped believing in you, Annie. And they never stopped loving you."

Holding her elbows close to her sides, she folded her forearms across her waist and rocked back and forth until the shivering stopped. She sensed rather than saw that John was watching her with increasing concern, but she could do nothing to reassure him.

"Dammit, Annie, don't do this to yourself," he said a moment later. "Go ahead and cry it out."

She knew what he meant. During their marriage he'd been constantly handing her his handkerchief because she'd been such a sentimental slob. But that had changed drastically the day she'd watched a family get murdered.

Anne often *wanted* to weep. Sometimes she feared she would start and never be able to stop again. But it was as if the pain and shock had gone so deep that day her tear ducts had been welded shut. Though she would mourn her parents until the day she died, she didn't have any tears to shed for them.

"It isn't like you to be so unfeeling," John muttered, staring at her in outraged disbelief.

Rising slowly to her feet, she returned his gaze with the impassive expression she'd learned to wear on the witness stand. "I do all my crying on the inside now, John. It doesn't mean I don't feel anything."

He stood, shoved his hands into his pockets and glanced away as if looking at her made him feel uncomfortable. The silence between them thickened like summer humidity in Mississippi.

Finally John said, "I can't understand why the government didn't tell you. Surely they knew."

"Of course they knew," Anne snarled, nearly choking on the rage surging up inside her. "Those lousy bastards didn't want to risk upsetting their only credible witness."

"That's pretty cynical, Annie."

"Think so? Duke Donner's first trial started about eighteen months after I entered WITSEC. The other one, Frankie Costenzo's, started a year later. Does that timing strike you as a coincidence?"

"It could be."

"Not likely! The prosecutors would hardly even let me go to the bathroom by myself until the trials and the appeals were over. They wouldn't have let me risk breaking my cover over something as unimportant as my parents' funerals. They wanted their convictions so bad I doubt they'd have told me if you or one of the girls had died."

John raised an eyebrow at that, but he didn't say anything. Though Anne knew her bitterness must have surprised him, she didn't regret her angry words. The sooner he understood she wasn't the same naive, compliant woman he'd known, the better they would get along.

"What about your folks?" she asked a moment later. "Are they all right?"

She saw pain flash into his eyes in the instant before he looked away again. Then he slowly shook his head.

"Mom died of a stroke three years ago."

"Oh, John," Anne murmured, aching for him and for Mike. "I'm so sorry. Your mother was a dear, dear lady."

"Yeah, she sure was. We've all missed her."

Anne slid her hands into her jeans pockets. "Whenever I used to read a letter to Dear Abby complaining about an evil mother-in-law, I always felt so lucky."

"She thought a lot of you, too," John said quietly, folding his arms over his chest. "You know, she took your side when you divorced me."

"She didn't!"

"You don't think so?" He grinned, as if at a fond memory. "She gave me dirty looks the whole week I was here with the girls. And when I was packing to go back to Chicago, she pulled me aside and said she wouldn't have put up with my nonsense for half as long as you did, and I'd better be prepared to crawl and beg for your forgiveness."

"That sounds like Irene, all right," Anne said, smiling a little. "How's Mike?"

"He's okay. Bossy as ever. I know he misses Mom, but it helps having the girls around."

"You've been through a lot in the past six years."

Nodding, John raised his left hand and gently brushed the backs of his knuckles over her cheek. "I guess we all have, Annie. For whatever it's worth, I'm damn glad you're safe now."

Anne closed her eyes against the exquisite sensations his touch invoked. They were a long way from resolving their differences. But as bad as things were between them, that simple, reflexive act was like a healing balm for her wounded spirit. She wondered if John had any idea how much this moment of tenderness meant to her.

Feeling as if her heart had climbed right up into her throat, she looked into his eyes and felt her insides turn to warm mush. Beneath all that infuriating stubbornness, he was a kind, decent man. She might have to whack him over the head to get him to listen, but once he *did* listen, there wasn't a better man to have in her corner.

"Thanks," she whispered, forcing a shaky smile. "You'll talk to the girls today?"

"As soon as they get off the school bus. There are two more things I want to say, and then I'd better go."

"All right."

"If you've been hoping for a happy family reunion, I'm afraid you're going to be disappointed. The girls will need plenty of time to get used to you again. I want you to give them that."

"Of course I will. I didn't come back to disrupt your lives. You set the pace and I'll follow."

"Good. The other thing is, if you're going to come back into their lives, I want you to plan to stay. You can't pop in and out on them whenever you feel like it."

"I told you I'm planning to move here," Anne protested. "Where else would I go?"

"I don't know. I'm not really sure what you're expecting, but they've both got abandonment fears. Especially Rachel. I'll smooth the way for you as much as I can, but you'll have to be patient."

"I'll do my best, John. I promise."

He picked up his hat. She handed him his jacket and went to unlock the door while he put it on. Pausing beside her, he asked, "Are you sure you're going to be all right here by yourself?"

"I'll be fine. When you leave, I'm going to take a nap and then go apartment hunting."

"Sounds like a good idea. I'll call you later, Annie."

She closed and locked the door behind him, then leaned back against it and blew out an exhausted sigh. What a day. Since meeting John for coffee, she'd experienced anger, grief, despair—just about every violent emotion it was possible to feel. But along with sustaining the major losses of her parents and her mother-in-law, she'd also made some major progress.

John was finally talking to her. Despite his warnings about the girls, she had high hopes that her daughters would accept her again. If not now, they would have to do it eventually, because once she moved up here from Denver, she wasn't going anywhere. Not ever.

If John would just understand about Chad...

"That's a pretty big if," she whispered.

Her throat tightened and her stomach clenched. She crossed the room to the window, arriving in time to see his Suburban pull out of the parking lot. She probably should have told him about their son today, but she didn't see how either of them could have handled one more issue. Especially one as emotionally charged as the issue of Chad was going to be.

"It'll be okay," she murmured, hugging herself. "Once he meets Chad, he'll love him as much as I do."

That was never the question, the little voice inside her head mocked. *The question is, once John finds out you've hidden his son from him all this time, will he ever be able to forgive you?*

Chapter Four

Flushed with the victory of finding an apartment, Anne hurried into her room later that afternoon. The phone rang before she could shut the door. Hoping it was John, she lunged for the receiver and sighed with disappointment when the voice she heard belonged to Steve Anderson, instead.

"I've been trying to reach you for two hours," he said. "Where have you been?"

"Renting a place to live," Anne replied with a smile. "You wouldn't believe how hard that is when the college kids are all in town."

"Things are going well for you, then?"

"About as well as I expected." Knowing how worried Steve had been about her taking this trip alone, Anne quickly filled him in the latest developments with John.

"You should have let me come with you," he scolded before she'd finished.

"No way, pal. It's time I learned to stand on my own two feet, and Chad needs you there. How's he doing?"

A warm, rich chuckle came over the line. "He's fine. I don't know how you keep up with him, though. That kid's got so much energy he's wearing me down to a nub."

"Oh, you poor old man," Anne teased him, though at thirty-six he was, in fact, two years younger than she was. Steve had been her labor coach during Chad's delivery and had come to love the rambunctious boy almost as much as she did. "May I talk to the little darling?"

"Sure. He's practically stomping on my head trying to get the phone away from me."

"Hey, Mom, guess what," her son said a moment later. "Barry ate his hot dog too fast at school yesterday and puked all over his desk."

"That sounds exciting," Anne said, marveling as always at the things he found interesting. "Are you having a good time with Steve?"

"Yeah. He's teachin' me to throw a football, and we're goin' to see a movie tonight with monsters in it. Tomorrow he's gonna teach me to play poker if I don't act like a mangy little varmint."

"You'd better behave yourself, then."

"I will. When are you coming home?"

"It won't be too much longer. Just a couple of days."

"Good. I miss you, Mom."

"I miss you, too, Chad. Let me talk to Steve again now, okay?"

"I told you he was fine," Steve said when he came back on the line.

"This monster movie better not be too scary, or he'll be up all night with his eyes bugged out," Anne said. "And why are you corrupting my son with poker, Anderson?"

"Hey, a Montana boy's got to have a lot of skills. Poker's one of 'em."

"Yeah, well, I guess you'd know if anyone would. Why do I get the impression you're just trying to find a way to make Chad sit down for a while so you can rest?"

"I was hoping you wouldn't figure that out." Steve fell silent for a moment. When he spoke again, a somber tone had entered his voice. "I hate to tell you this over the phone, but I finally got a report on your folks."

"It's all right. John told me. I'm, uh..." She paused and cleared her throat. "I'm handling it okay."

"I'd have told you, but I swear, I didn't know."

"I never thought you did, so don't worry about it."

"I'm really sorry, anyway. And you shouldn't have to be alone. Sure you don't want me to come up there? Chad and I could catch the morning flight."

"John doesn't know about Chad yet."

"Anne, you've *got* to tell him. The sooner the better."

"I know. I'll do it after I see the girls. I don't want to give John an excuse to put me off."

"The longer you wait, the harder it's going to be."

"I said I'll tell him, and I will. Listen, I've got to get off this phone. John may try to call any minute."

"All right. Take care, Anne."

"You, too. Hug Chad for me, will you?"

"Nah. I don't hug mangy little varmints. Good luck with the girls and call me tomorrow."

Anne agreed, then hung up the phone. The instant the connection was severed, a cloud of loneliness closed in around her. She ached to have Chad with her. No matter how depressed she got, his sunny smiles and exuberant hugs always fixed her right up.

And Steve. Dear, dependable Steve, who'd become her friend, as well as her protector. He'd violated all kinds of rules that could have cost him his job just to make life easier for her. Whenever she'd had to move, he'd moved with her, and she suspected he'd stayed in the Colorado office of the U.S. Marshals Service longer than he'd wanted, so he could continue to be there for her.

Now he'd be able to get on with his life and career, and she supposed she should be glad for him. But at the moment, she was painfully aware how much she would miss him when she moved to Bozeman. It would hurt as much as losing a brother. Or her parents. Or her mother-in-law.

Dammit, she'd already lost so much and it was so unfair. She hadn't done anything wrong. And yet, along with the inevitable grief, she felt incredibly guilty for all the anguish her family had suffered on her account.

Her eyes burned and her throat ached. She longed to throw herself across the bed and weep out her pain and frustration and rage. But she couldn't. Even if she could, it wouldn't change the past. And if she fell apart now, she might destroy whatever chance she had of building a future.

When John *did* call to tell her she could see Rachel and Holly, she would need every scrap of strength, every last dollop of poise and self-control, if her daughters rejected her as John had suggested they might.

She picked up her purse and dug out the photograph John had given her that morning. Then she took out Chad's latest picture and laid it beside the one of the girls. Talk about chips off the old block. They all had John's black hair and green eyes, his nose and stubborn chin.

It would really be something to see him with all three of the children. Even the most casual observer would have to recognize that those four people belonged together. Though she wouldn't fit into the picture the same way John and the kids did, she belonged, too. Surely God or fate, whoever or whatever was in charge of the universe, wouldn't be cruel enough to leave her out.

"Hold that thought," she whispered, holding the photographs against her breast.

The phone rang. Anne eyed it warily for a second, took a deep breath and snatched the receiver off its cradle.

"Annie," John said, the tone of his voice giving no indication of whether he had good news or bad.

"Yes, John. Have you talked to the girls?"

"Yeah. Why don't you plan to come out to the ranch in the morning? Say, nine o'clock?"

Anne's heart sank at the prospect of spending another evening alone in this motel room. "Why not tonight?"

"Well, they're a little upset. I want to give them more time to digest it all and talk to them again before they go to bed. Are you all right?"

She nodded, then realized he couldn't see her and said, "Disappointed, but fine. I'll see you in the morning."

Sighing, she hung up the phone, put the pictures away and looked at the digital clock on the nightstand. Fifteen more hours. She had to wait only fifteen more hours to see her girls. After six and a half years, she could do that without going crazy. No sweat.

Taking a pen from her purse and the newspaper she'd bought on her way up to her room, she crawled onto the bed and used the remote control to turn on the news. Then she propped the pillows behind her back and located the classified ads. She had a place to live, but she still needed to find a job.

Ruthlessly pushing grief, loneliness and worry from her mind, she found the Help Wanted listings. It took all of five minutes to circle every ad for which she was even marginally qualified. She filled another ten minutes by reorganizing her suitcase and choosing an outfit to wear in the morning.

Determined not to sit and brood, she went out for a sandwich, dawdling as long as she could before returning to the motel. Then she showered, shaved her legs, conditioned her hair and gave herself a manicure. By the time she'd finished all that, she still had twelve hours to go.

Staring at the clock in disbelief, she groaned. "It might as well be twelve years."

After a miserable night of disquieting dreams about Annie during the brief stretches he'd actually been able to sleep, John dragged himself out of bed later than he'd intended the next morning. He shaved, showered and dressed in record time, telling himself that he'd decided to wear his "hunk T-shirt," as Rachel called it, only because the girls had given it to him for Father's Day. Annie hadn't had a thing to do with his selection.

That twitchy feeling in the pit of his stomach wasn't anything like the eager sense of anticipation he'd always felt when he was going home to Annie after a business trip. Not really. It was simply the natural result of a slight case of nerves and a need for food and coffee.

Combing his hair for the fourth time, he eyed the pack of cigarettes on his dresser with longing, shook his head and hurried downstairs to the kitchen. Mike handed him a mug of coffee and went back to pouring pancake batter onto the griddle. The girls sat on either side of the round oak table, scowling at each other over breakfasts that had barely been touched.

John took a fortifying gulp, sighed inwardly and took his regular place at the table beside Holly. How two sisters who looked so much alike could have such different personalities, he would never know.

While Rachel had reacted to the news of Annie's return with every bit of the sullen attitude he'd expected, Holly had declared she couldn't wait to see her mother again. She'd flown into a frenzy of housecleaning with the purpose of making a good impression on Annie. Judging by their outfits, he figured nothing had changed during the night.

Rachel wore a red, short-sleeved sweater that left no doubt about her physical maturity, a pair of jeans so tight they looked as if the seams might explode if she sneezed and three times more makeup than she usually did. Holly, on the other hand, could easily go to church and fit right in.

Given the situation, both girls' reactions were probably perfectly normal. Though he'd told them their lives weren't really going to change just because their mother had turned up, he knew they didn't believe it. He didn't blame them, because he didn't believe it, either. And how could he reassure them when he was just as uncertain as they were?

Sighing again, he accepted a plate of pancakes from his dad. Rachel pushed the syrup across the table at him and went right back to scowling at Holly.

"Make her go change, Dad," Holly said, crossing her arms over her chest. "Mom's gonna think she's a hooker."

"Why do *you* care what she thinks?" Rachel demanded. "You don't even remember her."

"I do *so.*"

"Do *not.* You were only four when she left."

"So what? She's still my mom and I love her."

Rolling her eyes toward the ceiling, Rachel mimicked her sister in a singsong voice. "'She's still my mom and I love her.' I can't believe you're acting like such a geek over somebody who doesn't even care about us."

Holly shoved back her chair and stormed around the table. "She does *too* care! And you'd better go change and wash that gunk off your face right now. Make her do it, Dad!"

Rachel jumped to her feet and pushed Holly back a step. "I don't give a rip *what* she thinks, you stupid little—"

"That's enough," John said. Striding across the room, he stepped between the two girls. "You have every right to feel nervous about seeing your mother again, but don't take it out on each other."

"I'm not nervous," Rachel grumbled.

"Then you're doing better than the rest of us." John rested one hand on her shoulder and gave it a gentle squeeze. Poor kid, her muscles felt even tighter than his own did. "If you're done eating, why don't you clear your dishes and go out and visit the horses? We'll call you when your mother gets here."

Drilling him with a mutinous glare, Rachel shrugged off his hand and left the room, ignoring her dishes altogether. Deciding not to push the issue, John cleared her place and carried everything over to the sink. Mike scowled at him as he passed the stove.

"That kid's gettin' quite a mouth on her," Mike said. "We're all gonna have to listen to it for a long time if you don't start clampin' down on her."

John silently counted to ten. "Cut her a little slack today, will you? She'll come around."

"Hmph. If she'll talk that way around you, I hate to think about how she'll talk around Annie."

"Annie's just going to have to be an adult and handle it. Leave Rachel alone."

"Okay. Fine. Forget I said anything," Mike said, punctuating his words with jabs of his spatula. Then he scooped up the last batch of pancakes, slapped them onto a plate and shoved them at John's midsection. "Put these in the fridge. I'm not hungry anymore." With that he strode out of the room.

Irritated to his toenails, John turned toward the table and saw Holly standing where he'd left her, her eyes wide with dismay, her chin quivering.

"What's the matter with everybody today?" she asked. "Shouldn't we be celebrating, instead of fighting?"

John set the plate on the counter, crossed the room and pulled her into a hug. "It'll be all right, babycakes. We're just . . . nervous."

"But why does Rachel have to be so mean? She acts like she knows everything."

"Aw, Rachel's just as confused as the rest of us, but she's trying hard not to show it. Teenagers do that sometimes. Don't take it personally, honey."

Holly gulped, then nodded. "I'll try, Dad. But is it really dumb to want Mom to like me?"

"Of course not. And you don't have a thing to worry about, Hol. You're a pretty darn likable little gal."

Holly wrinkled her nose at him, then nearly jumped out of her black patent leather flats when a car door slammed outside. "Omigosh, she's here." She smoothed the skirt of her best Sunday-school dress. "Do I look okay?"

Stepping back, John squinted one eye and studied her for a second. "You'll do," he said with a smile. "In fact, you look downright gorgeous."

His heart contracted when she threw herself against him and hugged his waist with all the strength her skinny little arms possessed. Holly was his sweet one. It seemed as if she'd come out of the womb ready and eager to love and be loved. Her sunny disposition and wacky sense of humor had frequently reminded him of Annie—the Annie he remembered, anyway.

Holly was also extremely sensitive to feelings, both her own and other people's. She hated conflict. Couldn't stand to see anyone hurting or unhappy. Couldn't tolerate the thought that someone didn't like her. Just the way Annie had been.

Holly was eager to please, generous to a fault and easily wounded. Because she couldn't help showing that, she was also terribly vulnerable. She could give as good as she got when Rachel provoked her, and John supposed she would eventually toughen up in self-defense. But right now, he honestly feared for her if she couldn't establish a decent relationship with her mother.

Releasing him, Holly ran to the back door and bellowed for Rachel. Then she raced about, calling her grandfather. At last she went to the entryway of the house, and John stood behind her, resting his hands on her shoulders. Mike hurried out of the living room and stood to John's left. Rachel strolled into the hall a moment later, her expression clearly indicating that she would do this to be polite, but that she found the whole scene incredibly boring.

Inhaling a deep breath, John turned and looked outside. Annie was coming slowly up the walk, wearing jeans and a purple Windbreaker. She looked up, halting in her tracks when she caught sight of the tight little group waiting in the doorway.

John saw her throat contract. Her shoulders rose and fell in a sigh. Her mouth curved into a tentative smile. He wanted to smile back at her, but the curtain of tension surrounding him, his dad and the girls made it impossible. They were all holding their breaths, all desperately searching for something to say, all paralyzed with anxiety and maybe a little excitement.

"This is weird," Holly finally said. "Isn't anybody gonna talk?"

Her question triggered a round of relieved laughter. Annie started walking toward them again, her gaze darting from one daughter to the other. A lump grew in John's throat as she approached Holly. Her eyes filled with wonder and anguish, Annie raised one hand, fingers outstretched and shaking with a fine tremor, as if she desperately wanted to touch the child, but didn't quite dare. Holly stared at her mother for a second, then smiled in encouragement.

"Hi, Mom," she whispered.

Annie's eyes misted over, and John noted that she'd worn her glasses, instead of the brown contacts.

"Hi, Holly." She bit her lower lip as if to hold in a sob, then gave Holly a crooked grin. "It's good to see you again, honey."

"Yeah. Me, too, Mom."

After squeezing Holly's hand, Annie made a quarter turn to her right. "Hello, Mike."

Clearing his throat, Mike shook the hand she offered. "Welcome home, Annie. Glad you're okay. We've missed you."

"Thanks. I've missed you, too."

She made another quarter turn, coming face-to-face with Rachel. Her eyes cool and remote, Rachel stiffened and stepped back. John cringed inside for Annie's sake. At the same time, he hurt for Rachel. Could Annie see past their daughter's hostility to the frightened kid inside?

He hoped so. It wasn't that Rachel didn't care about her mother or about Annie's opinion of her—it was that she cared too much to let it show. Annie searched Rachel's face for a moment, then gave her a gentle, loving smile.

"Hello, Rachel," she said, casually lowering her hand to her side. "I didn't believe your dad when he told me you were almost as tall as I am. You've really grown up."

"Kids grow whether their parents are around or not," Rachel replied, her voice dangerously close to a sneer.

Deciding this was not an appropriate time to let Rachel start venting her hurt and anger, John stepped back, bringing Holly along with him. "Come on in, Annie."

"Yeah," Mike said, picking up on John's cue. "Let's all go take a load off in the living room. Can I get you a cup of coffee, Annie?"

Declining politely, Annie sat at one end of the sofa, smiling when Holly sat beside her. Mike plunked himself into his battered, beloved recliner. John took the chair across the coffee table from Annie, and Rachel perched beside him on the arm.

Before another excruciating silence could take hold, Mike said, "So, uh, Annie, it's been a while."

She shot him a grateful smile. "Yes, it has, Mike. I guess it'll take time to get used to all the changes."

She had *that* right, John thought.

"Are you going to stick around long?" Rachel asked.

John considered nudging her in reprimand, then decided against it. Rachel had a right to her feelings. If Annie intended to become a permanent part of the family again, she might as well see what she'd have to deal with.

"I'll be moving to Bozeman," Annie said quietly. "I'm looking forward to being your mother again."

"We don't need a mother," Rachel said. "Dad's got a neat girlfriend now, and they'll probably get married."

John watched Annie closely for any sign of a negative reaction, but her expression remained pleasant and interested. Well, that answered one of his questions. She'd come back only to see the kids, which was just dandy with him. No matter how she tried to rationalize the decisions she'd made, he didn't think he'd ever be able to forgive her for the heartaches she'd caused.

Holly scowled at her sister. "Paula would be our *step-*mother, Rachel. We can still have our own mom, too."

Rachel tossed her head, swinging her long hair behind her shoulders. "Paula's a gourmet cook and she knows all about makeup and clothes, and she can sew anything. I don't know why we'd want another mom around."

"I'll try not to clutter up the place too much, Rachel," Annie said with a wry chuckle. "I'd just like to see you girls whenever you've got the time."

"Well, we won't have much," Rachel said. "We're pretty busy."

"And what keeps you so busy?" Annie asked, her interested smile still firmly in place.

John had to give her credit for refusing to rise to Rachel's baiting. From the thunderous expressions on their faces, however, Holly and Mike weren't going to tolerate much more of her snide attitude. Sure enough, the ten-year-old sent her sister a scathing look and jumped into the conversation.

"We're both in 4-H, and Rachel's a cheerleader. I'm in beginners band."

"That's wonderful, Holly. What do you play?"

"The flute. I like it 'cause it's easy to carry on the bus. I'm still taking piano lessons, too, but Rachel quit because she was too lazy to practice."

"That's not why I quit," Rachel protested. "I just never had time. Wait'll you get to junior high and see how much homework *you* have."

"If you weren't so busy flirting with the boys—"

Mike gave them both a quelling look. "All right, you two, don't start that now. I'd like to hear more about your mother. John hasn't told us much, Annie. Was it pretty bad for you?"

Her smile was so sad and yet so sweet John had to steel himself against it. He couldn't help feeling a certain amount of sympathy for her, but dammit, he couldn't let her get to him again. He just couldn't.

"It was bad enough," she said. "The worst part was having to be away from all of you."

"Oh, *right,*" Rachel muttered.

Annie raised an eyebrow at her daughter, but her voice and expression maintained the quiet dignity John had found so unsettling when she'd first come to his office.

"Why don't you go ahead and get whatever it is you want to say off your chest, Rachel?" Annie said. "I can see you're awfully angry with me."

"What did you expect?" Trembling with rage, Rachel jumped to her feet, fists at her sides. "You think you can just walk back in here and pick up where you left off? Well, I've got news for you. You gave up your place in this family and we don't have room for you anymore."

"That's not true!" Holly wailed. Tears rolling down her cheeks, she frantically clutched at Annie's arm as if she feared her mother would leave at any second. Annie patted her hand, then stood and faced Rachel with an unflinching gaze.

"I understand how you feel, Rachel, but—"

"No, you don't! Grandma Liz *loved* you. She never would have left you no matter what happened to her."

"I didn't want to leave you, baby—"

"I'm not a baby!"

"Well, you're sure as hell actin' like one!" Mike snapped. "I'm ashamed of you, Rachel. Can't you even give your mother a chance?"

Tears puddled in Rachel's eyes as she faced her grandfather. She dashed them away with the back of one fist. "A chance to do what, Grandpa? Hurt Daddy again? Hurt all of us? No thanks. I don't trust her and I don't want anything to do with her."

John surged to his feet and put his arm around Rachel. "Calm down, honey," he said softly. "Nobody's going to make you do anything. Do you want to go to your room?"

She looked up at him, pain and resentment written all over her face. Then she gave a jerky nod and fled. A moment later her footsteps thumped up the stairs, her bedroom door slammed and a painful silence filled the living room. Annie gulped and ducked her head.

Mike and Holly scowled at John, as if Rachel's outburst had been all his fault. And maybe it had been, he thought, angry at himself now for not cutting Rachel off at her first snotty remark. But what would that have done but force the kid's resentment underground?

"I'm sorry, Annie," Mike finally said. "You didn't deserve that. I'll go talk to her."

She shook her head at him. "It's all right, Mike. Rachel's entitled to feel angry with me."

"She shouldn't be allowed to talk to any adult that way," Mike retorted, shooting John a disapproving frown.

"Stay out of it, Dad," John said. "Annie's going to have to deal with Rachel on her own."

"That's right," Annie agreed. "She'll only resent me more if anyone tries to interfere. When she's had more time to think things through, I'll talk to her."

"She's your kid," Mike grumbled, crossing his arms over his chest. "I just hope you know what you're doin'."

Holly stood and looked up into Annie's eyes. "I'm not mad at you, Mom. You're not gonna go away again, are you? I really want to get to know you."

Cupping both hands around Holly's face, Annie kissed her forehead. "Oh, honey, I want that, too. More than anything. I think it would be best if I left for now, but I've already rented an apartment in Bozeman. As soon as I get my things packed up, I'll be back, I promise."

"Cross your heart and hope to die?"

"You betcha."

Unbearably touched by the love shining in Annie's eyes, John cleared his throat. She looked over at him, her eyebrows raised in query.

"I, uh, think I'd better go check on Rachel," he said. "But I need to talk to you about something before you go back to Denver. I'll come and see you at the motel this afternoon. Say, one o'clock?"

"That's fine, John. My flight's not until four. There's something I need to discuss with you, too."

John detected more than a hint of anxiety in her voice at that last bit, but a crash overhead prevented him from thinking about it much. Whatever she wanted to discuss would have to wait. Rachel needed him now.

Chapter Five

Desperately wishing she could be the one to comfort Rachel, Anne watched John leave the room. Then she turned and found Mike standing beside her, his weathered face filled with sympathy.

"She'll be all right, Annie. C'mon. I'll walk you to your car."

"Can I come too, Grandpa?" Holly asked.

"Not this time, pumpkin. I need a minute alone with your mom, okay?"

Holly looked so disappointed Anne wanted to protest. The glint in her father-in-law's eyes told her that wouldn't be a good idea. She opened her arms to her daughter, inviting a hug. To her intense pleasure, Holly accepted the invitation without a second's hesitation.

Oh, to be able to touch this child and feel her warm, little body pressed so close to hers was enough to make Anne giddy. Rubbing her cheek over Holly's dark, glossy hair, she closed her eyes and savored the moment. It took every bit of willpower she possessed to release Holly. The second she did, her arms literally ached to hold her baby again. And to hold Rachel.

"I'll see you soon, honey," she whispered.

Holly's eyes glistened like rain-drenched emeralds, but she valiantly held back her tears. "'Bye, Mom."

If Mike hadn't taken her arm at that instant, Anne doubted she would have been able to leave at all. The warm, fresh air outside steadied her emotions, however, and when they reached her rental car, she managed to smile at him. Her heart contracted when he smiled back. It seemed so odd to see him standing there without Irene.

"You hang in there, Annie," he said, his voice gruff with affection. "Rachel and John will come around."

"I hope so, Mike. But I'm afraid they'd both be happier if I stayed in Colorado."

"You're not really thinking about..."

Anne shook her head. "No. I couldn't. At least not until I've done everything I can to win their trust again."

"That's the spirit. And don't you worry about Paula, either. John would've married her a long time ago if he'd really wanted to."

The mention of John's girlfriend pierced Anne's heart, but she wasn't about to encourage Mike's tendency to interfere. She knew he meant well, but if she didn't squelch any matchmaking ideas he might be entertaining right now, he was bound to cause trouble. Carefully maintaining a bland expression, she looked up at him.

"I don't have any claim on John. His relationship with Paula is none of my business."

Mike tipped his head to one side and studied her, a thoughtful frown furrowing his forehead. "Sounds like you've already given up on him. Don't you want him back?"

"I don't know. We're different people than we were before, and God knows we had plenty of problems then. I never expected him to stay celibate all this time. If he's found someone who makes him happy, I can't object."

"Aw, c'mon, Annie. This is *me* you're talkin' to. You really think you can let him go?" Mike snapped his fingers. "Just like that?"

She gave him a rueful grin. "I didn't say it would be easy. But I don't know if he'll ever be able to forgive me, and I'm not going to spend the rest of my life apologizing for doing what I had to do. I'm not even sure he'd accept an apology if I offered one."

"Sounds to me like what you're really sayin' is that it all depends on whether John wants *you* back."

"He's a big boy, Mike. If he wanted to try to put our marriage back together, I'd probably be willing to listen. But he's got to make his own decisions about his future."

"It's your future, too," Mike insisted. "And Rachel's. And Holly's. Dammit, you're a family."

"We *were* a family," she said, struggling to hold on to her patience. "But sometimes things happen that can't be fixed. It may be too late for us to be a family again."

"It's never too late when you love somebody, Annie. Not until one of you dies. And I can't believe you're just gonna give everything up without a fight."

"I didn't say that. But I refuse to raise anyone's hopes, not even my own. We've all been hurt enough."

Sighing, Mike rubbed the back of his neck and gazed off into the distance. "Well, that's true. But, Annie, don't give up too soon. No matter what John and Rachel would have you believe, we need you, gal."

"You've all survived just fine without me."

Mike shook his head, then scowled at her. "You're wrong about that. Dead wrong. You were the linchpin that held everybody together. We all fell apart when you disappeared. Especially John. He lost forty pounds and he couldn't sleep for months. For a while there, I thought we were gonna lose him, too."

"And Rachel?" she asked softly.

"She withdrew from everybody. Walked around here like a little ghost. Holly kinda cried it all out in a few weeks, but Rachel's never been quite the same, Annie."

"Did she have any counseling?"

"She and John both went for a couple of years. It helped some, but neither one of 'em seemed happy until Paula came along. It was like . . . she filled a hole inside 'em that nothing but a warm, caring woman could fill."

"Then I'm glad she came along," Anne said. "And I wouldn't dream of doing anything that might upset her. Maybe someday Paula and I can even be friends."

He shot her a doubtful glance, then smiled knowingly. "Uh-huh. Well, she's a likable little gal, Annie. But I'm tellin' you, John doesn't love her the way he loved you."

Smiling fondly at him, Anne sighed and gazed off toward the mountains. "I appreciate your support." She looked back at him again. "I really do. And I know you only want what's best for all of us."

"But?" he prompted when she paused to search for the right words to express her doubts.

"But the thing is, I'm not the woman John loved. Once he gets to know me again, he may not even like me."

"Aw, baloney. You look a little different, but I'd bet this ranch you're still Annie inside."

"Annie's a little girl's name, Mike. It fit when I was married to John because I'd never been on my own before."

"You went to college."

"It's not the same thing. My dad was still paying my bills, and the dorm was a sheltered environment. When I got married, it seemed natural to let John make the big decisions. But I've grown up. I don't believe in happy-ever-after endings anymore."

Mike gazed into her eyes for a long moment. "You really mean that, don't you?"

She shrugged one shoulder. "At this point, I'd be happy to settle for a friendship with John and a chance to be included in whatever pieces of the girls' lives they're willing to share with me."

"Good Lord." He stared at her as if she'd just said the most appalling thing he'd ever heard. "What have they done to you, Annie? What *really* happened to you?"

The thought of describing the murders and their aftermath racked her with a shudder of dread. "I don't talk about it anymore, Mike. It's just too... horrible."

"Aw, Annie." Mike pulled her into a protective embrace that reminded her of her own father so much it brought a painful lump to her throat. "Maybe if John and Rachel really understood..."

Backing away, she shook her head vehemently. "No. Absolutely not. Especially not Rachel. I don't want any of you sharing my nightmares or feeling sorry for me. If I'm going to be accepted back into this family, it has to be because you like the person I am now."

"All right, hon," he said, his voice somber and subdued. "Just remember I'm here if you ever need me."

"I will." She grasped his hand and held it tightly between her palms. "I'm sorry about Irene."

"Yeah. And I'm sorry as hell about your folks, Annie. They would've been damn proud of you."

"I hope so." She squeezed his hand before releasing it. "I'd better go now."

After promising to let Mike know if he could help with the chore of moving, she climbed into the car, started the engine and made a U-turn in the graveled driveway. She looked back at the big, old, two-story house that had sheltered John's family for three generations and saw a curtain twitch at one of the upstairs windows.

Was that Rachel's room? she wondered. Was her daughter standing there staring down at her? Hating her? Needing her?

Her teeth gritted with determination, Anne drove away. Getting through to that kid wouldn't be easy, but she'd do it somehow. For Rachel's sake as much as her own. And no matter what her family ultimately decided about having room for her in their lives, by God, she'd make sure they *made* room for Chad.

Her son needed to know John and Mike, Rachel and Holly. He needed to interact with people other than his paranoid mother and a vigilant deputy U.S. marshal. He needed to have a place where he would always be welcomed, where he could run free, play like other little boys and be safe.

Unfortunately, in order to get all that for Chad, she had to tell John he'd fathered another child. Which would, no doubt, completely reverse the slight softening she thought she'd detected in his attitude toward her. No doubt about it, the man was going to be royally ticked off.

He eventually might have been able to forgive her for her decisions about entering WITSEC. But she didn't believe he would ever forgive her for keeping his son from him for more than six years. She tightened her grip on the steering wheel, bracing herself for the coming showdown. She'd already handled John's wrath twice this week. She could handle it again, right?

"Right," she muttered. Then she looked up into that big, blue Montana sky overhead and sighed. "But why me, Lord? Why me?"

Drained from the emotional whirlwind Annie's visit had unleashed at the ranch, John parked beside the motel, switched off the Suburban's engine and leaned his head against the back of the seat. Closing his eyes, he released a heartfelt sigh and wallowed in a moment of peace.

The counselor he and Rachel had seen for a while had told him repeatedly that in a healthy, functional family, everyone felt free to express negative emotions. If that was true, the Miller family must be pretty damn healthy and functional. He hadn't seen so many negative emotions flying around the house in years.

The counselor would also have told him Annie's return was good for the girls because it allowed them to deal with any unresolved feelings they had about their mother. While he understood that, John dreaded the process. Because now he had to deal with his own unresolved feelings for Annie, too. Analyzing his feelings ranked about as high on his list of fun things to do as visiting a proctologist.

It wouldn't be so bad if he could just hang on to his anger. By any reasonable standards, Annie had given him plenty to be angry about. But underneath his righteous indignation lurked a demon named guilt.

Try as he might to deny it, he had to accept responsibility for his own part in the decisions Annie had made. If he'd been a better husband, she might have trusted him more. Might have included him in those decisions. Might never have been placed in that impossible situation.

As if guilt wasn't enough, he had another demon to contend with—fear. Stark, paralyzing fear. Rachel had articulated it for him when they'd talked in her bedroom that morning.

"Okay, so what if I trust her, Dad?" she'd said, looking at him with anguished eyes that had damn near broken his heart. "What if I let myself get to know her again and I love her again, and then she leaves again? I couldn't stand that a second time. It would hurt too much."

Would it ever, John thought. Short of losing one of his kids, he couldn't imagine anything that would devastate him more. Well, it didn't have to be a problem.

He'd loved Annie once, but that didn't mean he had to love her again. He was forty years old, not some green kid who couldn't control his thoughts and emotions. Hell, Annie didn't seem to be interested in trying to rekindle any old sparks, anyway, so he didn't have a thing to worry about, right?

A knock on his window startled him half out of his wits. Bolting upright, he looked to his left and felt his heart turn a somersault. There was Annie, grinning at him like a mischievous kid enjoying a practical joke. Chuckling in spite of his racing heart, he rolled down the window.

"Sorry I woke you up," she said, sounding about as sorry as a lottery winner.

"I'll bet. Anyway, I wasn't sleeping. Just thinking real hard."

"You'd better be careful about that, John. You might sprain something important."

Damned if she wasn't cute, he thought. She'd always had a sassy mouth, and though he'd given her heck for it on occasion, he'd always enjoyed it when she'd teased him like this. Then the laughter faded from her eyes.

"How's Rachel?" she asked softly.

"All right. Took her horse out for a ride after lunch. That always seems to calm her down when she's upset."

"I'm glad. She's a good rider?"

"Yeah. She's a heck of a ranch hand, too. Since Dad doesn't have any grandsons, I think he's just about decided to turn the place over to her when he retires."

A funny, stricken sort of expression passed across Annie's face. She cleared her throat, glanced at the ground, then looked up at him again.

"So, do you want to come in and talk?" she said before he could ask her what was wrong.

John considered the idea, but Annie's face was so pale and strained, he figured some fresh air and sunshine would probably do her good. "It's too nice a day to waste inside. Why don't we go to a park?"

"All right. I'll go get my purse."

She turned and ran into the building. As John watched her trim little behind switch back and forth under her jeans and felt a swift, automatic tightening below his belt buckle, he was doubly glad he'd suggested the park. Annie could use some sun, all right, but the truth was, he didn't want to be confined in the intimacy of a motel room with her again.

Not that he expected any hanky-panky, but a man couldn't be too careful. Where sex and Annie were concerned, his past record for restraint was nothing to brag about. They'd had plenty of problems during their marriage, but not in the bedroom. *Never* there.

He couldn't even think about the last night they'd spent together without breaking into a sweat and wishing he'd bought his jeans a size larger. Man, oh, man, Annie had been something else that night—tender, playful and at times so intense in her passion, she'd scorched his soul.

Glancing down at his lap, he cursed under his breath and muttered, "Well, *now* you've done it, you damn fool."

Of course, that was the exact moment the woman came bopping out of the door. His mouth went dry. His neck and ears grew hot. The throbbing in his groin increased.

Cursing again, he adjusted his fly, sat up straighter and inhaled a deep breath, forcing himself to focus his attention on the pop cans she carried and away from the more interesting parts of her anatomy. Then he leaned across the seat and opened the passenger door for her. She climbed inside, handed him a can of pop and stuck her own can between her legs while she hunted for her seat belt.

Hell, he was really in trouble now. Big trouble. For crying out loud, Annie wasn't even trying to be sexy, and that was all he could think about. Who said he wasn't a green kid?

Clenching his teeth, he slammed the Suburban into gear, headed down the road and turned onto Main Street. Annie didn't say a word, but she kept shooting perplexed, anxious glances at him that made him feel like a jerk. The Saturday-afternoon traffic was heavy enough to claim his attention, however, and by the time they arrived at Lindley Park on the east side of town, he'd regained most of his equilibrium.

They climbed out of the vehicle and strolled across the lush grass. Annie produced a couple of candy bars from her purse, and they ate them in reasonably comfortable silence while they walked and absorbed the sunshine. Then, spotting a picnic table, she suggested they sit down and talk.

John settled onto the wooden bench across from her, wondering why she suddenly looked tense enough to start gnawing off all her fingernails. Before he could ask what was wrong, she insisted that since he'd requested this meeting, he should go first.

"All right," he said, bracing one elbow on the table. "I just wanted to tell you about the financial arrangements your dad made for you before he died."

Her eyebrows shot up beneath her bangs. "He made arrangements for me?"

"You'd better believe it. I told you he never gave up on you, didn't I?"

"Well, yes, but I never thought... I mean, I just assumed that if he had any money to leave anyone, he would have left it to the girls."

If he had any money to leave, John thought, shaking his head in amusement. Annie was in for quite a surprise, but this time, it would be a nice one.

"Oh, he took care of the kids just fine," John said. "They can go to college anywhere they want, and he set up hefty trust funds they can claim when they're thirty. He made me promise not to tell them about that until they've had a chance to earn their own living for a while, though, and I think that's a good idea."

"Are you serious?"

"Yup. He left me a nice retirement nest egg, too."

"Where on earth did he get that kind of money?" Annie asked. "I know he did okay in the real-estate boom Billings had during the oil crisis, but our house wasn't a showplace and he always bought used cars."

John laughed out loud. "That's how he got all that money, Annie. And he did more than okay. He got out of real estate just before the boom ended and studied everything he could find about investing in the stock market. He was pretty damn good at it. He left you enough that you'll never have to work again if you don't want to."

Annie shot him an incredulous look, then gaped when, as the estate's executor, he quoted the latest figures he'd received.

"Lord, he *was* good, wasn't he?" she murmured, her eyes slightly dazed. Then she sipped from her pop can and set it on the table. "What if I'd never come back?"

"Ten years after his death, your trust fund would have gone to the girls. We'll have to go down to Billings to sign some papers. If you need a loan in the meantime for moving expenses or anything, I'll be glad to help you out."

She bit her lower lip and studied her hands for what felt like an eternity to John. Her utter stillness worried him, especially since he'd thought she'd be ecstatic over her good fortune.

"What about Mom and Dad's house, John?"

"It's in your name with the same ten-year provision as your trust fund. The last time I was in Billings I rented it to a professor from Rocky Mountain College. He's got another year left on his lease, but I think he'd probably agree to move out if you want him to."

"No, I don't want to live in Billings now, anyway. I'm just glad it wasn't sold."

"Your dad wanted you to have it. I didn't know what you'd want of your parents' personal stuff, so I put everything in storage. Maybe you can go through their things when we go down to handle the paperwork."

Her eyes glistening with unshed tears, she managed a wobbly, hopeful smile. "Is there anything of Mom's?"

"Everything but her clothes, Annie," John said. "Your dad was as big a pack rat as you are."

The brief laugh she uttered had a bitter tinge to it. "I'm not a pack rat anymore, John. I haven't accumulated much since I went into the program. But thanks for handling everything. You must have had a big job on your hands."

He shrugged. "Your folks helped me a lot when you disappeared. I was glad to return the favor."

"Dad couldn't have found a better man to trust."

Her voice was a husky whisper, as if her emotions were close to the surface and she couldn't speak any louder without risking a breakdown. Dammit, he wished she'd cut loose and let those tears fall. She seemed so bereft, so alone, and he wanted to hold and comfort her. As if she could read his thoughts in his eyes, however, her chin came up to an angle that said she wouldn't welcome any sympathy from him.

She picked up her pop can, carried it over to a trash barrel and dropped it in. The resulting clang was a harsh, discordant note in the otherwise peaceful setting.

"I don't understand what's going on with you," John said when she returned to the table. "I know nothing can replace your folks, but most people would be happy to find out they're independently wealthy."

"I'm not unhappy about it. It just doesn't quite seem real somehow." She raised one shoulder in a halfhearted shrug and looked off toward the Bridger Mountains. "After what happened with Rachel this morning, I was afraid you wanted to tell me I shouldn't move to Bozeman. I sure didn't expect you to offer me a loan."

John sighed and rubbed the back of his neck. "Look, I know I haven't exactly welcomed you, Annie. And I don't agree with the decisions you made, but I don't hate you."

"I'm glad to hear that. We're going to have to try to get along for the girls' sakes."

"I agree. We'll have to take it slow and easy for a while, but I think it'll be good for the kids to get to know you again."

"How slow and easy?" she asked. "May I come to their birthday parties? Take them on outings? How do I fit in?"

"That'll have to be up to the girls. I'd like for you to clear any invitations you want to offer them with me first. I think if we work together and are honest with each other, we can head off a lot of problems."

Though he wouldn't have thought it possible, her complexion paled even more and he saw her throat work down what looked like a painful gulp. What the heck was the matter with her? What more could he do to be pleasant and reasonable? What was she so damned afraid of?

"I appreciate that, John, and I'll cooperate any way I can." She paused and gulped again, then took a deep breath and continued, the words coming slower and with more hesitation—as if she was having to force every syllable out of her mouth.

"But, there's, um, something I have to tell you, too. I would have told you before, but it seemed like we all had more than enough to handle just with my coming back, so..."

"What is it, Annie?" he asked, unable to bear watching her tie herself into knots like this.

"When I move up here next weekend, Steve Anderson will be coming along to help me get settled."

"Okay," John said, feeling the hairs on the backs of his forearms prickle, though he still wasn't sure where she was headed. "What's the big problem?"

She hesitated so long this time he wanted to shake her for scaring the whey out of him.

"Well, there's ... um, there's someone else I haven't told you about who'll be coming with me, too."

"You mean like a boyfriend?" he asked, finding the thought completely distasteful. "I don't want you parading your lovers in front of the girls."

She stared at him. Then a rosy flush climbed out of the collar of her blouse and into her face. Her eyes flashed with temper and suddenly her speech became fluent again.

"I don't *have* a lover, John, not that it's any of your business. But if I did, I don't think you'd be in any position to complain after what Rachel said about Paula. I didn't get the impression that was a platonic friendship."

"Hey, *you're* the one who left *me*. Don't expect me to feel guilty about Paula, because I won't. With two little kids to take care of, I was lucky to have any opportunity for a love life at all."

"And I'm glad you have one, John. I don't want you to feel guilty."

"Then what the hell are we fighting about?"

"I was trying to explain to you about this other person. If you'll be quiet for five seconds and stop making nasty assumptions—"

"All right, all right, I'll shut up. Just get on with it, will you? Who is this mysterious other person?"

"He's, um . . ." As if all of her anger-fueled bravado had wilted, her shoulders slumped and her eyes suddenly looked bigger and darker than he'd ever seen them before. She cleared her throat and took a deep breath, visibly bolstering her courage before finally spitting it out. "He's your son."

Chapter Six

You sure handled that one with a trainload of finesse and sensitivity, Anne told herself as she watched the color drain from John's face. If he didn't stop gaping at her and remember to breathe soon, she'd have to whack him between the shoulder blades.

She needn't have worried. In the next instant, a crimson flush raced up his neck to the top of his forehead. He shut his mouth with an audible snap. Nostrils flaring, he inhaled so deeply the Montana State bobcat printed on the front of his T-shirt stretched sideways over the muscular expanse of his chest.

"My *what?*"

A shout, a bellow, an indignant roar—any of those reactions would have been preferable to the deadly quiet tone he'd used to ask that question. Suppressing an instinctive shudder of apprehension, Anne forced herself to maintain eye contact.

"Your son, John," she said. "Remember the night before you took the girls to stay with your folks?"

His eyelids lowered to half-mast and there was a sharp break in his breathing that told her he remembered every vivid detail, just as she did. Shoot, she *still* dreamed about that night. Then he shook his head slightly, as if he wanted to shake the memory out of his brain. "You were supposed to be taking the pill."

"Evidently I hadn't been taking it again long enough for it to work. His name is Chad. He had his sixth birthday last month."

John's eyes narrowed to slits, focusing his anger on her as effectively as a laser beam. "And you kept him from me all this time? Damn you, Annie."

"I didn't know I was pregnant until I'd been in the program for almost three months. By then it was too late."

"Oh, right. You've always been so regular."

"I was too busy trying to stay alive to think about the calendar at first," she argued. "And then I thought the stress was messing up my cycle."

"My God," John muttered. He squeezed the bridge of his nose between thumb and forefinger and glared at her again. "How *could* you? What did I ever do to deserve—"

"You didn't *do* anything. And neither did I. We've all been victims of circumstances beyond our control."

He smacked his palms on the table. "Dammit, Annie, it wasn't beyond *your* control. *You* made the decision to leave me and the girls behind. You didn't have any right—"

"Lower your voice or you're going to attract a crowd," she said in a furious whisper. Jabbing her index finger at the bobcat on his chest, she continued, "You don't know what it was like, John. You don't know what I went through. And you still don't know beans about listening."

"If it was all that bad, he would have been safer in Montana. You should have sent him to me."

"I probably should have," Anne admitted quietly. "But it would have meant risking my cover and endangering the whole family."

"That wasn't your decision to make, either. I can't believe it was legal for the government to deny me knowledge of my own son. How did you manage that?"

"I didn't put your name on Chad's birth certificate," she explained. "I said I didn't know who his father was."

The look he gave her could have stripped the hide off a steer at forty yards. He flexed his hands, as if warming them up to wrap around her throat. His voice returned to its former, deadly quiet tone, but now it sounded gritty, as if he'd swallowed a wad of sandpaper.

"I'll never forgive you for this. Of all the dirty, low-down, underhanded . . ."

Bracing both hands on the table, Anne rose from the bench and glared at him. "Look, I understand how you must feel, but you had the girls, your folks and mine. Chad was all I had. He was a *baby* and he needed me. There were times when he was my only reason to go on living."

Imitating her stance, John brought his nose to within an inch of hers. "Oh, yeah? Well, what would have happened to Chad if you *hadn't* gone on living? Would anyone have told me I had a son, or would he have ended up in foster care? Maybe they would have put him up for adoption. Did you ever think of *that?*"

"That wouldn't have happened," Anne said. "Steve and Ben Thorn knew you were Chad's father. They're honorable men—"

"Honorable, my rear end! This whole thing stinks, Annie. It just plain stinks and you damn well know it."

Unable to refute his statement or bear the accusation in his eyes a moment longer, Anne slowly lowered herself onto the bench and covered her face with both hands. She could hear John's harsh breathing, feel the hurt emanating from him, sense the disillusionment tearing at his soul.

The silence stretched out between them like a hundred miles of bad road. The table wobbled as the opposite bench accepted his weight. He heaved a ragged sigh and Anne looked up in time to see him rub one hand down over his face. When he spoke, his voice reeked of weary resignation.

"Where is my son?"

"In Denver. Steve's taking care of him. Would you like to see a picture?"

John nodded. Holding her breath, Anne opened her wallet and pulled out the picture she'd taken of Chad just after he'd lost his top front teeth. She looked at it, drawing strength from the sight of her son's exuberant smile, and slid it across the table. John picked it up, stared at it, then blinked and stared at it some more.

He sucked in a deep breath and his face became slowly and magically transformed. The hard ridge of muscle that had been standing out along the line of his jaw relaxed. The grim slash that was his mouth softened, curving up slightly at the corners. A wistful, hungry expression chased the fury from his eyes.

His reaction didn't surprise Anne. Chad was an adorable little boy. His grin expressed an impish delight in himself and the world around him, and it was the best therapy for depression and despair she'd ever found. John might be livid with her, but she knew he didn't own a hard enough heart to resist Chad.

The knot of tension in her stomach eased slightly. "I mentioned the Miller genes before," she said. "See any family resemblance?"

John glanced at her, then back at the photograph. "If you put my first-grade picture next to this one, I'm not sure anyone could tell us apart."

"He was born on April fifteenth."

"Dad's birthday?"

She nodded. "I think Mike'll get a kick out of that."

"He'll go nuts over this kid." John smiled at the photograph, sighed again and shook his head before focusing his attention back on Anne. His smile evaporated like raindrops on a hot sidewalk. "For God's sake, if you've got any more bombs to drop on me, do it now."

"That was the last one." Ignoring his snort of disbelief, she tucked her wallet back into her purse and waved his hand away when he tried to give the picture back. "Keep it. Mike and the girls will want to see it."

"Does Chad know about me?"

"Of course. Steve's been wonderful about spending time with him, but Chad's been asking about his dad ever since he started preschool. He's anxious to meet you."

"Why didn't you bring him along?" John asked.

"Because this is his last week of kindergarten and I didn't want him to miss it."

"Uh-huh. Sure you didn't want to save him for a bargaining chip in case I wouldn't let you see the girls?"

"I didn't need one, remember? Another reason I didn't bring him with me was that I want him to like all of you. He's protective of me, so I didn't want him to see us fighting like this."

After checking her watch, she closed the zipper on her purse and slung the strap over her shoulder. "I'd better get back to the motel."

"Not so fast." John reached across the table and grabbed her wrist before she could stand. "How do I know you won't disappear again?"

Anne blew out an exasperated sigh. "I'll be back by the end of the week, John. Saturday at the latest. Will you stop being so damn suspicious?"

"Hey, for all I know, you don't even live in Colorado."

Anne jerked her arm out of his grasp, unzipped her purse and dumped its contents onto the table. Muttering under her breath, she tossed her wallet, her checkbook, her airline ticket, a notepad and a pen in front of John.

"Take a look at that stuff, find all my ID and write down anything you want. Go ahead and be damn quick about it. I've got a plane to catch."

John went to work, tossing each item back at her when he'd finished with it. Seething, Anne shoved them into her purse and started walking to the parking area while John tucked the paper he'd written on into his hip pocket. Neither spoke until he'd parked in front of the entrance to her motel.

One hand on the passenger-door latch, Anne turned to him. "I'll call you when my plans are finalized. For whatever it's worth, I never meant to hurt you or anyone else. Have a good week."

Before John could respond, Annie jumped out of the Suburban and slammed the door. He waited until his ears stopped ringing, then drove away, cursing her and himself and the whole damn situation six ways from Sunday. By the time he reached Main Street again, he'd blown off enough steam to breathe normally again. By the time he pulled into the driveway at the ranch, he was ready to think rationally. At least he thought he was.

He unfastened his seat belt, pulled out his wallet and flipped through the plastic holders until he found Chad's picture. The sight of his son's face aroused a host of emotions. Pride. Joy. Anger and grief for all the time he'd lost with the boy, time he could never reclaim.

Though he adored his daughters and wouldn't trade either one of them for all the boys on earth, he had to admit there was something mighty special about seeing this small, masculine version of himself. The kid looked like he was all boy—probably chock-full of energy and mischief.

Damned if he wasn't the cutest little stinker John had ever seen. It wouldn't be hard to love the kid. But would Chad find it easy to love him?

An emotion that came dangerously close to fear filled John's chest. In a bizarre, detached sort of way, he almost admired the slick method Annie had used to trap him. He had possession of the girls. She had his son. A son, she had taken pains to point out, who was protective of his mother.

"In other words, bucko," John grumbled, "don't mess with the kid's mom if you want him to like you."

Oh, she'd said she hadn't planned to use Chad as a bargaining chip, but he didn't believe it. Not after the way she'd betrayed him. And to think he'd actually started to like her again. To feel sorry for what she'd been through. To want to help her regain Rachel's affection.

He could rip out his tongue and stomp on it for that sappy little speech he'd made about working together and being honest with each other. That woman wouldn't know honesty if it bit her on the butt.

Well, he knew things about little boys she could never hope to learn. He'd play along with Annie until Chad got to know him. Then she'd better watch her step. It would be one frigid day in hell before he'd ever trust her again.

But even as that last thought finished echoing through his mind, his conscience reared up and forced him to stop right there and take another look at what he'd been thinking.

Annie's actions had hurt him more than she would ever know. But whatever else he chose to believe about her, he knew damn well she would never do anything to harm her children. And deep down inside, despite all the wounds she'd inflicted, he couldn't honestly believe that she had intentionally set out to hurt him, either.

The one sure way to hurt the kids—all three of them—would be to start a war with their mother. He didn't have to trust Annie as a wife anymore. He didn't have to love her again, God forbid. But no matter how much it galled him, he *had* to establish a working relationship with her.

She still seemed like a stranger in lots of ways, and there were bound to be plenty of problems ahead. But he'd treat her with civility if it killed him. Yeah, that was the ticket. Work with Annie, instead of against her, for the kids' sakes, and avoid any kind of emotional involvement for his own.

That shouldn't be all that hard. Other than being his children's mother, Annie meant nothing to him now. He wouldn't want to resurrect their marriage, even if there was a snowball's chance in hell of doing that, right? Well, *right?*

Unable to honestly answer that the way he wanted to, John climbed out of the Suburban. Then, slamming the door hard enough to make the big vehicle shimmy, he stomped toward the house, muttering about fools and idiots.

* * *

Anne returned to Denver to be met by an ecstatic Chad and a weary Steve. When she'd finally managed to tuck her son into bed and Steve had left for his own apartment, she started listing all the things she needed to accomplish. Being able to plan a move was a pleasant change.

The days zipped by at an incredible pace. She should have been exhausted by Thursday night, but she was too wired to sleep. Unable to tolerate lying in bed or even sitting on the couch, she wandered aimlessly through her apartment. With no personal possessions lying around, the rooms looked bleak, and a crushing sense of loss filled her heart.

The apartment had never been luxurious, but it had been the best home she could make of it. Chad had learned to print his letters and colored a million pictures for her at that table. While she hadn't been deliriously happy here, she'd managed to find a measure of contentment.

Was she crazy to leave? To start all over again with no guarantees that life in Bozeman would be any better? When it could, in fact, be much worse? She'd love spending time with Holly and Mike, but what if Rachel and John never forgave her? Was she setting herself up for a disappointment that would shatter her heart for good?

She wrapped her arms around herself as she gazed into the darkness beyond her kitchen window. "It's too late to go back, Anne. You have to go forward."

By the time morning arrived, she was more than ready to leave. With Steve along to share the driving and help her entertain Chad, the first day of the trip was easier than she'd expected. She enjoyed seeing the plains and mountains of Wyoming, and told herself that if the pioneers could cross this barren, rugged terrain in covered wagons with no towns to offer comfort on the other end of their journey, surely she could survive whatever lay ahead in Bozeman.

Still, it felt odd to be out on the open road. All the traveling she'd done since entering WITSEC had been by air. Though Steve maintained a relaxed, confident attitude, she kept a close eye on the rearview mirror, watching for signs of a vehicle tailing them. Old habits died hard.

They spent the night in Jackson Hole, hit the drive-through window at a fast-food restaurant for breakfast the next morning and headed north through Grand Teton and Yellowstone national parks. His nose pressed against his window, Chad spotted elk, moose, deer and a small herd of buffalo with five new calves.

They stretched their legs at Old Faithful, watched the famous geyser erupt and got to West Yellowstone by eleven o'clock. Eager to reach Bozeman and get settled, Anne bought doughnuts and sodas and drove the final sixty miles through the Gallatin Canyon. She called the ranch from the Kountry Korner café at Four Corners.

Mike answered the phone. "Annie? You're already here? Well, that's great. John took Rachel into town for a haircut, and Holly and I are bakin' cookies. Come on out and have some with us."

"We're not going to stop in right now," she said. "I just wanted to let you know we'd arrived."

"Aw, Annie," Mike wheedled. "I want to meet my grandson. We'll whip up some lunch."

"My apartment's unfurnished, Mike, and I don't have any furniture. If I don't get into Bozeman and buy some beds, we'll be sleeping on the floor."

"Well, shoot, you don't have to buy anything. John's got everything from your house in Chicago stored in the old barn. Come and take a look, and I'll haul anything you want in the pickup."

"You don't think John would mind?"

"Why should he? He's not usin' any of it."

Despite the logic of his statement, Anne hesitated. "I don't know. Maybe I'd better wait and ask him."

"It's not like you're gonna sell any of that stuff. Where's the harm in your borrowing a few things? Lord knows we've got plenty of furniture around here."

"Well, okay. Besides, I *would* like to see what's stored from my folks' house before I buy anything."

"I'll see you in ten minutes," Mike said, hanging up before she could answer.

Chuckling to herself, Anne returned to the car and related the change in plans to Steve and Chad. When they got to the Flying M, Mike and Holly greeted them effusively at the front door. Unused to accepting so much attention from strangers, Chad hung back, clutching Steve's hand.

Mike acted as if he hadn't noticed and led the group to the kitchen. While everyone else attacked the chocolate-chip cookies cooling on the counter, he grabbed a set of keys from a Peg-Board and a box of rags from under the sink.

Accepting the impossibility of slowing down her mule-headed father-in-law, Anne followed Mike out to the truck, helped Chad onto the high seat and climbed in beside him. Holly and Steve climbed into the pickup's bed. After a bone-jarring ride over a rutted path to the south of the house, Mike parked in front of a weathered barn.

Laying one hand on Chad's shoulder, Mike gazed at the building for a long moment. "My great-grandpa helped his daddy build this old barn back in 1870, Chad. There's been a Miller man workin' this place ever since. You could be the next one to take over if you're interested."

"Really?" Chad asked.

Ruffling the boy's hair, Mike chuckled. "You're a Miller man, aren't you?"

"No, my last name's Martin."

"Well, you're a Miller man all the same," Mike said. "And you've got as much right to this land as anyone."

Remembering the heated arguments John and Mike had had over this very issue, Anne frowned at her father-in-law. "Chad's got plenty of time to decide what he wants to do when he grows up."

Giving her an oh-so-innocent grin, Mike shrugged. "It won't hurt him to have a little sense of his family's history, Annie."

Then he opened the barn doors, the rusty hinges creaking in protest. Wrinkling her nose at the musty smell, Anne paused in the doorway while her eyes adjusted to the dim light inside.

"I tried to get John to go through all this stuff, but he never had the heart to do it." Mike gestured toward a tower of boxes standing beside a jumbled stack of furniture. "The movers piled everything up like that. I covered it all in plastic in case the roof leaked, but I imagine the mice have done some damage. Good thing I put the mattresses in the attic at the house."

Anne gulped at the enormity of the task Mike had presented to her. She hadn't taken much with her when she'd moved into the apartment in Chicago because she hadn't intended to stay in it very long. That plastic-shrouded mountain contained the physical remnants—a history of sorts—of her marriage to John.

She could never go through all of it in one day, but she could get an idea if there was anything worthwhile left. Pushing the sleeves of her sweatshirt to her elbows, she waded into the mess, kicking up a blizzard of dust motes.

John turned into the ranch driveway half an hour later and felt a nervous, fluttering sensation in the pit of his stomach when he saw the little blue car with Colorado plates parked in front of the house.

"Oh, great, they're already here," Rachel grumbled, scowling at the car as if she'd like to kick its tires.

"Don't you want to meet your brother?" John asked.

"Why should I?" she demanded. "Everybody I know who's got one says little brothers are a pain in the butt."

"Watch it, Rach," John said mildly. "Be mad at your mom if you have to, but Chad's just a little kid. None of what happened is his fault."

She shrugged and climbed out of the Suburban without a reply. John followed, taking a deep breath as he stepped into the entry.

"Dad? Annie? Where is everybody?" he called, hanging his Stetson on a peg by the door.

He checked the living room, then the dining room, feeling more and more puzzled when no one answered him.

"There's a note out here from Grandpa," Rachel shouted from the kitchen. "They're at the old barn. He wants you to bring the Suburban."

Impatient to meet his son, John put his hat back on. "Come on, Rach. Let's go."

She walked into the hallway, a cookie in each hand and a mutinous look in her eyes. "Do I *have* to, Dad?"

"Yeah." John snatched one of the cookies and nudged her out the front door. "Stop whining and get a move on."

By the time he'd parked beside his dad's pickup, the critters in John's stomach had gone from flutters to great, swooping swan dives. The barn doors stood wide open as if in invitation, and a jumble of conversation and laughter came from inside. His gut knotted and a drop of sweat slid down the side of his neck. He caught a glimpse of a small face with curious green eyes and a mop of dark hair, heard a child's voice.

"Mom, there's a guy out there. And a girl, too."

There was an instant of silence. Then Annie appeared in the doorway, holding a little boy's hand. John was vaguely aware of some other people coming out of the barn behind them, and of Rachel stepping close to his side, but he couldn't focus on anything but Annie and Chad.

They looked . . . right together. He could almost see the aura of love and trust surrounding them as they approached him. Between wary glances at John, Chad looked at his mother. She didn't say a word, but whatever silent reassurance she gave the boy obviously satisfied him.

John's chest and throat felt tight and the backs of his eyes stung. Dammit, *he* wasn't supposed to be the emotional one in this family. Annie was. But she looked as cool and serene as the spring wildflowers in the meadow behind the barn. The reversal of roles made him feel too vulnerable and exposed, and he resented it to the heels of his boots.

They stopped two feet in front of him. Chad tipped his head way back and gazed into John's eyes for a gut-wrenching moment. "Is that *him,* Mom?"

Annie nodded. "Yes, honey. This is your dad."

"Really?" Chad asked, studying John again, his voice hushed with awe. Then he whipped his head around and looked at his mother. "He's the wonderful man?"

"Gee, I hope so," John said, trying to smile as he squatted on his heels in front of Chad. Tipping back his Stetson, he offered his hand to the boy. "I'm glad to meet you, son."

Chad hesitated for a moment, then cautiously placed his hand in John's. "I'm glad to meet you, too."

"What's all this about a wonderful man?" John asked.

Digging the toe of one sneaker into the grass, Chad leaned back against Annie's legs and gave John a bashful grin. "Whenever I ask about my dad, Mom always says he's the most wonderful man in the whole world."

"She does?"

"Uh-huh. Are you really wonderful?"

John cleared his throat. "Well, I do my best, but I make mistakes like anyone else. It was nice of her to say that, though."

"Oh, my mom's real, *real* nice," Chad said earnestly.

"Yeah, I know," John replied. Straightening to his full height, he smiled down at Chad. "That's why I married her. I'll bet you're pretty nice, too."

A gleeful light danced in Chad's eyes and he scrunched his mouth up to one side as if seriously considering the truth of John's statement. Then he firmly shook his head. "Steve says I'm a mangy little varmint."

"Why does he call you that?" John asked.

Chad shot a smug grin at a tall blond man standing behind him, then said, " 'Cause I won't let him win at poker. He really likes me, though."

"I do not, shorty," the blond man said, reaching out to ruffle the boy's dark hair.

Then he offered his hand to John, along with a broad, genuine smile. "I'm Steve Anderson. Glad to finally meet you, Miller. You've got yourself quite a boy here."

John looked into Anderson's clear gray eyes and shook his hand. The other man had a solid grip, but he didn't get into any strength contests. John thought he might have liked the guy under other circumstances, but there was something about the way Anderson hovered close to Annie and Chad that irritated him.

"Yeah, he sure seems to be," John said.

Chad turned and playfully pummeled Steve's midsection. Steve scooped him up in one arm and slung him over his shoulder. Flailing his arms and legs, Chad shrieked with delight. Steve spun him around a few times, then turned him upright and set him on his feet.

"Behave yourself or I'll dangle you by your heels, kid," he threatened good-naturedly.

"I dare ya," Chad shouted. "C'mon, Steve, I dare ya!"

"Not right now," Anne said firmly.

"Aw, Mom!"

"No, Chad. Your other sister wants to meet you."

John nudged Rachel forward. "This is Rachel, Chad."

Chad tipped his head way back again and studied her. "Wow, you're a babe, too," he said, gravely shaking her hand. "Just like Holly."

Rachel's mouth quirked at the corners, then slowly turned up in a reluctant grin. "You're not so bad yourself, little bro."

"Bro? Is that anything like a bra?" Chad asked, wrinkling his nose as if the idea disgusted him.

Giggling, Rachel went down on one knee and gently smoothed down the hair Steve Anderson had ruffled. "No, it means brother. It's kinda like a nickname, you know?"

"Oh. I guess it's okay, then. I've never been a brother before. I'm not sure what I'm s'posed to do."

"Well, I've never *had* a brother before, so I'm not sure, either. We'll figure it out together, okay?"

"Okay." Chad glanced back and gave Holly a charming grin that made her giggle. "Holly, too?"

"Yeah. Holly, too. She's never had a brother, either."

Chad pointed his thumb over his shoulder at the barn. "Want to help us find stuff in there? We don't have any furniture, so my mom's borrowin' some. It used to be hers or something."

Rachel stiffened at the reminder of Annie. Shaking her head, she got to her feet. "No. I have homework to do, Chad. I'll see you later, though."

"Is it okay if I play with your old toys? Holly found a whole box of 'em."

"You can have 'em if you want." She turned to John. "I'll walk back to the house, Dad."

"Don't you want to stick around?" he asked quietly.

She shot a resentful glance at her mother and shook her head. "No. I've got finals next week."

It was a lame excuse and they both knew it. Rachel despised studying as much as she loved horses. Though he hated to see her isolate herself from the rest of the family, John decided not to force the issue. She'd warmed up to Chad fine and he was proud of her for that. Maybe she just needed more time to get used to Annie.

"All right, Rach. We'll see you later."

"Well," Mike said as she walked away, "we'd better get back to work. Steve, why don't you give me a hand with the bed frames?"

Steve nodded and the two men went back into the barn. Holly held her hand out to Chad. "I found something else you're gonna like, Chad. Wanna come see?"

Chad eagerly accepted her invitation, taking her hand without hesitation. John's heart contracted as he watched him scamper off with his sister.

"You handled him beautifully," Annie said softly.

"Did I?" John asked. "It seemed like he was scared of me."

"It wasn't you personally, John. Mike got the same treatment." She shrugged one shoulder. "Chad's learned to be wary of strangers, especially men."

"He's not wary of your friend Anderson."

"He's known Steve since the day he was born. Give Chad a little time. He'll come around."

John sighed and rubbed the back of his neck. "All right, I'll try to be patient. But dammit, it just seems so unfair."

"That's how I feel about Rachel."

Her simple, heartfelt statement, coupled with the empathy in her eyes, eased his frustration. For the first time that day, he really studied her appearance. She wore her glasses, jeans, sneakers and a pink sweatshirt with blue and green letters across the front that read, "If MAMA ain't happy, ain't NOBODY happy." And there were lighter, golden streaks scattered through her hair now. It looked softer, more like the way he remembered it.

Suddenly he wanted to touch her, to hug her and comfort her and reconnect, if only on a physical level. To thank her for telling his son he was "the most wonderful man in the whole world," even though she obviously hadn't believed it. If she had, she would have taken him into the WITSEC program with her.

The thought cut deep. Shoving his hands into his jeans pockets to prevent himself from doing something stupid, he inclined his head toward the barn. "I'm surprised you want any of that old stuff."

"Until I have a chance to go shopping, it will really come in handy," she said. "We really don't have any furniture."

"Why not? I thought the government took pretty good care of people like you."

"They pay a subsistence, John. And they help with emergency moving funds, but they expect you to earn your own living as soon as possible."

"Have you been teaching?"

She shook her head. "A new profession is part of your cover. I worked as a waitress and a motel maid until we got to Denver. And then, thanks to you, I was able to start my own business.''

"Thanks to me?''

"You taught me a lot about computers. Steve lent me the money for a PC, and I've been doing free-lance word processing. I've loved being able to stay home with Chad.''

"Could you make enough to support yourself?''

"We got by,'' she said with a shrug.

"Then why don't you have any furniture?''

"I never knew when I might have to move at a moment's notice, so we always rented furnished apartments. If you don't mind my borrowing this stuff, it'll be nice to have some familiar things around me again.''

Good Lord, what kind of a life had Annie and Chad been living? It sounded like something out of a movie, and he didn't like to think of her and Chad going without the basic comforts he'd always provided for his family.

"We never got around to dividing it up after the divorce,'' he said, his tone more curt than he'd intended. "Take whatever you need, Annie. Half of it's yours.''

"Well, um, I guess I'd better get back to work then. Maybe you should come along and make sure I don't take anything you want.''

"If I'd wanted anything from our marriage, it wouldn't be sitting out here.''

For an instant, pain flashed in her eyes. Then, without saying a word, she straightened her shoulders, turned on her heel and walked into the barn. Feeling like a jerk for letting his irritation run away with his mouth, John cursed under his breath and followed, telling himself he'd better watch his step.

If he wanted to get acquainted with his son, he couldn't afford to alienate Annie. But he didn't understand why his careless remark had hurt her feelings. She'd been the one who had ended their marriage. What difference did it make to her whether or not he wanted any of the stuff they'd collected together?

Chapter Seven

Telling herself that since John didn't want anything from their marriage, she might as well pack up the whole mess and take it with her right now, Anne marched into the barn. The stack of boxes she had yet to investigate brought reality crashing down on her. She would never be able to fit even half this stuff into the two-bedroom apartment she'd rented. And when she brought her parents' things back from Billings...

Well, maybe she'd start looking for a house. A big one with a fenced yard so Chad could finally have a dog. She'd soon have enough money to buy whatever she wanted. The more she thought about it, the more she liked the idea.

Owning her own home would give her a sense of permanence and security. Maybe she'd buy a brand-new one, make a really fresh start. For now, she'd take only the things that had the most sentimental value to her.

A squeal of laughter drew her attention to the play area Holly had set up for Chad. John and the kids were hunched over the old hockey set Rachel used to love. The sight of those dark heads so close together brought a lump to Anne's throat.

How many times had she imagined such a scene? A hundred thousand, at least. And wouldn't she love to go over there and join them? Knowing John would welcome her about as much as he'd welcome a rattler at a backyard barbecue, she sighed and went back to work.

Ten minutes later, Chad appeared at her side. "Whatcha doin', Mom?"

"I'm still going through boxes, honey," she replied.

"How long's it gonna take?" he asked.

Rubbing the small of her back, Anne straightened and surveyed the mess waiting for her. Lord, it didn't look as if she'd made any progress at all. "I don't know. Another couple of hours, anyway."

"But I'll starve to death before then," he protested.

She glanced at her watch and noted that it had been hours since he'd had a snack. "Give me another twenty minutes and we'll see about finding some food, okay?"

John approached her with a neutral expression on his face. "Looks like you could use some help. If Chad and I opened the boxes, that would speed things up for you."

"Yeah," Chad agreed, gazing at his father with a broad grin. "I like to open boxes. It's kinda like Christmas."

"I'll go up to the house and make some sandwiches," Holly offered. "Then you won't have to stop for too long."

"Good idea, Holly," John said, fishing a pocketknife out of his jeans. "Get some chips and drinks, too, and have Rachel help you carry it all down here."

Determined to act as if John's presence had no effect on her, Anne reached for the next box. John followed suit, and before long, she had to admit the work went twice as fast. By the time Holly returned with Rachel, followed by Mike and Steve, who had taken a load of furniture into town, the mountain had shrunk to a hill.

Everyone washed up in the creek, then gathered around the cooler Holly had packed. Chad plunked himself down beside Rachel, and to Anne's relief, the girl patiently answered his continuous stream of questions. Though the atmosphere in the barn remained congenial, Anne felt too uptight to eat more than a few bites.

Taking her soda can with her, she unobtrusively went back to the boxes. The conversation of the others flowed around her, and she listened as she worked, smiling at Chad's shameless efforts to charm his sisters. Then she opened a carton marked "Basement" and couldn't prevent a delighted gasp when she saw its contents.

"Whad'ja find, Mom?" Chad asked.

Feeling her face grow warm at the sudden attention she was receiving, Anne tried to shrug off her discovery. "Just some keepsakes, honey."

Chad scrambled to his feet and ran across the room. "Lemme see," he demanded, yanking a chunk of the mover's wrapping paper out of the way.

Before she could stop him, he picked up a chipped ashtray and frowned at it. "You don't even smoke, Mom. What's so special about this?"

"It, uh, well, came from the hotel where your dad and I spent our honeymoon, Chad."

"Really?" Holly asked, hurrying over for a look.

The next thing Anne knew, Chad and Holly were taking turns removing everything from the box and asking about each item. John and Rachel came over to watch, as well, standing to Anne's right and slightly behind her.

Chad waved an empty champagne bottle under Anne's nose. "How come you saved this?"

"The hospital gave that to us the night Rachel was born, Chad. The little pink bow was on her bassinet."

"Is this me?" Holly asked, her voice squeaking with excitement as she handed Anne a framed photograph.

Anne looked at it, then smiled and nodded. "You're the squalling baby. And that's Rachel holding you in my room the day after you were born."

"Didn't you save anything from when I was borned?" Chad demanded.

"Of course I did, honey," Anne assured him. "Your keepsakes are in the car because you were born later."

Satisfied with her explanation, he continued pawing through the box, coming up with some things even Anne had to admit were a little ridiculous—a swizzle stick from her drink at a fancy restaurant John had taken her to for their anniversary, the hideous lamp she hadn't been able to part with because it had been a wedding present, a pretty rock she'd found on a camping trip.

She didn't tell the kids that that particular camping trip had resulted in her first pregnancy, but judging by the lusty gleam in John's eyes, she knew he remembered. And then, ever so subtly, the tension between them eased. As more and more treasures came out of the box, John began contributing to the conversation.

Before long, their sentences started with "Remember when..." and ended with nostalgic sighs and chuckles. It was as if the silly, sentimental items contained in that cardboard box held magical powers that leached out the old hurts and misunderstandings and left behind only the warm, sweet memories of their life together.

Holly held up a slender photo album bound in white leather. "Wow, check this out. These are from your wedding, aren't they?"

Oh, dear, Anne thought, giving Holly a jerky nod. She wasn't ready to look at that particular keepsake. She glanced over her shoulder at John. He'd leaned closer to see what had caught Holly's interest. When he recognized the book, his gaze flew to meet Anne's and held it.

The barn, the boxes, the children all faded into the background of her consciousness. The years dropped away and she could almost smell the flowers, hear the soft organ music, feel the excitement and anticipation, the glowing hopes and dreams that had filled them both the day those pictures had been taken. John's eyes had burned with the same green fire she saw burning in them now, and for a heartbeat, they became that earnest young couple again, solemnly vowing to love, honor and cherish each other forever.

"You look like that was the happiest day of your life, Mom," Holly said, her voice sounding to Anne as if she was standing yards farther away than she actually was.

Unable to blink, much less look away from John's eyes, Anne whispered, "It was, Holly. Believe me, it was."

More shaken than he wanted to admit, John forced his gaze away from Annie's and cleared his throat. "Well," he said, his voice sounding so thick to his own ears he cleared his throat again. "We'd, uh, better finish up here and get on with the moving part."

From the corner of his eye, he saw Annie shiver and shake her head as if she'd been released from a trance. Suddenly she was all business. Setting the keepsake box aside, she reached for the next one and shooed the children back to their sandwiches.

John waited until they were out of earshot, then hooked one finger under her chin, tipping her head up so he could see her face again. Her fingers crumpled a wad of wrapping paper and her eyes held a wary expression when she finally met his gaze.

"I guess our marriage meant something to you, after all," he said softly.

She pulled her chin out of his grasp and looked down at her hands. "Of course it did. I don't know how you could ever have thought otherwise."

"The divorce might have had something to do with it."

She shot him a scowl, then chucked the paper onto the floor. "You know damn well I didn't want to go through with it. If you hadn't been such a stubborn cuss . . ."

"Yeah, I acted like a jerk," he admitted, smiling to himself when she looked at him again, her eyes wide with surprise. "If you'll think back for a second, you'll remember I was trying to make things right with you again."

"I remember."

The softening in her voice encouraged him to ask the question that had haunted him since she'd returned. "If you hadn't gotten tangled up in that mess, would you have married me again, Annie?"

"Come on, you know the answer to that."

He shook his head. "I know what I believed at the time. What I wanted to believe, anyway. But after you disappeared, I was never really sure."

A thoughtful, faraway look entered her eyes. Then one side of her mouth twitched as if she was fighting a grin. "Let me put it to you this way," she said. "You know where I went shopping the day I got tangled up in that mess?"

"You said at the mall."

"That's right, but which store at the mall?"

"How should I know? You liked Marshall Field's—"

"Nope. I only hit one store that day and it wasn't Marshall Field's."

"So, which one was it?" he asked.

"You want a hint?" She was obviously enjoying his inability to solve her little mystery.

"Why don't you just tell me?"

"I like tormenting you, John. You want a hint or not?"

"All right, give me the damn hint," he grumbled, though he wasn't nearly as irritated as he was trying to sound. The truth was, it was nice to see Annie's impish sense of humor again.

"You bought my Christmas present at the same store the year after we moved to Chicago."

With that, she picked up the box she'd been sorting and carried it outside. Too busy trying to figure out her hint, John didn't pay much attention. Rachel had been three when they'd moved to Chicago, so that must have been the Christmas before Holly was born. What the heck had he bought Annie that year? The Chicago cutlery?

No, that couldn't be right. A set of knives wouldn't have put that sparkle in her eyes—unless she'd been planning to cut his throat with one. The kids all laughed at something, and he glanced across the room at them. The second he laid eyes on Holly, he knew the puzzle had something to do with her.

Holly's birthday was on September twenty-fifth, nine months to the day after Christmas. Annie had teased him about giving her a baby with her Christmas present, so that must have been the year he'd bought the black, slinky negligee.

Smacking his forehead with the heel of his hand, he laughed, and like an idiot, practically shouted the answer. "Of course! Frederick's of Hollywood!"

Everyone else in the barn suddenly stopped talking and gaped at him as if he'd just sprouted horns.

"What did you say, Dad?" Rachel asked.

"Nothing," John muttered, feeling his neck get hot.

The memories that flashed into his mind raised his temperature another ten degrees and sent an embarrassing rush of blood below his waist. Then he heard a whoop of laughter from outside and found himself chuckling in spite of his discomfort. Now, *that* sounded like his Annie.

The rest of the day passed in a blur of activity. Though there was still plenty of rearranging and putting away to do, Anne was pleased with what had already been accomplished. The beds were set up and made. The kitchen and bathroom were scrubbed and stocked with the essentials. Best of all, the whole family had worked together without any major blowups.

While Rachel had kept her distance from Anne, she'd come into town and helped Holly entertain Chad. Even if it hadn't been a spectacular start on a new relationship with her firstborn, Anne told herself she'd expected far less. The kids appeared to like each other, and Chad had loosened up with John. Wasn't that enough for one day?

Mike drove the girls home at eight o'clock, and after receiving his first real hug from Chad, John announced that he needed to leave, too. Steve offered to supervise Chad's bath, freeing Anne to walk John out to his Suburban.

Neither spoke until they reached the vehicle. The neighborhood was quiet, the evening air cool and refreshing.

Though they hadn't exchanged a cross word for hours, Anne felt tension growing inside her with every step.

John paused at the front bumper and turned to her with a lopsided smile that made her suspect his emotions were every bit as ambivalent as hers. Would it always be like this whenever they didn't have other family members present to act as buffers? The prospect drained her of optimism, much like the approaching night drained the vivid red and purple hues of the sunset radiating from behind the mountains.

"Thanks for all your help today," she said.

He gave her an I'd-do-the-same-for-anybody shrug. "No problem. It was a great way to get acquainted with Chad."

"I'm glad it worked out." Feeling excruciatingly awkward because she couldn't think of another thing to say, she stepped back, inclining her head toward the apartment triplex. "Well, uh, thanks again, John. I guess I'll be seeing you . . . sometime."

He reached for her arm before she could turn away. "Annie, wait a minute."

Her muscles tensed at his touch, though there was nothing threatening about his attitude. It was silly and she knew it, but even with the thick fabric of her sweatshirt between his skin and hers, she suddenly felt connected to him—and she wasn't ready to feel that way about him again. Muttering a curse under his breath, he released her and shoved his hands into his pockets.

"I'm not going to hurt you," he said.

"I'm sorry. It just surprised me, that's all. Did you, uh, want to talk about something?"

Eyeing her skeptically, he leaned back against the vehicle and crossed one booted foot over the other. "I just wanted to thank you for telling Chad I was wonderful. It helped a lot that he was prepared to like me."

"He needs a father, John. I wanted him to like you for his sake as much as yours."

"It was still a nice thing to do. A lot of divorced women turn the kids against their dads, and I didn't handle your coming back very well. I was afraid you wouldn't show up today after the way I acted when you told me about Chad."

"I didn't blame you for being upset," she said softly.

"Well, I'm sorry if I've made this harder for you than it had to be. I know you've got a lot to cope with now."

"Forget it. No matter what kind of problems you and I have, I really want us to work together where the kids are concerned."

He pulled his hands out of his pockets and crossed his arms over his chest. "That's the only reason you came back? For the kids, I mean?"

She hesitated before answering, wishing she could decipher from his expression how he felt about asking that question. No such luck. He'd always been good at hiding his emotions when he wanted to. It seemed that the years of separation had honed his skills.

"Basically," she said, opting for caution until she knew where he was heading.

"What about me?" he asked. "You didn't have any thoughts at all about us getting back together?"

She looked off toward the mountains. "You've got a girlfriend, John. I don't intend to interfere in your relationship with her, if that's what you're worried about."

"We're not talking about Paula. We're talking about us. What did you have in mind when you came back?"

God, how humiliating it would be to admit how much she'd wanted him back and then have him reject her! Refusing even to glance at him for fear she would betray herself, she asked, "What difference does it make?"

"None, I guess," he said. "But I'd kind of like to know. We meant a lot to each other once, Annie."

"Yes, we did," she agreed slowly. "I'll admit that I wanted to see you as much as I wanted to see the girls. But I didn't expect you to be unattached after all this time."

"But if I had been?"

Damn, he was worse than the defense attorneys who had grilled her without mercy at the trials. Well, she hadn't lied then, and she wouldn't lie now, but that didn't mean she had to spill her guts.

"I honestly don't know. But I've learned to accept things as they are. Paula obviously means a lot to you and the girls, and I wouldn't dream of interfering."

"You really mean that, don't you?"

"Of course. Isn't that what you wanted to hear?"

It was John's turn to look away. "I don't know what I wanted to hear," he said. "The truth is, Paula and I broke up the other night."

"Because of me?" Anne asked, horrified at the thought. He would always resent her for this. So would Rachel.

"She thought you deserved a chance to get your family back." He glanced at Anne and shook his head. "Don't look so appalled. Paula never believed I was really over you. It wasn't like we were engaged or anything."

"I'm sorry, John. I'll talk to her if you think it'll do any good."

Turning to face her, he crammed his hands into his pockets again. "What would you say? That there isn't any hope of a reconciliation between us?"

She raised her chin and returned his challenging stare with one of her own. "Well, there isn't, is there?"

To Anne's surprise, he hesitated before answering, tracing a crack in the sidewalk with the toe of one boot. "I don't know," he said, his voice suddenly husky. "I didn't think so at first, but now . . . well, I just don't know."

Her heart started pounding and her stomach took a nervous little jump. "Are you serious?"

She watched one side of his mouth kick up in a rueful grin as he studied her undoubtedly incredulous expression. Then he moved closer and raised one hand to the side of her face. Her nerve endings tingled wherever his rough fingertips brushed her skin.

"The thought of trying again scares you, doesn't it?"

She nodded. "Doesn't it scare you?"

"Oh, yeah. Scares the hell out of me if you want to know the truth. But I'm not sure we have any choice."

"Why wouldn't we?" she whispered, barely able to breathe, much less think when he was so close.

Instead of answering with words, he raised his other hand and slid his fingers into her hair. Then he lowered his lips to hers in a tentative kiss that made her feel as if the ground had suddenly dropped away beneath her feet. She gasped at the pleasure of it, parting her lips in an invitation to take it deeper.

He pulled away slightly, studying her through slitted eyes. Then, uttering a guttural moan, he wrapped his arms around her waist, pulled her flush against him and kissed her with all the desperate, driving hunger of a starving man. It was everything she'd remembered, everything she'd dreamed of in all those lonely motel rooms while she'd been waiting to testify, everything she'd literally ached to feel and taste and experience again.

Kissing him was like knocking back a shot of tequila on an empty stomach—fiery, disorienting, so exciting it robbed her of breath and turned her brain to putty. Her response to him was automatic, uncontrollable and achingly familiar. While she reveled in it, even rejoiced that her sexuality hadn't died during their separation, a part of her resented the effect he had on her.

The physical side of their relationship had always been good. Perhaps *too* good. When John had been home, she'd felt close to him because they spent so much time romping between the sheets. But the glow from that kind of passion lasted only so long in any relationship.

After the children were born, it was impossible to jump each other's bones whenever the urge hit. His absences became longer and more frequent as his career progressed. Missing him desperately, Anne had gradually realized that her perfect marriage wasn't so perfect, after all. Though it was rich in physical intimacy, it was poverty-stricken when it came to emotional intimacy.

No matter how long it had been since she'd known the pleasure of John's kisses, the joy of being in his arms, the excitement of feeling his big, aroused body pressed against hers, it wasn't enough. If it hadn't satisfied her before, it sure as heck wouldn't satisfy her now. Shuddering with the effort, she stepped back, pressing her palms against his shoulders when he tightened his arms around her.

"That's enough, John."

Chest heaving, he raised his head. Lord, his eyes—his marvelous, sexy green eyes—were nearly black in the fading light. They drilled into her with an intensity that scorched her soul and sent a shiver down her spine. When he spoke, his voice was as low and rough as the five-o'clock shadow on his chin.

"Dammit, Annie, I don't think I'll ever get enough of you. I tried so hard to forget you, and now..." He shook his head, cursed under his breath and turned away.

Anne gulped, feeling cold and exposed, as bereft as the moment she'd finally given up hope of ever seeing him again. She stared at his broad back, the rigid line of his shoulders, the hands clenched at his sides. And suddenly a well of anger broke open somewhere deep inside her.

Anger at him. At herself. At everyone and everything that had brought them to this agonizing moment.

John whirled to face her, propping his fists on his hips like an avenging warrior. "Well? Say something!"

"What do you want me to say?" she demanded.

"You could admit you still want me."

"I still want you. So what?"

"What do you mean, so what?"

"It doesn't solve anything, John. It never did."

He shrugged, whether in agreement or dismissal, she couldn't say. "Maybe it doesn't have to solve anything. Maybe all we need is to get each other out of our systems—"

She cut him off with a disgusted huff. "Oh, right. Just climb in bed, scratch the old itch and go on about our business. Thanks, but no thanks."

"I didn't mean it like that."

She arched both eyebrows at him. He grinned and shrugged again.

"Okay, maybe I did," he said. "But I can't live in the same town with you, see you all the time and pretend I'm not attracted to you, so what are we gonna do, Annie? Do you want to try to get back together again?"

She looked away, forcing herself to resist the temptation to simply say yes and let nature take its course. She didn't want to let sexual frustration cloud her judgment. There were too many important questions she couldn't answer yet.

Was John merely turning to her on the rebound from Paula's rejection? How did she really feel about knowing he'd had a sexual relationship with another woman? Would she be able to live in the same town with him if they tried to reconcile and didn't make it? How would it affect the kids?

Taking a deep breath, she said, "What about Rachel? Have you told her about Paula yet?"

"She was upset enough without hearing that, too."

"Then we'd better think about this. She already resents me. If she thinks you've betrayed Paula, she'll resent you, too."

"Yeah, you're right about that." Rubbing the back of his neck, he sighed. "But... well, shoot, Annie, what the kids all need right now is some stability. Maybe we ought to get married again so we can give it to them."

"No. Absolutely not. Don't even *think* about it."

He raised an eyebrow at that, then smiled wryly. "You don't have to be insulting. It's a logical solution."

"It's a recipe for disaster," Anne said. "I've changed more than my hair color, John. I don't think you realize how much more."

"Oh, come on. It wouldn't be that hard to patch our marriage back together. You said you didn't want to go through with the divorce."

"But I *did* go through with it. Remember that, because if I ever get married again, to you or anybody else, I won't accept the same kind of marriage we had."

"It wasn't all *that* bad, was it?"

Rolling her eyes, Anne turned her back on him and silently prayed for patience. Why did it have to be so blasted easy to slide right back into the same old dysfunctional patterns of behavior? This kind of argument was so familiar they might never have been apart.

She heard the soles of his boots scrape the sidewalk, then felt his hands close over her shoulders and his chin brush the top of her head.

"Will you at least think about it?" he asked quietly.

Sighing, she turned to face him and sadly shook her head. "I can't. I don't want to settle for a patch job or go back to the way things were before."

"We don't have to, Annie. I've changed, too, you know. I think if we really try, we can work out our problems and start a whole new relationship."

"Maybe we can. But if we're going to have a new relationship, we'll have to start from scratch like any other strangers. That's what we really are."

"Okay, so we'll have to get to know each other again. I still don't see why you're making such a big deal—"

"To me, it *is* a big deal," she said. "I'm not afraid of being alone anymore, John. I've found out I can support myself even without my inheritance to fall back on."

He stiffened and his coaxing smile became a grim, straight line across his face. "Is that the only reason you stayed with me? Because I was a meal ticket?"

"You know better than that. I'm just telling you we're not going to get married again out of a misguided sense of obligation to the kids, or because we'd benefit financially or any of the other logical reasons you're cooking up to throw at me. I'll never marry you again unless we're really in love with each other."

He studied her for a moment, then slowly nodded his head. "All right. I see where you're coming from now."

She seriously doubted that he did, but decided to let it pass for the moment. "Why don't we just take it one day at a time and see what happens?"

"How do we do that?"

"I'll be going to Billings at the end of the week to see Dad's lawyer, but maybe we could all do something together after I get back," she suggested. "Maybe a picnic or a camping trip?"

"Or, we could all go to Billings with you. The girls will be out of school for the summer on Wednesday. They can watch Chad while we're at the lawyer's office, and I can help you load up your parents' stuff. If we leave Thursday morning, we can get the work done by Friday and play for the rest of the weekend. How does that sound?"

"It sounds fine. I'll see you Thursday morning." She turned to leave. When she reached the bottom step leading up to her apartment, John called to her again.

"Annie? Remember one thing, will you?"

"What's that?"

"Whatever we have left between us, one way or another, we've got to resolve it. For good this time."

Chapter Eight

John stood on the sidewalk, holding his breath while he waited for Annie's response. Maybe it had been seeing her interacting with the kids or sharing the mundane tasks that went along with moving, but he'd felt more comfortable with her today than he had since the first time she'd come back to Bozeman. In fact, it had almost seemed like old times, and he hated to let go of those feelings.

But suddenly, in the space of a heartbeat, he could see what she had meant when she'd said they were strangers to each other. Yes, there were traces of the Annie he'd known and loved, but the woman staring back at him now appeared to be self-possessed, certain of what she wanted and absolutely determined to get it. His pulse thumped loudly in his ears as she silently studied him, her gaze unnervingly direct.

"Yes," she said quietly, "we *do* need to resolve whatever we have left between us. For good this time."

Then she marched up the steps without so much as a backward glance and let herself into the apartment. John climbed into the Suburban and drove home, the image of her walking away from him playing over and over in his mind like a cassette tape on auto reverse.

"What the hell is the matter with you, Miller?" he muttered, smacking the steering wheel with his fist as he waited for the light to change at an intersection. "How could you even *think* about a reconciliation, much less talk about it? Since when did you get so damned impulsive?"

A woman in the passenger seat of a van stopped in the next lane raised her eyebrows at him, grinned and said something to the driver. Realizing she must have noticed him talking to himself, John gritted his teeth and willed the light to turn green.

His emotions remained in an uproar all the way to the ranch. He wanted a beer, a smoke and an hour of privacy to sort himself out, but Rachel shot that idea full of holes the second he stepped inside the front door. Practically breathing fire, she charged out of the living room before he'd even hung up his hat.

"What's going on, Dad?" she demanded, ramming her fists onto her hips.

"What do you mean?"

"I called Paula when we got home. She said you won't be seeing each other anymore. I want to know why."

Barely stifling a groan, John forced a note of calm into his voice. "It's complicated, Rachel. And frankly, I'm not sure it's any of your business."

She reared back as if he'd slapped her. "Well, ex*cu-u-u-se* me. I thought Paula was *my* friend, too."

Rachel turned toward the stairs, but John grabbed her arm before she could take one step. Feeling the agitated trembling in the girl's muscles, he led her into his den. He closed the door and indicated the wing chair in front of his desk, propped one hip on the side of the desk closest to her and leaned forward, digging deep into his soul for patience.

"All right," he said. "I've had a long, hard day, just like you have. I'm willing to talk about this, but I'm not going to listen to that snotty tone of voice, and I'm not going to put up with any tantrums. Understand?''

Lips tightly pursed and chin quivering, Rachel glared at him. John straightened his spine and folded his arms across his chest, making it clear that he was prepared to wait forever to get her agreement. As he'd expected, it didn't take long for the resentment to fade from her eyes and the confusion she was feeling to take its place.

''I'm sorry,'' she mumbled, twisting her fingers together in her lap. ''I just don't want to lose Paula. Sometimes I need to talk to a woman, and since Grandma Irene died, Paula's the only one I can trust, you know?''

''Yeah, I know. But I can't do anything to change the situation. It was Paula's choice to end our relationship.''

''It was because of *her*, wasn't it?''

The venom in Rachel's voice told John exactly who she meant, of course. There were times when having smart, intuitive kids was nothing but a trial.

''Paula thought it was the best thing to do for all of us, Rach. She said your mother deserved another chance with me and with you girls.''

''You're not gonna take her *back*, are you?''

''It's a possibility if she wants to come back,'' he said.

Rachel's eyes widened with horror. ''But, Dad, she *left* us! You can't just forgive that, can you?''

Settling himself squarely on the desktop, John braced his elbows on his knees and held out his hands to her. ''As I said, it's complicated. I'm still angry in a lot of ways, but there were circumstances beyond her control.''

''Baloney!'' Rachel shot out of the chair and paced to the bookcase, stabbing at the air with her fingers to emphasize each word. ''She didn't *have* to testify. She could've come home if she'd really wanted to.''

''I'm not sure that's true, Rach. Drug dealers and hit men don't leave potential witnesses running around loose. But that's not really the point, anyway.''

''Well, what *is* the point, then?''

"The point is, no matter how you and I might feel about what your mother did, she's still your mother, and Holly's and Chad's. We have to learn to get along with her again, because she's going to be a part of our lives from now on."

"I don't *want* her to be a part of my life," Rachel insisted, shoving her hair back over her shoulder with one hand. "I don't trust her and you shouldn't, either. When she gets tired of playing mommy, she'll probably take off and dump Chad on us to raise."

"I thought you liked Chad."

"He's all right, I guess. For a little kid. But are you sure he's yours? Maybe you should have a blood test done."

John snorted in exasperation. "Come on, Rachel. All you have to do is look at him to know he's your brother."

"Well, maybe. But what about that guy who came with her? I mean, he's a *hunk*. A major babe. And didn't you see the way he watches her all the time? Like he just can't stop lookin' at her? I think he's got the hots for her."

"I think you're letting your imagination run away with you," John said, though he had to admit he'd noticed Anderson's good looks and his interest in Annie more than once today.

Annie might think of the guy as a good friend, but there wasn't a doubt in John's mind that Anderson wanted to be a hell of a lot more to her than a friend. He didn't like the idea one bit, and he didn't like the insinuating note in Rachel's voice when she spoke again, either.

"He's spending the night in her apartment. Do you really think he's gonna sleep on the couch?"

"That's enough, Rachel. Your mother and I have been divorced for a long time. Her love life is none of my business or yours. Maybe you should try giving her a chance for a change."

"No way," she said, shaking her head and giving him a pitying look as she walked to the door. "Be as gullible as you want, Dad, but I know I'm right about this. I'm gonna watch her like a hawk and prove it to you."

Her words haunted him long after she left the room. While Rachel's bitterness toward her mother didn't surprise him, he couldn't help worrying about it. And he had to wonder if maybe she wasn't right to call him gullible. *Was* something going on between Annie and that marshal?

John didn't want to be paranoid, but he didn't want to be a sap, either. Rachel had always been awfully perceptive. Every one of her suspicions about her mother had already occurred to him, and it had been downright spooky to hear the kid giving voice to his own fears. Because that was what all this anguish and emotional churning boiled down to— fear of trusting Annie again.

That was when the truth hit him. His throat and chest tightened, and a fine sheen of sweat broke out on his forehead. He could say from now until Christmas he'd just been testing the waters tonight, that he didn't know if he really wanted to reconcile with Annie. But he'd be lying.

He knew what he wanted, all right. It was time to admit it, if only to himself. If he didn't sincerely want another chance with Annie, he wouldn't feel so relieved about Paula's decision to break up with him. He wouldn't remember in such graphic detail that kiss he'd shared with her. And he sure as hell wouldn't be sitting here with his guts twisted into knots, wondering where Steve Anderson was going to sleep tonight.

Dammit, he *wanted* to trust Annie again. To love her again. He just didn't know if he dared.

Anne locked the front door, then followed the sound of Steve's voice into Chad's bedroom. Steve was sitting on the bed with his long legs stretched out in front of him, reading Chad's favorite story aloud. Chad was snuggled as close to the big man's side as he could get, pointing at the drawings and chiming in with the lines he'd memorized so well he could have recited the whole book.

They looked adorable together, and the realization that this was probably the last time Steve would be reading Chad's bedtime story yanked at her heartstrings. Lord, how was she ever going to be able to say goodbye to this man who had provided virtually all the safety, friendship and moral support she'd known since entering WITSEC? As if sensing her distress, Steve glanced up, smiled at her and quickly finished the book.

She helped him tuck Chad in and followed him out to the kitchen. He accepted the beer she offered him and went to work installing a new lock on her back door. Anne carried a beer for herself over to the dinette table and collapsed onto one of the chairs.

"I like your family," Steve said without looking up from his work. "Holly's a real sweetheart and your father-in-law reminds me of my uncle Bud."

"Is he the one who lives up around Wisdom?"

"Yup. Born and raised on the Big Hole and still running the ranch. I worked for him every summer when I was in high school and college. He's quite a character."

"What about Rachel?"

Steve shot her a sympathetic look. "You've got your work cut out for you there, I'm afraid. That's one scared, hostile kid."

Anne gave him a wry grin. "Tell me about it. There were times today when I wasn't sure whether I wanted to hug her or turn her over my knee. What did you think of John?"

"You really want to know?"

"Yeah. Didn't you like him?"

Steve straightened and turned to face her. Taking a swig of his beer, he studied her with an expression that suggested he was trying to decide how much he should say.

"He's all right, I guess." He shrugged, as if his opinion didn't matter much. "I liked the way he handled Chad."

"Come on, Anderson, that's not all of it," Anne said.

"It's hard to like someone who hates your guts, Anne."

"That's silly. Why would John hate your guts?"

Steve laid his screwdriver on the counter, then strolled across the room and straddled the chair at a right angle to hers. "You really don't know, do you?"

"Well, I suppose he could be dumping some of the blame for my decisions on you, but I don't think that means he hates you personally, Steve."

"It doesn't have a thing to do with WITSEC. C'mon, Anne, even *you're* not that naive. Your ex is jealous."

"Oh, really, now..."

Hooking one arm over the back of the chair, Steve leaned forward, all amusement fading from his eyes. "I'm not kidding. He's jealous of my relationship with Chad, and he thinks there's something going on between you and me. I could feel it every time he looked at me today."

"But I already told him we're just good friends. It doesn't make any sense."

"It doesn't have to. It's not a rational thing," Steve insisted. Then he clasped his hands together and dropped his gaze to the tabletop. "He probably picked up on my feelings for you."

Staring at him, she shook her head in confusion. Was he saying what she thought he was saying? "What are you talking about? We've been through so much together, we're closer than most friends, but..."

He raised his eyes to meet hers, and the stark, painful honesty she saw there silenced her. "But I've always wanted a lot more than friendship. I've been in love with you from the first time I met you. Surely you've sensed that."

Too stunned to speak, she shook her head again, then cleared her throat. "You've always been so professional. When we were cooped up in all those motel rooms together, you never said or did anything...."

"It wasn't because I didn't want to," he admitted quietly, a wistful little smile tugging at his mouth. "I've bitten more holes in my tongue and taken more cold showers than any man should have to. But you had more than enough to cope with, and I always knew you'd go back to John if you ever had the chance."

"I'm sorry," she whispered.

He reached out and ruffled her hair in a brotherly kind of gesture, exactly the kind of gesture she'd come to associate with him. "Don't be. You never led me on. I always knew you didn't feel the same way about me."

"Why are you telling me this now, Steve?"

"Because I want you to know that if things don't work out for you here, you've got another option. I know you need to find out for yourself if you can put your family back together, but I'd be happy to have you and Chad back in my life on any terms you want to name. I'll only be a phone call and a plane ticket away."

"No," she said, though she was deeply touched by his offer. "It'll be months before I have any idea whether or not things are going to work out. It's not fair for you to have to wait."

"I've waited more than six years to tell you this. I don't mind waiting a little longer."

"You need to get on with your own life," she said softly, reaching out to squeeze his hand. "You've taken care of us for a long time, but no matter what happens here, we'll be fine now."

"I know you will, and I don't think John's dumb enough to let you go again. But I'll be coming back to Montana to see my folks in July or August, and I'm going to check in on you then, okay?"

"I don't know. You're one of the most attractive men I've ever known," she said earnestly. "But even if things don't work out with John, I can't promise I'll ever feel what you want me to feel."

"All I want you to feel is happy. Whatever happens with John, I don't want to lose your friendship. And you'd damn well better remember that I'll be here for you anytime you need me."

She tried to smile, but figured she probably failed miserably. "The same goes for you."

He got to his feet and looked down at her. "Will you do me one favor?"

"Name it."

"Right now, while we're alone, I want you to kiss me goodbye. I promise it won't go any further than that."

She nodded, then rose, her palms suddenly growing damp with nervousness. Oh, my, she thought, suddenly seeing his thick blond hair, his gray eyes and his strapping, muscular body in a whole new light. She'd always thought Steve was handsome, but she'd never allowed herself to think of him as a potential lover.

He opened his arms to her as he had so many times before. But that had only been to comfort her when she was scared out of her mind or lonely or discouraged. The look in his eyes told her this time would be different.

Hesitantly she wrapped her arms around his waist and rested her cheek against his broad chest. He held her close, cupping the back of her neck with one big palm while he gently kissed the top of her head. His heart thumped heavily beneath her ear, and when she looked up into his stormy gray eyes, she wanted to weep for the pain she had caused him. Would, no doubt, continue to cause him until she got her life straightened out.

Caressing her chin with one finger, he whispered, "I want a real kiss, Anne. Not a little peck."

She complied willingly, partly because she needed to give him *something* for all he had meant to her, partly because she wanted to know if his kiss could ignite the passion in her that John's had.

Steve shuddered when she opened her lips for him and touched the tip of her tongue to his. He tilted his head to the right, expertly searching out the most intimate corners of her mouth. Her lips tingled and her blood hummed and she enjoyed kissing him. It was warm and, yes, passionate.

But no matter how completely she tried to immerse herself in the moment, in Steve himself, she couldn't summon up the same kind of response John had so effortlessly drawn from her. The fierce, sweet magic, that special link from her soul to his, simply wasn't there with Steve. Perhaps, if she ever truly got over John, it could be.

But it wasn't there now.

As if he had heard her thoughts, Steve abruptly ended the kiss and gazed deeply into her eyes. "Thanks," he said, his voice hoarse and a little breathless.

"You're, uh, welcome."

He dropped his hands to his sides. Turning away, she hugged herself, hating the new awkwardness that had sprung up between them, but not knowing what to do about it. She heard him sigh. Then his hands descended on her shoulders and squeezed them gently.

"It's all right," he said with a quiet chuckle. "I didn't expect an earthquake and fireworks. You didn't hate it *too* much, did you?"

"I didn't hate it at all."

"Well, good." He turned her toward the hallway and nudged her into motion. "Go on to bed before I forget how to be noble."

Feeling the force of his gaze in the middle of her back, she strolled across the room, then turned and propped one shoulder against the wall. He raised an eyebrow at her and folded his arms over his chest.

"All right. What is it?"

"Number one, you couldn't forget how to be noble if you tried, Anderson," she said.

"Don't count on it," he said with a wry grin. "What's number two?"

"Number two is a friendly piece of advice. You deserve to expect an earthquake and fireworks. Forget me and go find the woman who can give them to you. She's out there somewhere."

"Think so?"

"Uh-uh. I *know* so. Do yourself a favor and don't settle for anything less."

That said, she retreated to her room. Too restless to sleep, she stood at her bedroom window and gazed out at the quiet neighborhood, wondering what John was doing. Was he really jealous as Steve had suggested?

Did he still consider her to be his wife? Their divorce had gone through on paper, but she'd never really felt divorced.

Maybe that was why she'd never allowed herself to sense Steve's attraction to her. Was it the same way for John? If so, did he want to resolve whatever was left between them so they could heal their relationship? Or because he really wanted to be free of her? For good this time.

The questions haunted her long into the night. By the time she finally dragged herself into bed, she hadn't come up with any answers. All she could do was hope and pray that their trip to Billings would start them in the right direction. Whatever that was.

Chapter Nine

"They're here! They're here!"

"Okay, let them in," Anne called, smiling at Chad's excited shout.

She crammed her curling iron into the tote bag, zipped it and took one last look in the mirror. She'd had her hair highlighted again, hoping the lighter strands would make the transition back to her natural, sandy-blond color less noticeable. She wasn't sure she liked the effect the hairdresser had achieved. Before she could decide, Holly poked her head into the bathroom.

"Hi, Mom. Ooh, I like your hair."

Anne kissed her daughter on the tip of her pert little nose. "Ah, the joys of having a daughter who notices things like hair. How are you this morning, Miss Holly?"

"Glad to be out of school. Are you ready to go?"

"You bet. I guess we'd better get out there before your father starts getting antsy."

Holly wrinkled her nose in amusement. "Yeah, he's like that whenever we're going on a trip."

"Does he still bellow the line about burnin' daylight?"

"Uh-huh." Holly looked at her watch. "It oughtta be coming any time n—"

"C'mon, gals, get a move on," John shouted. "We're burnin' daylight."

Anne slung one arm around Holly's shoulders, picked up her bag and walked down the short hallway, her chuckles becoming hoots of laughter when Chad shouted in a near-perfect imitation, "Yeah, c'mon. We're burnin' daylight."

"Don't you dare teach my son that miserable habit," she said, smiling as she entered the living room.

John winked at Chad, then turned toward her, giving her a brief but thorough once-over. She returned his scrutiny, feeling a slow, curling warmth invade the pit of her stomach. He wore a green-and-white-striped dress shirt with a pair of black pleated slacks and shiny wing-tip shoes. Mercy, but he was a handsome man, she thought, especially when he smiled at her as if he liked the way she looked in the navy-and-white knit dress she'd chosen for their visit to the lawyer's office this morning.

"Morning, Annie," he said, reaching for the tote bag.

She gave it to him, hoping he wouldn't notice how flustered she felt when their fingers brushed. Honestly, she'd better get a grip, or this could turn out to be an awfully long weekend. Searching for composure, she looked away and realized they were missing a family member.

"Where's Rachel?" she asked.

Instead of answering her, John asked Holly to take Chad to the car and get his seat belt fastened. When the kids were out of earshot, he said, "Rachel's not coming. I tried to talk her into it, but I didn't think it was a good idea to insist. I'm sorry, Annie."

Though her heart sank at his explanation, Anne dredged up a smile. "It's all right. I'm glad you didn't force her. Well, I guess we'd better get on the road, huh?"

While John carried her luggage outside, she double-checked all the locks, telling herself she'd swallowed so many disappointments what was one more? If John had

forced Rachel to come along, the girl would have felt obliged
to act like a sullen teenager. Maybe it was just as well she'd
stayed at home. Still, when John pulled away from the curb
and headed for the interstate, there was an aching spot in the
center of her chest with Rachel's name written on it.

The drive proved a welcome distraction. Holly enter-
tained Chad, obviously relishing her role as big sister. Anne
made a mental note to make sure Holly didn't spoil him too
much and settled back to observe the scenery.

She had driven this stretch of road so many times it
should be easy to spot the changes. If there'd *been* any
changes, she thought with an affectionate grin for her home
state. Montana had never been and never would be on the
cutting edge of innovation, and that, along with its snow-
capped mountains, sparkling rivers and lush green valleys,
was a large part of its charm as far as Anne was concerned.

With each passing mile came memories, some happy,
some sad, but each one reaffirmed her growing sense of
connection to this place. It was the kind of place where
strangers still smiled and spoke to one another on the streets.
Where neighbors brought cookies to newcomers and
watched out for one another's kids. Where each member of
the community was valued, quirks and all, and friendships
often lasted from the cradle to the grave.

Montana wasn't just a place; it was an attitude, a mind-
set, a way of life you had to experience to understand. You
had to be tough, resilient and self-sufficient to survive the
climate and the rugged landscape. But you had to be willing to stop and help the owner of that stalled car along the
side of the road on a cold, snowy day, because you might be
the only one to pass along for hours, maybe even days in the
more remote areas. And you never knew when you yourself might need help in a similar situation.

You could take people who'd been born and raised in
Montana away, but you could never completely take the
spirit of Montana out of those people, no matter how far
they'd traveled or how long they'd been gone. Anne con-

sidered herself a prime example of that. Steve was another, which was probably why she'd always felt at ease with him.

"Yo, Annie," John said, startling her out of her reverie. "Big Timber's coming up and we've got plenty of time. Want to stop at Fry's?"

"Does Montana have sagebrush?" she retorted, her mouth automatically watering at the thought of the huge, succulent cinnamon rolls dripping with melted butter that had made the café a traditional rest stop for her family and John's.

They all enjoyed the treat and a chance to stretch their legs, and when they piled back into the Suburban for the last 140 miles of the trip, John appeared ready for some conversation.

"So, what've you been doing all week?" he asked, signaling to pass a black pickup hauling a horse trailer.

"You noticed I haven't unpacked those boxes stacked all over my living room?" she said, smiling at him with feigned innocence.

"They're a little hard to miss."

She chuckled at his dry tone and turned toward him, tucking her left foot under her right thigh. "I haven't unpacked because I've been house hunting."

He shot her a surprised look. "You're planning to buy a house?"

"Uh-huh. I've found the one I want, too."

"Jeez, Annie, you just got here. Don't you think you're rushing things a little?"

"I'm sick of living in an apartment, and since money's not a problem, what's the point of waiting?"

"Buying a house is a big decision. You don't just buy the first thing you see that appeals to you, and you should talk to an accountant about taxes. There may be some other things you could do that would be wiser financially."

"I don't care if buying a house is the wisest financial move or not," Anne said, grinning when John gave her an appalled look that said she was talking heresy. She glanced over her shoulder and noted that both kids had their headphones on and were immersed in music. "Don't give me that, John. Chad and I need a home of our own. A real one where we can have pets and—"

"Annie, be practical for a minute, will you? What if we get back together in a few weeks or months? Dad needs me on the ranch and the girls won't want to live in town."

His words about the possibility of their getting back together pleased her, but the note of husbandly condescension in his voice and his assumption that she should plan her life around him irked her even more. She reminded herself to be tolerant, however.

After all, she'd usually allowed John to handle their finances and make most of the major decisions before. It would take him a while to understand that she intended to make her own decisions now.

"I'll sell the house or rent it out if that happens," she said.

"But think of the hassle involved," he insisted. "Think of the time and the expense."

Despite her good intentions, her patience slipped a notch and her voice took on a sharper edge. "It's not your problem, John. And I don't think it's any of your business."

A chagrined expression flitted across his face. But to his credit, he smiled a moment later. "So, thanks, but no thanks for the advice, huh?"

"That about covers it." Smiling back to take the sting out of her words, she changed the subject. "Are you going to teach summer school?"

"Nope. Sometimes I'll write a journal article or a freelance article for a computer magazine. And I play at designing computer games, but my summers belong to the girls. We usually help Mike with the ranch and go camping and fishing whenever we can. I'd like Chad to come with us if he wants to."

"He'll want to," Anne assured him. "I want to take him on some day trips this summer, too. I'd love to have the girls come with us when you don't have other plans."

"Why don't we all go together?" Holly asked, taking off her headphones. "It'd be a lot more fun that way."

"Maybe we can sometimes, Holly," John said, glancing at Anne as if checking her reaction.

She shrugged in response. "Sure. Why not?"

Then it seemed as if the mountains were starting to shrink, the land flattening out into the vast, open prairies of the eastern half of the state. The little towns along the Burlington Northern Railroad's tracks zipped past the windows. Reedpoint. Columbus. Park City. Laurel.

Each road sign brought her a step closer to Billings. A step closer to home. Only the people who had always made it home were no longer there. She winced at the thought and found she couldn't push it away. A lump grew in her throat at the familiar sight of the Yellowstone River valley, stretching out between the rimrocks on the north and the river on the south.

"Are you okay?" John asked softly.

"I'm fine." She cleared her throat. "Just a little ambivalent. I'm anxious to see everything again, but I'm, uh, not looking forward to facing some of the changes."

He reached over and squeezed her hand. "You don't have to face them alone, Annie. That's why I came with you."

She looked at him, and the empathy in his eyes comforted her as much as anything could have at that moment. "I know," she whispered. "And you'll never know how much I appreciate it. Thank you for... well, you know."

John knew what she was thanking him for, all right, and it made him angry that she would even think she might have had to make this trip by herself while he was alive and kicking. Annie had made it plain that she wanted to be independent, but this was the day when she was going to have to face the reality of her parents' deaths. She was going to need a friend, and he wanted to be that friend. Maybe it would make up for a few of the times she'd needed him and he hadn't been there for her.

Unfortunately his visions of being a strong shoulder for her to lean on while she dealt with her grief dwindled with each passing hour. At the attorney's office Annie conducted herself with a stoic dignity that worried John, even while it impressed him.

The only time she faltered was when the man gave her the letters from her parents, which had been left in his keeping before they had died. She accepted the envelopes, tracing the handwriting on the outsides with the tip of her index finger, and John saw her throat contract with a hard gulp. He moved closer, ready to hold and comfort her the second she lost control of her emotions.

But she didn't lose control. She raised her chin, squared her shoulders and faced the attorney head-on while she stuck both envelopes into her purse, as if she were a war veteran who had learned to accept death without flinching. As if showing the emotions anyone would feel in this situation would shame her.

John knew plenty of men like that. Shoot, he'd been like that himself before he and Rachel had gone to counseling. Though he didn't break down openly or often, he'd cried at his mother's funeral, for God's sake.

Annie's rigid poise was about the spookiest damn thing he'd ever seen. Even the lawyer was reacting to it. The guy kept shooting her funny looks, as if he wasn't sure whether he was grateful not to have to deal with an hysterical woman or appalled that she was showing so little feeling for his former clients. Jeez, he probably thought she hadn't loved her folks, but John knew that wasn't true.

If Annie noticed anything amiss, however, she gave no sign of it. After thanking the lawyer for his time, she preceded John from the office and greeted the children, who had waited in the reception area. Then she suggested that they check into their motel, change into casual clothes and buy some hamburgers for a picnic in Pioneer Park.

Of course, the kids loved the idea. John went along with it, but it seemed pretty bizarre to see her acting as if this were just an ordinary day and they were just an ordinary family planning an ordinary outing.

After lunch, she asked him to drive by her parents' house, saying she wanted to show Chad where she'd grown up. John obliged her, hoping that seeing her home would crack the emotional barrier she'd wrapped around herself. Instead, she eagerly led Chad up the front steps, rang the bell and convinced the tenant's wife to give them a tour.

Then she wanted to stop at a greenhouse to buy flowers before they went to the cemetery where her folks were buried. John obliged her again, thinking surely she wouldn't be able to look at that marble headstone without some kind of emotional reaction. Surely she would have to lean on him just a little to get through this experience.

But she didn't.

Oh, her eyes got a little misty when she laid the pink roses she'd bought on her parents' graves. And there was sincere affection in her voice when she told Chad and Holly a few heartwarming stories about their grandparents. But she didn't crack, she didn't weep, and she sure as hell didn't need him or anyone else to lean on.

As he drove back to the motel, John began to feel disillusioned and detached from the woman sitting in the passenger seat. She wasn't Annie, that was certain. He wished he'd stayed in Bozeman, and it didn't take him long to figure out why.

He'd been more angry and hurt since Annie had returned than he'd ever been in his life. But despite all the things she'd done—divorcing him, leaving him and the girls behind, hiding Chad's existence from him—he'd been holding on to the belief that somehow, given sufficient time, they would be able to find enough remnants of their old relationship to put it back together.

He'd desperately wanted a chance to redeem himself in her eyes and in his own, to prove that he could be a good husband to her, that he could be the man she'd wanted and needed all those years ago.

He'd hoped that by healing his relationship with Annie, he could heal the wounds Rachel still carried, and the wounds he and Annie had inflicted on each other, as well.

No matter how many times she'd told him she'd changed, even *shown* him she'd changed, it had never occurred to him that there really might not be any remnants of their old relationship left to pick up. Who *was* this woman sitting beside him? He'd thought he'd seen glimpses of his Annie, especially when she was with the kids.

Had he imagined those glimpses because he'd wanted, maybe needed, to see them? Was it possible for a person to change that much? The question chilled him clear through to the marrow. If the answer was yes, there was no hope for a future with Annie. Because the Annie he'd known and loved was as dead as her parents.

Late that night, John lay on the hard motel mattress, staring at the ceiling and listening to Chad's soft snores from the other bed. The door between this room and the one Holly was sharing with Annie stood open in case Chad woke up during the night and needed his mother, but it had been quiet over there for what seemed like hours. Though he was physically and mentally exhausted, John wasn't anywhere near falling asleep.

He'd watched Annie closely since they'd returned to the motel, and he felt more confused and discouraged than ever. She'd been warm and loving with the kids all evening, and Holly had certainly basked in her mother's attention. Before the lights had gone out next door, he'd heard them giggling like a couple of little girls at a slumber party.

Maybe he was making a big deal out of nothing. Maybe Annie really did do her crying on the inside now. Or maybe she'd cried for her folks when she'd gone back to Colorado. And who was he to judge her, anyway? God knew he'd changed a lot in the past few years. Why should it bother him so much to realize that she had, too?

Then he heard a faint noise from the other room, a hinge creaking maybe, followed by the sound of water running in a sink. He sat up and rubbed one hand over his face, ears straining to catch any other sounds. A moment later, Holly appeared in the doorway. With the aid of Chad's night-light, John could see her peering anxiously toward the beds, as if she were trying to figure out which one he was in.

"What is it, honey?" he whispered.

"I think you'd better come in here, Dad," she whispered back. "There's something wrong with Mom."

He swung his legs over the side of the bed, grabbed his jeans and yanked them on, buttoning the fly as he crossed the room. From his bed, he'd been able to hear only the water running, but when he stepped into the other room, he heard another sound, the one that had, no doubt, wakened Holly. She grabbed his hand and squeezed it.

"What should I do, Daddy?" she asked.

"I'll take care of her, Hol," he said, gently guiding her into his room. "Why don't you crawl into my bed so Chad won't be alone?"

"Will she be all right?"

"Yeah. Go back to sleep. I'll call if I need you."

He shut the connecting door, switched on a lamp and hurried to the bathroom. A strip of light shone at the bottom of the closed door, and he could still hear the water gushing from the tap. And Annie was still weeping.

The sound was raw and filled with pain, but he'd never been so relieved to hear anything in his forty years of life. He hesitated a moment, wondering if he should knock, fearing she would stop when she realized her privacy had been invaded. Then he heard her moan, "Oh, Mama," and another gut-wrenching sob, and he knew he couldn't let her suffer alone any longer.

Letting himself in, he found Annie huddled on the floor beside the tub, one hand clamped over her mouth, the other clutching a thick sheaf of papers against her chest. So, he thought, she'd finally read the letters. Her eyes were closed, her face contorted with agony. Tears streamed from beneath her lashes, spilling over the fingers covering her mouth, dripping onto her raised knees.

She gasped when John scooped her into his arms and carried her back to the bedroom. He set her on one of the rumpled beds, crawled to the center and propped the pillows behind his back, then hauled her onto his lap. Her breath hitching with uncontrollable sobs, she turned into his embrace like the wounded child she was.

He rocked her, rubbed her back and stroked her hair, murmuring her name over and over. Her tears scalded his chest, and she clutched at his shoulder with her free hand as if she feared she would drown. Her other hand maintained a death grip on the now crumpled wad of papers.

John tried to take them from her, but she muttered in protest and curled her arm between them in a protective gesture that damn near broke his heart. Though the letters scraped his bare skin, he let her keep them, knowing she needed whatever small comfort they represented. Resting his head against the padded headboard, he held her close, hoping she found comfort in his arms, as well.

Five minutes later, she swiped at her cheeks with the back of her hand and pulled slightly away. "I'm s-sorry," she said. "I d-didn't mean to b-bawl all over you."

John pushed her head back down on his chest and kissed her soft hair. "You need to cry for them, baby. Go ahead. I won't melt."

To his intense gratification, she accepted his invitation, burrowing into him as a fresh onslaught of tears overwhelmed her. He didn't know how long she sobbed, and he didn't care. His Annie might have changed, but she wasn't dead, and it felt damn good to hold her again.

Gradually the hitches in her breathing smoothed out. The tears slowed to a trickle. Annie released her death grip on the letters and lay against him, limp with exhaustion. He brushed her back in long, soothing strokes, and she finally began to talk in a soft, raspy voice.

"I was the luckiest kid in the whole world, John. They were the best parents anyone could ask for."

"They were special folks, all right," he agreed.

"They loved me so much. They could forgive anything. God, I miss them."

He kissed the top of her head, then continued stroking her back. "I do, too, honey. Your dad especially."

"You do?"

"Uh-huh. He understood why I had to leave the ranch a lot better than Mike ever did. And he never said a harsh word to me about the divorce, even after you disappeared. He refused to believe it had anything to do with me."

"Yeah, that was Dad, all right. Always looking for the most positive approach." She sighed and rubbed her cheek against John's chest. "Know what I feel the worst about?"

"What, Annie?"

"That I haven't been able to give my own kids the kind of security my folks gave me. I tried so hard when the girls were little...."

"And you did a wonderful job with them. I think that's why Rachel took it so hard when you were just...gone. She hardly knew me, and it was impossible for her to accept that you really weren't there anymore."

Her shoulders trembled, and John felt a new batch of tears trickling down his chest. "She must have felt so betrayed. God, she's never going to forgive me, and you probably won't, either. I had everything I ever wanted within my grasp. And because I was so damned stupid and greedy, it's all gone and I can never, ever get it back."

"What do you mean, greedy?"

She pulled away and looked at him. Her eyes were swollen and bloodshot, and there was such grief in them he felt his own eyes misting over.

"I wanted it all with you. I acted like a spoiled little girl demanding a fairy tale. I was trying to make you be the perfect husband and f-father, like a damned knight in sh-shining armor. And I wrecked our marriage and destroyed our family, and now nothing will ever be the same again. Will it?"

"No, it won't be the same," John said softly, "but maybe that's not such a bad thing, Annie. What we had before wasn't that great in some ways, and you sure didn't wreck our marriage all by yourself. Believe it or not, some good things have come out of all this.''

"Oh, right. Like what? You lost your career...."

He clasped the sides of her head and wiped her tears away with his thumbs. "And you know what? I found out I really like teaching. And if I'd gone on traveling all the time, I'd be one of those fathers who never took the time to know his own kids. I would have regretted that later."

"But you had such awful fights with Mike about leaving the ranch. I know you didn't want to go back."

"No, I sure didn't. But I've made peace with my dad now, which was something I never thought I'd be able to do. And the girls love it out there. Especially Rachel."

Studying him intently, Annie pulled away until he dropped his hands to his sides. Then she slid off his lap, yanked a tissue out of the box sitting on the nightstand and blotted her eyes. "Are you telling me you're not angry with me for going into the program by myself anymore?"

"Not necessarily," John admitted with a rueful grin. "I don't know if I'll ever really understand why you did that, but maybe it doesn't have to be an issue. Maybe we can agree to disagree."

"Do you think that's possible?"

"What other choice do we have? We can't change anything that happened. It seems to me the only thing we can do is try to put it all behind us and get on with the future."

Nodding thoughtfully, she wadded the tissue into a little ball, carried it across the room and tossed it into a wastebasket. "I, uh, need to go wash my face, John. My eyes hurt from all that crying."

Taking that as a signal she wanted to be alone, John climbed off the bed. He stopped in front of her and gently tucked a strand of her hair behind her ear. Her eyes widened at his touch, as if she was suddenly aware that they were alone in a motel room in the middle of the night. He'd been doing his best to ignore that fact himself, but he couldn't ignore it now, not when she nervously licked her lips and stared at his chest as if she wanted to touch it.

Come to think of it, he really liked that nightshirt she was wearing. It looked a little bit like a baseball player's uniform shirt, and he could easily imagine himself lingering over each button, sliding it out of the buttonhole, kissing each new patch of soft skin....

"I really am sorry I cried like that," she said, licking her lips a second time. "It won't happen again."

"Don't worry about it," he said, hearing a husky note in his voice he'd swear hadn't been there a second ago. "Your tears have never bothered me, Annie. Why did you fight them so hard today?"

"It's a habit, I guess. While I was in WITSEC, I couldn't afford to lose control or show any weakness. I always had to be tough because there wasn't anyone else to take care of Chad if I fell apart."

Unable to resist, he leaned down and stole one quick, sweet kiss, then another and another. Her lips clung to his during the last one. Wanting to wrap his arms around her in a crushing embrace, he forced himself to pull away.

Though he felt they'd gone a long way toward reestablishing emotional contact, he knew she was too vulnerable tonight to carry this any further. But soon—at least he hoped it would be soon—they'd have to see what they could do about reestablishing contact on a more physical level. If the rush of blood into his groin was any indication, that wouldn't be at all difficult.

"I've gotta go, Annie," he whispered, opening the door to the other room.

She glanced at his fly and smiled up at him, the knowing look in her eyes nearly undoing his noble intentions. "Thanks, John. Thanks for everything."

Then she turned and walked into her bathroom. John watched the gentle twitch of her little fanny under that nightshirt for an instant, then sighed and shut the door behind him. Both kids were sound asleep, and the digital clock on the television read one forty-five. Rather than disturb

Holly by sending her back to the other room, he stretched out beside Chad and closed his eyes.

For the first time in a very long time, John felt a sense of peace wash over him. Logically, he knew that there were still problems ahead for him and Annie and the kids. But there was hope, too. Real hope for a reconciliation and a future together. For now, that was enough.

Chapter Ten

The month of June was a hectic, productive time for Anne. After so many years of concentrating on day-to-day survival, of feeling stuck and helpless to change anything because of the threats hanging over her head, she couldn't resist the urge to make up for lost time. Suddenly her life was changing at warp speed, and she moved through each day with a giddy sense of euphoria.

As if she'd found a magic charm to break an incredibly long chain of rotten luck, everything started to go her way. A sales manager who had hired a contractor to build a four-bedroom house in a wonderful new subdivision was unexpectedly transferred. Anne made a generous cash offer, and they closed the deal within two weeks.

The contractor installed extra locks and a security system the day after the closing. Anne and Chad moved into their new home the day after that. A neighbor mentioned that her brother had German shepherd puppies for sale. By nightfall, Chad owned a wiggly best friend named Rex.

Another neighbor owned a car dealership. Though John and Mike were aghast that she'd bought a house and a dark blue minivan by herself, she calmly informed them that she was satisfied with her choices. They backed off without a fuss and appeared to be somewhat mollified when she asked them to help her buy a horse for Chad.

From the moment her son met the fifteen-year-old black mare named Dolly, Anne knew she would be making daily trips to the Flying M. Chad badgered his father and grandfather for riding lessons constantly. Every night he came home filthy, exhausted and bubbling over with descriptions of all the neat "man stuff" he had learned to do that day. He copied John's mannerisms to the point that Holly and Rachel started calling him Ditto.

While it was difficult to relinquish so much of her son's life to his newfound heroes, there was ample compensation in watching him form strong bonds with the rest of the family. There were other compensations, too. When Anne dropped Chad off, Holly frequently came home with her. And by the middle of July, Anne thought she'd sensed a gradual thawing in Rachel's attitude toward her.

Hoping to speed the process, she planned a surprise slumber party to celebrate Rachel's fifteenth birthday. She combed through cookbooks, made decorations and hit every junior-clothing store in town. After watching several mothers and daughters battling over outfits, she bought a gift certificate from Rachel's favorite teen shop.

Cautioning herself not to expect too much from one party, Anne met the rest of the family at a restaurant for the birthday dinner. When they had all finished eating, she invited everyone to her house for cake and ice cream. Rachel shot her a wary glance, but didn't object.

Anne raced home ahead of the others on the pretext that she wanted to put on a pot of coffee. The look of sheer delight on Rachel's face when her giggling friends poured into the living room brought tears to Anne's eyes. John handed her a clean white handkerchief with a smug grin that made her laugh.

Mike eventually took Holly and Chad back to the ranch, but John stayed to help Anne with kitchen duty and crowd control. At ten o'clock, they collapsed onto chairs at the dinette table. He laughed when she told him she envied his easy rapport with the teenagers.

"I've driven in a lot of car pools with that bunch," he said, his eyes warm with fond memories. "Dance lessons, 4-H, soccer practice—you name it, I've hauled them to it."

"I'd be happy to take over some of that for you," Anne offered. "That's why I bought the minivan."

"You're a brave and foolish woman," he said, shaking his head at her. "They're all nice kids, but you won't believe how noisy they can be."

A piercing shriek of laughter echoed over the music blasting from the living room. Anne grinned at John. "I think they're having a good time."

"If they have any better time, you won't have a house left by morning."

"Did I rent the right movies?" She hopped out of her chair and rushed to the work island, rearranging platters of snacks the girls would trash in seconds. "What about the food? Do I have enough?"

"You've got enough food to feed the Bobcat football team. Sit down and relax, will you?"

"I don't think I can," Anne admitted with a helpless shrug. She walked back to the table and perched on the edge of the chair. "I'm hoping that if her friends like me, Rachel will, too."

John reached over and squeezed her hand. "They *do* like you. You did a great job organizing this, and I don't think Rachel will ever forget it. Mike'll do almost anything for the kids, but he can't stand slumber parties."

"But am I really making progress with her, John? Or am I just imagining it?"

"You're doing fine. The gift certificate was a stroke of genius. The way that kid loves to shop—"

Anne cut him off with a shake of her head. "But maybe I went overboard. I don't want her to think I'm trying to buy her affection."

"You've hit exactly the right chord, Annie. You made an obvious effort to show her you care about her, and that's the way she'll interpret it. You haven't done a thing her friends' parents haven't done before."

Anne stuck out her lower lip and blew a puff of air straight up, ruffling her bangs. "I've been so nervous."

"Stop worrying so much. In fact, I wish you'd stop worrying about the kids and think about me for a change."

"Oh, really?" Anne propped her chin on the heel of her hand and wrinkled her nose at him. "Why, you poor man. Have you been feeling neglected?"

He gave her one of those droll, masculine looks that said he was willing to put up with her teasing—to a point. "I know you've been busy, Annie. But you're settled in now, and things are going okay with the kids. Don't you think it's time to start sorting out our relationship?"

"What did you have in mind? We haven't had much privacy to talk."

"Shoot, we haven't had *any* privacy," John said. "And we're not gonna get any unless we demand it. I think we should start going out on dates."

"Dates?"

"Yeah. You know, something you do together on Saturday nights? Dinner and a movie? Dancing? Bowling?"

"Are you serious? Like in high school?"

"We've figured out how to work together as parents, but how are we going to be a couple again if we don't spend any time alone?"

"I don't know. I know we'll have to eventually, but—"

"Jeez," he grumbled. "You make it sound like a chore on a to-do list."

"I didn't mean it that way," she chided him. "I'm just not sure how the kids will react. Rachel's barely starting to tolerate me."

"We can't let the kids dictate our relationship." Resting one elbow on the table, he leaned closer and brought his other hand to the side of her face. Brushing her cheek with the backs of his fingers, he gave her a smile that made her toes curl. "C'mon, Annie, you know we'll have fun together. We always did before."

Which was precisely the problem, Anne thought, feeling a whole herd of lusty urges responding inside her. She knew he wasn't talking about dinner or movies, dancing or bowling, and the wretch knew she knew it. What was it about this ex-husband of hers that made her so susceptible to his charm?

During the past six weeks John had been helping Mike with branding, moving cattle onto the land they'd leased for summer grazing, cutting and baling alfalfa for winter feed. Whenever she'd seen him, he'd been as filthy and exhausted as Chad. There hadn't been any more kisses, gentle touches or sexy smiles like the one he'd just given her.

She suspected something other than busy schedules had kept them apart, however. After that intensely emotional weekend in Billings, they'd both needed time to regroup. Evidently John was finished regrouping.

She wasn't at all sure *she* was, however, and wasn't that typical of men? John's brain worked with the efficiency of a computer. When making a decision, he would list his options and choose the most logical one, without allowing extraneous factors like emotions to get in the way.

Anne approached decisions from the opposite direction, starting with emotions and coming around to logic at the end of the process. That didn't mean she couldn't make a logical decision; it simply meant that it took her longer to arrive at one she felt comfortable with, which was something John had never understood when they were married.

Because John's method was quicker, he'd considered his way to be the superior one. It had driven him nuts to wait for her input when he already had a reasonable solution to a problem, whatever it was. She'd usually taken the easy way out and let him have his way. She had also frequently resented him, because she'd ended up feeling like a less-than-equal partner.

It had taken her dozens of self-help books to figure all this out, to understand and accept her own responsibility for the breakdown of their marriage. When she looked at it unemotionally, it seemed like an easy thing for two intelligent adults to fix. But how could she look at it unemotionally when he was drumming his fingertips and bristling with impatience?

Well, if she wanted to spend the rest of her life with this man, she'd better learn to stand up for herself. She couldn't change John, but she *could* change her reactions to him, and there was no time like the present for getting started. Taking a deep breath, she forced herself to smile.

"I'll have to get back to you on that, John," she said. "I'd like to think it over."

"What's there to think about?" he asked. "You said we're going to have to do it sooner or later. Why not now?"

"Because I'm not comfortable with now."

"Annie—"

"It won't do any good to badger me," she said. "I'll get back to you when I'm ready."

"Gimme a break, Annie."

"I'll get back to you when I'm ready, John."

He crossed his arms over his chest and studied her with a puzzled frown. She held his gaze, trying to communicate with her eyes her intention to stand firm. After a long, breathless moment, he pushed back his chair and stood.

"All right. Since you've got everything under control here, I guess I'll head for home."

Anne walked him to the door, thanked him for his help and waved him off. Then she turned on the security system, leaned against the door and hugged herself before hurrying back to the kitchen.

She had loved John Miller to the depths of her soul. She'd respected his ambition and found his hard-charging, aggressive personality exciting both in and out of bed. In all honesty, she still felt that way about him. She wanted a *man* for a husband, not a weakling.

On the other hand, she didn't want to live with a steam-roller, either. That was how she'd felt the day she'd filed for a divorce—as if John was always flattening her whenever she tried to explain why his workaholism made her so un-happy. What had made the whole situation so painful was that she'd known all along that he wasn't intentionally try-ing to hurt her.

He was simply doing what he thought needed to be done to ensure his family's security. She hadn't been able to slow him down long enough to make him understand that there were other, more important things she and the girls needed from him. Things like his time and attention and affection.

John could have used better listening skills. She could have used better communication and assertiveness skills. It had mattered back then, and it mattered now. And by golly, this time she was going to get it right. She was going to act like an adult. She was going to use her head, as well as her heart, whenever she dealt with him.

Getting John to agree to wait until she was ready to make a decision might seem like an insignificant thing to anyone else. He'd probably laugh himself sick if he knew how ex-cited she was about it. But to her, it represented nothing less than hope for their future together.

She didn't have to let him roll over her like a tank. If she could stand up for herself with John Miller once, she could do it again. She *could* be an equal partner. Things really *could* be different this time. What a concept!

After checking the clock, she paced around the room for another five minutes, wanting to make sure John had had enough time to get home. Then she grabbed the phone and punched in the Flying M's number.

"Hi," she said, smiling when she heard the surprise in his voice at hearing from her so soon. "I've made my decision. Are you free next Saturday night?"

"Whatcha puttin' that gunk on for, Dad?"

John grinned at the boy standing beside him. Chad had

spent the day at the ranch and had come upstairs to keep him company while he got ready for his first date with Annie. The kid questioned every move he made, from why he had to shave again to how come he made such funny faces while he did it.

He remembered grilling his own dad exactly the same way. While he might have preferred to carry on the tradition at a less nerve-racking moment, he didn't have the heart to send Chad downstairs. He'd already missed too much time with this kid as it was.

"Women like you to smell good," he said, holding the bottle of after-shave under Chad's nose.

Chad took a whiff, made a face and giggled. "I know. Steve had lotsa girlfriends. He told me if ya want a gal to get close to ya, ya can't smell like a goat. Are you tryin' to get close to Mom?"

"Yeah," John said. "Is that all right with you?"

Tipping his head to one side, Chad scrunched up his mouth and thought about that for a moment. "I guess so. You'll take good care of her, won'tcha?"

"You bet." Grabbing the tie he'd draped over the bathroom doorknob, John slung it around the back of his neck. "A man always takes good care of his date."

"Are you gonna *kiss* her?"

"Maybe." John muttered under his breath at the cockeyed knot he'd produced, yanked it free and started over. "If she'll let me."

"You *like* kissing girls?" Chad demanded, scrunching up his whole face this time.

Laughing at the disgust in the boy's expression, John ruffled Chad's hair. "It's what they call an acquired taste, son. You'll like the idea better when you're older."

"No *way,*" Chad said, shaking his head. "I watched this movie with Steve one time, ya know? And these people were kissin' and this lady stuck her tongue right in the guy's mouth! Barf city, man!"

"What happened then, Chad?"

"I dunno. Steve said I was too young for that stuff and changed the channel."

Thank God for *that,* John thought. Despite his tender years, Chad was nobody's fool. With all the time he was spending around the ranch animals, it wouldn't be long before they'd have to have a man-to-man talk about sex. John hoped he wouldn't turn as red in the face as Mike had. He slid the new knot up to his collar button, nearly strangling himself at Chad's next question.

"So, are you gonna sleep in Mom's bedroom tonight?"

John hooked his finger under the knot and loosened it, then tried to force a casual note into his voice. "I doubt it. Why do you ask?"

Chad propped both elbows on the counter and plunked his chin onto his palms. "That's what moms and dads do on TV."

"You're supposed to be married to do that. Remember when I explained that your mom and I aren't married now?"

"Yeah, I remember," Chad grumbled. "That's how come we don't live at the ranch with you guys."

"Would you like to live here?"

"Well, I'll tell ya, Dad. It'd be neat to be able to see Dolly any time I want to, but I gotta take care of Mom. She gets kinda scared sometimes at night."

"What does she get scared about?"

"Those bad guys that were tryin' to hurt her."

"You know about them?" John felt guilty to be pumping a six-year-old kid for information, but not guilty enough to stop. Annie sure hadn't told him much. Whenever he brought the subject up, she always made an excuse to avoid it.

Chad stuck his hands into his jeans pockets and looked down at the dusty toes of his boots. "I'm not s'posed to talk about it. It's not safe."

John went down on one knee and crooked a finger under Chad's chin, coaxing the boy to look at him. "That's all right, buddy. I'm proud of you for taking care of your mom the way you do. It hasn't been easy for you, has it?''

Shaking his head, Chad bit his lower lip. John's heart clenched as tears puddled up in the boy's eyes in spite of his obvious effort to hold them back.

''I get kinda scared at night, too, Dad,'' Chad whispered. ''I know those guys are dead and everything, but sometimes I forget and I have bad dreams. Like, if I see Mom's scar or something.''

''What scar, Chad?''

''The one where that Donner guy shot her.'' Chad pointed to a spot on the left side of his chest, an inch below his clavicle. ''Right here. That's how come she won't wear a swimming suit anymore. 'Cause her scar's too ugly.''

Feeling as if he'd been punched in the face, John stared at his son. Now that he thought about it, Annie hadn't worn a tank top or a sundress or any kind of outfit with a scooped neckline all summer—not around him, anyway. And she'd told him she didn't have any more bombshells to drop on him. Didn't she consider her having been shot a bombshell, for God's sake?

The rage he felt must have shown on his face. Chad's chin quivered and his tears spilled down his cheeks. Dashing them away with the back of one fist, he bolted for the door. John grabbed a belt loop on the back of his jeans and hauled him into his arms.

''It's okay, son. I just didn't know, that's all. I'm glad you told me.''

''I thought you were mad at me for bein' a scaredy-cat.''

''Heck, no, I'm not mad at you. And you're not a scaredy-cat. Shoot, I'd be scared, too.''

''You would?''

''Darn right. Only an idiot wouldn't be scared of guys like that. Can you tell me one more thing?''

Chad gulped, then nodded. ''I'll try.''

''Has anything happened to scare you or your mom since you've been here in Bozeman? Strange guys coming around or anything like that?''

"I don't think so. Mom watches for cars that don't be-long all the time, but everybody's been real nice to us. We just both have bad dreams sometimes."

"Well, don't worry about it. Nobody expects you to con-trol your dreams. I have bad dreams, too."

Chad smiled as if a burden had been lifted from his shoulders. "Oh, yeah? What do you have bad dreams about?"

John straightened and made one more attempt with his tie. "Dumb things, usually. Getting up in front of a class and forgetting my lecture. Stuff like that."

"That doesn't sound very scary."

"Well, I don't want to tell you the really scary ones. You'll be up all night with your eyes bugged out."

"I will not."

"Will, too."

The conversation degenerated into teasing at that point. By the time they rounded up Rachel, who had agreed to baby-sit, and headed for town, Chad's sunny disposition had returned. John envied his son's ability to switch his mind to other topics.

Every time he thought about Chad's revelation, he felt like gnashing his teeth. Dammit, Annie should have told him she'd been shot. On the other hand, he couldn't escape the guilty knowledge that he hadn't exactly encouraged her to confide in him when she'd first come back, or the realiza-tion that there'd been plenty of clues that her time in the WITSEC program had been rough.

For God's sake, he'd seen her gun! And that state-of-the-art security system she'd had installed wasn't exactly stan-dard equipment in a little town like Bozeman. He'd thought the cellular phone in her minivan was just a convenience she'd chosen because she had plenty of money, but now he wondered if she hadn't had a more serious motivation for that purchase, too.

How was he going to get her to talk about those lost years? He could always confront her, but he doubted they'd have a pleasant evening if he did. No, he wanted her to trust him enough to volunteer the information. The only way that would ever happen was if they learned to relax with each other again.

Which put him back to square one—showing Annie a good time without any pressures or hassles. He needed to charm and woo her, just as he'd planned to do all those years ago in Chicago. With that thought firmly in mind, he parked in her driveway and followed the kids to her front door.

Annie greeted them with a welcoming smile that turned a shade nervous when she looked up at John and caught him checking out her legs. Well, good, he thought, grinning to himself. At least he wasn't the only one who felt like an awkward teenager tonight.

Wearing a black silk blouse with a knee-length, aqua skirt and high-heeled sandals, she looked cool and elegant. He was glad he'd struggled with the damn tie and made reservations at The Pasta Company, a quiet restaurant in the Baxter Hotel.

"I guess we can go now," she said when Rachel had demonstrated—twice—her proficiency with the security system.

"Better watch him, Mom," Chad advised with an impish grin. "He said he was gonna kiss you if you'd let him."

Annie shot John a startled glance, then chuckled and sailed out the door ahead of him. Reminding himself to have a talk with his tattletale son, John hurried to catch up with her. He helped her into the front seat of the Buick sedan he'd borrowed from his dad for the occasion, and hurried around to the driver's door.

"I'll have to watch what I say to that kid," he said as he settled in behind the wheel.

Annie shot him a rueful grin before chuckling again. "He's never seen me go out on a date before. I'm sorry he embarrassed you."

"I'll live. I don't think my intentions were a big secret, were they?"

She blushed and shook her head, but didn't say anything. Feeling a stifling sense of tension seep into the car, John drove downtown. Some charmer *he* was, he thought, wishing he could recall his last remark. Annie had always been such a chatterbox he hadn't realized how much he'd counted on her to keep a dialogue going.

The Baxter was a grand old hotel, decorated with lots of marble and dark wood to provide a hushed, luxurious atmosphere. He followed Annie through the revolving door, pausing for a moment beside her while their eyes adjusted to the subdued lighting. Then she smiled up at him, her pleasure in their surroundings shining from her eyes.

The simple gesture restored his flagging confidence. Placing a hand at the back of her waist, he escorted her to the restaurant. The hostess seated them in a private alcove at the side of the dining room. A bottle of good wine, steaming platters of pasta and great service went a long way toward easing any awkwardness between them.

Declining dessert, Annie took a final sip of her coffee and sat back with a sigh of repletion. "That was wonderful, John. Thank you."

"Feel up to some exercise?" he asked.

"A walk sounds nice."

"I had something a little more vigorous in mind." He laughed at the reproving look she shot him, then plastered what he hoped was an innocent expression onto his face. "Shame on you, Annie. I only had dancing in mind."

"Uh-huh."

"I *did*. Relax, honey. You don't have to be afraid I'll pounce on you without any warning tonight."

"Does that mean you won't pounce tonight?" she asked. "Or that you'll give me fair warning before you do?"

"Which do you prefer?"

Resting her chin on the heel of one hand, she studied him for a moment, her eyes glinting with amusement.

"That's an interesting choice, Professor. While the thought of being pounced on has a certain, shall we say, earthy appeal, it does tend to make a woman feel a bit skittish. On the other hand, it seems to me that a warning would take all the fun out of the pounce itself. Of course, it might also depend on what you would consider to be fair warning. If you were to define the term to mean . . .''

The little flirt rattled on in that ridiculous, pseudoscholarly vein until John had to laugh at her. Still, her message came through as clearly as if she had shouted it at him. *Don't rush me, John. I want you, too, but I'm not ready yet. Give me a little more time.*

Well, he could handle that, he told himself. As eager as he was to make love with Annie, he suspected that if he wanted to win her trust again, this was a test he needed to pass. Just like the one she'd put him through the night of Rachel's party—to see if he would respect her boundaries.

Yeah, he knew what she was up to, all right. He had Rachel's counselor to thank for that scrap of insight into the bizarre workings of the female mind. Resigning himself to a slower pace than he would have liked, he paid the check and escorted Annie out to the car.

He drove straight to Willy's, a popular night spot on the east end of town. The dance floor was already crowded, the band cranking out one country hit after another. A waitress helped them find a table in the back of the room.

Her eyes bright with interest, Annie looked around before smiling at John. "I could be wrong, but I think we're a little old and overdressed for this joint."

John raised an eyebrow at her. He'd been here before with Paula and had never felt out of place. Oh, *jeez,* he thought, quickly scanning the room. Wouldn't it just be dandy if Paula was here tonight?

Exhaling a quiet sigh of relief when he didn't see her, he studied the other patrons. Almost everyone else had on jeans, Western shirts and boots, and most of the men wore Stetsons or baseball caps. While he saw a few guys who were around his age and a couple who were probably older, most of the women looked like college girls.

Well, tough. Annie loved to dance, Willy's was the best place in town, and he wasn't about to let a dumb thing like age or clothes stand in the way of sharing it with her. She didn't look much older than the other women, and he thought she looked more feminine and sexy in her skirt and heels than the rest did in their skintight jeans.

Without waiting for the waitress to return with their drinks, he stood and grabbed Annie's hand. "Come on, honey, let's show these young pups how it's done."

Warily eyeing the wild action on the dance floor, she hesitated for a second, then laughed and allowed him to pull her to her feet. Their first steps together felt awkward, but as the band finished one song and ripped into another one, their timing began to mesh.

Suddenly it was as if they'd never been apart. They danced again and again, laughing and carrying on, trying new steps without the slightest concern for their dignity.

"I guess it's like riding a bike," she said when the band finally played a slow, sweet ballad.

John rubbed his chin against the side of her head, enjoying the silky feel of her curls against his skin. "Once you learn how, you never forget?"

"Uh-huh. I've had a wonderful time tonight."

"I'm glad, Annie. I have, too."

Which was the absolute truth. As far as he was concerned, however, the rest of the evening had only served to bring them to this point—the point where he could hold her in his arms again. There were other things besides riding a bike and dancing a person never forgot. He hadn't forgotten a blessed thing about Annie. Lord, but he'd missed being close to her like this.

He loved the feel of her body moving against his. Loved the musky, womanly scent of her that filled his nostrils. Loved the dreamy, unconsciously sexy look in her eyes as she gazed up at him. Shoot, he might as well admit it to himself—he just plain loved Annie.

It didn't matter what she'd done or why she'd done it. He'd only been going through the motions of living while she'd been gone. It had been as uncomfortable as having circulation restored to a foot that had gone to sleep, but her return had blasted his numbed emotions fully awake for the first time in years.

Dammit, she *belonged* with him. It didn't have anything to do with the kids or unfinished business left over from the divorce. He loved her. He wanted her. He needed her in his life the way she had once said she needed him.

Fear ballooned in his chest when he completed that thought. He'd always been the independent one in their relationship, the one who came and went as he pleased because that was what his job had demanded. Now, however, the tables had turned.

Annie wasn't saying she needed him anymore. Since her return, she'd gone out of her way to prove how independent she'd become. If they ever got back together, it would be on *her* terms.

He didn't like it much, but he thought he was finally beginning to understand why Annie had gone through with the divorce. It was frightening and humiliating to have your heart belong to someone who might not be as committed to the relationship as you were. Someone who might take off one day and never come back. Someone who might want you physically and even love you, but who acted as if she really didn't need you for anything.

That was exactly the way he'd treated Annie before she'd disappeared. He'd been so cocky and arrogant, so sure of her commitment to their marriage, he'd actually forced her to carry out her threat to end it. If anyone was to blame for this fiercely independent attitude of hers, it was probably him.

Sighing, he splayed his fingers across her slender back and pressed her closer. She snuggled into his embrace, laying her head on his shoulder as she followed his shuffling steps around the dance floor. Her action reassured him a little. But not enough. Not nearly enough.

She looked up at him and smiled. So much blood rushed to his groin it was a wonder he didn't pass out. The words "I love you," hovered at the tip of his tongue, but he couldn't say them. Annie was plastered so tightly to him she had to know how aroused he was. He didn't want her to think he was just trying to coax her into bed.

Damn. What a mess. Loving this woman should be the easiest thing in the world, but he felt as if he'd been caught up in a terrifyingly intricate dance with her. He'd done his part to complicate it, and he sensed that he'd already made too many false moves. One more, and she might give up on him for good.

He stopped dancing and kissed her forehead, her cheek, her sweet, luscious mouth. Her eager response made him want to drag her off by the hair and settle this matter the way his ancient ancestors would have. Instead, he slowly released her, led her off the dance floor and out to the car, feeling that he had no choice but to follow her lead.

Chapter Eleven

Still wrapped in a warm glow from the delightful evening with John, Anne reluctantly left the passenger seat of the Buick. She inhaled deeply as she accompanied him up the sidewalk, enjoying the scent of freshly mown lawns and the sweet perfume from her neighbor's flower beds after the smoky atmosphere of the bar.

Her nerves humming with anticipation of a good-night kiss, she felt young and carefree and eager. John took her hand while they climbed the steps and when they reached the top turned to face her, his eyes glittering with obvious intent as he pulled her close. The front door opened, startling them into jumping apart like a couple of guilty teenagers.

Rachel appeared in the doorway, arms crossed over her chest, a scowl on her face that would have curdled milk. "It's about time you showed up."

"What's the matter, Rach?" John asked. "Chad didn't get sick, did he?"

Shaking her head, she stepped back to allow them entry. "Ditto's fine. Do you have any idea how *late* it is?"

Anne exchanged an amused glance with John, then took a closer look at her outraged daughter. Oh, dear, the poor kid really was upset. "I'm sorry if you were worried, Rachel. I guess we were just having so much fun—"

John interrupted. "I don't remember giving you a specific time to expect us."

"Well, I sure didn't expect you to stay out till after one!" Rachel snapped. "Don't you think you're a little old for partying?"

"All right, maybe we should have called," he said. "But, Rach, we're adults. What's really bugging you here?"

Rachel lowered her hands to her hips and shot Anne a venomous glare. "Her boyfriend called tonight. Twice. He wants her to call him no matter how late she gets home."

"I don't have a boyfriend, Rachel," Anne said.

"Oh, *right.*"

"That's enough, Rachel," John said.

Anne silenced him with a look. "I assume you're referring to Steve Anderson, Rachel. What is it about him that upsets you?"

The girl rolled her eyes at the ceiling, as if the answer to that was ridiculously obvious. "Are you having an affair with him?"

"No. I've never had an affair with him or anyone else."

"You expect me to believe that?" Rachel stormed into the living room and whirled to face them when they followed her. "I'm not a little girl. I saw what a hunk he is, and I saw the way he looked at you when he was here."

"I'm not denying that Steve has a romantic interest in me," Anne said. "And I won't deny that I have a special friendship with him. He's been an important part of my life for a long time, and he always will be. But I don't feel the same way about him, and he knows that."

Crossing her arms over her chest again, Rachel raised both eyebrows at her father. "Are you buying this?"

"Steve has put his life on the line to protect me and your brother more than once, Rachel," Anne said before John could reply. "He was my labor coach when Chad was born, and he helped us both far beyond the call of duty. Please don't make his friendship with me into something ugly."

"But what about Daddy? Do you still love him? Are you guys gonna get married again or what?"

"How would you feel about it if we did?" Anne asked.

"It might be okay, I guess." Rachel stuck the tips of her fingers into the waistband of her shorts. "I just don't want Dad to get hurt again."

"And I don't want to hurt him. Can you trust us enough to believe we'll do what we think is best for everyone?"

Rachel shrugged one shoulder. "I don't know. It's not easy for me to trust you anymore."

Anne swallowed the lump in her throat. "Are you afraid I'll leave again?"

Biting her lower lip, Rachel nodded.

"I don't know what I can say to ease your mind about that, honey. The best I can do is swear that I won't lie to you, and I'll never make you or your dad any promises I'm not sure I can keep. Is that fair enough?"

Rachel studied her for a moment, her expression tinged with what Anne hoped was grudging respect. "I guess so."

It took a ton of willpower to prevent herself from hugging the girl, but somehow Anne managed to restrict herself to a smile. Rachel gave her a shy one in return, then turned to her father.

"Well, uh, I don't know about you guys, but Chad wore me out and I'm tired."

John put his arm around her and gave her a hug. "All right, Rach. Let's go home."

Anne followed them to the front door and picked up her purse from the railing in the entryway. "What's the going rate for baby-sitting, Rachel?"

Rachel held up one hand in refusal. "This one's on me, Mom."

"Oh, honey, I expected to pay you," Anne protested. "I know what a handful Chad can be."

"I didn't say I'd always baby-sit that little monster for free," Rachel said with a grin. "But I'd like to do it this time, okay?"

"Thank you," Anne said, feeling perilously close to tears. Since her tear ducts had started working in Billings, she hadn't had much success in turning them off again. "I appreciate that."

Struggling to hold on to her composure, she turned to John. He winked at her, silently telling her he understood just how much these past few minutes had meant to her. Then he leaned down and gently kissed her cheek.

"I'll see you tomorrow, Annie. Sleep well."

Sleep? Anne thought as she closed the door behind them and reactivated the alarm system. She wouldn't be able sleep for hours. Kicking off her high heels, she danced into the living room and on into the kitchen, where she found Rachel's note about Steve's telephone calls.

Wondering what had prompted him to call, she made a cup of tea, carried it over to the breakfast bar and punched in the number she'd memorized long ago. He answered on the first ring, his voice impatient, as if he'd been waiting by the phone for hours.

"Did you have a good time on your date?" he asked.

"As a matter of fact, I did," she answered. "How did you know about it?"

"Your daughter took great delight in informing me," he said dryly. "She doesn't like me much."

"I don't know about that," Anne said. "She called you a hunk tonight."

"You've got to be kidding."

She laughed, then quickly recounted the conversation she'd just finished with Rachel.

"Perceptive little wretch, isn't she?" Steve asked.

"You'd better believe it. But I'm sure you didn't call to hear about Rachel. What's up, Steve?"

"I wanted to remind you to keep your guard up. Don't get sloppy about security."

An icy finger of fear skated the length of Anne's spine. "What's going on?"

"It's nothing I can put my finger on at this point. Just an instinct."

"I've got a lot of respect for your instincts, pal," Anne said. "Come on, Anderson. Give. Something must have happened to set you off."

"It's nothing serious, Anne. I just heard from one of my DEA contacts today that they're getting ready to raid Manny Costenzo's operation." Steve's friends at the Drug Enforcement Administration had provided him with useful tips on many occasions.

"I remember him staring at me during Frankie's trials, but he never threatened me," Anne said. "Not even after Frankie died."

"I wouldn't have let you leave the program if he had. But I've always thought it was a little fishy. Frankie was the only family Manny had left. But, hey, the DEA boys will round him up and have him behind bars before long."

"Yeah, right," Anne muttered. She closed her eyes for a moment, remembering Frankie Costenzo's face contorted with rage and hatred as the bailiff dragged him from the courtroom after the foreman of the jury announced the guilty verdict. "Dammit, I shouldn't have come back here."

"Don't freak out on me, now. I'm so used to protecting you and Chad, I'm probably having separation anxiety or something. I just want you be careful, okay?"

"You're talking to the queen of careful."

"Which is why you and Chad are still alive, so keep it that way. I'll be in touch if I hear anything."

Her euphoria over the progress she'd made with Rachel deflated by Steve's warning, Anne hung up the phone, dumped the dregs of her tea down the sink and checked all the doors and windows to make sure they were locked. Then she wandered into the living room. She really should get some sleep. Chad would be up by six, but the thought of facing her empty bed was repugnant.

Her blood froze when the doorbell rang a moment later. She wasn't expecting anyone, and she didn't know a soul who would visit her so late. Every sense painfully alert, she crept silently to the front door. Her breath came out in a relieved whoosh when she looked through the peephole and saw John standing on her porch.

She deactivated the alarm and swung open the door, inviting him inside with a sweep of her hand. "This is a surprise. Is Rachel all right?"

"She's fine." John handed her his Stetson and waited while she hung it on a peg mounted on the wall behind her. "I just wanted to talk to you about something. I hope I didn't scare you by showing up so late."

Leading the way to the living room, she smiled over her shoulder at him. "A little. It might be a good idea to call first next time. Would you like something to drink?"

Shaking his head, he settled himself at one end of the sofa and crossed one long leg over the other. Taking the opposite end, she turned sideways and tucked her feet to one side, resting her elbow on the back of the sofa.

"What did you want to talk about?"

"I had a great time with you tonight," he said slowly, as if choosing each word with care. "And I really admired the way you handled Rachel. She was pretty snotty there at first."

"That doesn't bother me," Anne said. "I'll take snotty over indifferent any day. I thought we made good progress tonight."

"You did. She didn't say much on the way home, but I could tell she was impressed with your honesty. I was, too." He took a deep breath and sighed it out before he continued. "I guess that's really why I'm here, Annie. You see, uh, I wasn't entirely honest tonight."

"What do you mean?"

"Chad told me some things he said he wasn't supposed to talk about. I didn't tell you because I didn't want you to feel pressured to explain anything. I was hoping you'd tell me yourself before too long."

"What did he tell you?"

"That you've got a bad scar on your shoulder from getting shot. That you still have nightmares and so does he." John uncrossed his legs and leaned forward, clasping his hands between his knees. "The thing is, I still don't know what all happened to you. And I'm so damn jealous of your pal, Anderson, I—"

Anne swore in exasperation and hit the sofa with the side of her fist. "For heaven's sake, John. I'll swear on a stack of Bibles I never had an affair with him."

"I believe you about that, Annie," he said. "Honest. I don't have any trouble with your having him for a friend."

"Then why on earth are you jealous of him?"

"Why do you think? Chad talks about him all the time like he can walk on water or something. And now I find out he was your labor coach. I can't help feeling that it should have been *me,* dammit."

"I wish it *had* been you," she said. "But what's the point in tormenting yourself over something we can't change?"

"I'm not tormenting myself. It's just that Anderson was a part of your life without me. He knows things about you and about Chad that I don't. I feel shut out. Like I said, I don't even know what happened that day at the mall."

"It was so awful you really don't want to know," she whispered, closing her eyes against the anguish in John's.

"Maybe I don't *want* to. But I *need* to, Annie."

"Why? Why can't you just trust me on this?"

"Because I didn't handle it very well when Chad told me you'd been shot. He got upset and I don't want to do that to him again."

"All right. I'll tell you on two conditions," Anne said, her stomach churning with acid at the prospect of reliving that hideous scene. "Number one, you have to let me tell it without interrupting. It's the only way I'll be able to get through it."

"Fine. What's the other condition?"

"I don't want you to tell the girls. They don't need to have nightmares, too."

"All right. Go ahead."

Climbing off the sofa, she wrapped her arms around her waist and paced in front of the coffee table, working up the courage to begin. The prosecutors had always made her start with what had happened when she came out of the mall, but for John, she wanted to set the stage a bit earlier.

"It was hot that day," she said, forcing herself to pull up the details that were indelibly imprinted on her mind. "Miserably hot and muggy. The air-conditioning in my apartment wasn't working very well, so I decided to go shopping.

"After that last night we spent together, I was hopeful that we were going to be able to work things out. I thought it would be a nice surprise for you if I bought some nighties and underwear that weren't cotton or flannel."

"I would have enjoyed that kind of surprise, Annie," John said softly.

She shot him a wry grin. "You're not supposed to interrupt, Miller. Remember?"

"Yes, ma'am. I won't do it again."

The gentle, teasing light in his eyes reminded her that this was the man who had shared her secrets for more than a decade. He'd made mistakes during their marriage, but he'd never betrayed a confidence. Somehow it made the telling a little easier. Sliding her hands into her skirt pockets, she resumed her pacing and her story.

"Anyway, I went a little nuts and came out of the store with two big bags of stuff. I was excited and happy, and I didn't care that I'd just spent my entire month's food budget at Frederick's of Hollywood.

"It was about three-thirty. The parking lot was fairly quiet. Maybe that's why I noticed the family sitting in the car next to mine. The parents were in the front seat, and there were three little kids in car seats in the back. They were all eating ice-cream cones.

"They made me think of you and the girls, and I guess I must have smiled at the father. I remember him smiling at me. I thought he and his wife looked pretty young to have so many kids, but they were laughing over the mess the kids were making with their ice cream, and they all seemed . . . happy."

This was where it got difficult. Difficult to force herself to remember and difficult to describe an unspeakable horror with words. Anne inhaled twice and hugged herself again.

"I, uh, climbed into my car and rolled the windows down. Then I turned around and stuck my bags in the back, and I felt something poking my ankle from under the front seat.

"I turned back around and started feeling with my hand for whatever had poked me. It was one of the girls' coloring books. It was stuck tight. It must have jammed the seat mechanism, because I couldn't get the seat to slide in either direction."

Her breath and her words started to get choppy, just as they always had on the witness stand. Sweat trickled down her sides and the back of her neck. Her stomach curled into a tight little ball, like a porcupine prepared for battle.

"I couldn't get the coloring book out and I couldn't get it to go back under the seat, either. I slid over to the passenger side and knelt on the floor, thinking that if I could see what I was doing, it might help. I guess that's why Duke Donner thought he could do his job and get away with it. He couldn't see me because I was all crunched down behind the dash."

Unable to continue, Anne looked over at John and found him literally sitting on the edge of his seat, his hands still clasped between his knees. His eyes were filled with concern and intense interest and, dammit, sympathy. Well, she probably looked so pained and demented maybe he couldn't help it.

"Are you getting the picture?" she asked.

"Yeah. I think so. Keep going, Annie."

"I was yanking at the coloring book. Then I heard a man's voice right next to the window. He said, 'Whalen? I've got a present for you from Frankie Costenzo.'

"And then...oh, God, then I heard the man in the other car swear. His wife screamed. I looked up and saw this man...this perfectly ordinary-looking man...raise a pistol and start firing into their car."

"Good God, Annie," John murmured, rising off the sofa.

She waved him away and talked faster, wanting only to be finished. "He was using a silencer, so no one heard the shooting. I knew it was already too late for that family, but I reached over and started pounding on my horn, trying to attract somebody's attention. Donner just kept firing. Then he turned and looked in at me, and...

"He had dead eyes. Absolutely no emotion there at all. Steve told me the man who killed him in prison told the guards that he couldn't stand to look at those damn creepy eyes of his anymore. I don't blame him.

"When I have nightmares, that's what I dream about. Looking into Donner's dead eyes while he aims his gun at me and pulls the trigger. Twice. He got me both times. In the shoulder."

"How..." John said, his voice trailing off as if he couldn't complete a coherent sentence.

"How did I get away?" she asked. He nodded.

"I got lucky. Brad Whalen was an undercover DEA agent who'd come home on a leave of absence. A guy Brad worked with got wind of the hit and had tracked him to the mall with four other agents to warn him. They heard me honking and came running. Donner had to take off before he could make sure I was dead. They drove me to the hospital.

"When I came out of the anesthesia after my surgery, they were thrilled that I could pick Donner out of a photo lineup, and ecstatic that I could tie Frankie Costenzo to the hit. Nobody had ever been able to do either one of those things before.''

"So that's how you ended up being a protected witness."

"Uh-huh. They wouldn't have had a solid case without me, and everybody knew it. They treated me very carefully."

"Is that when they brought in Anderson?"

"No, I had a different marshal at first, but there were a few security problems in the DEA or the prosecutor's office—they never knew for sure where the leaks were coming from. Anyway, another hit man almost got to me the day after the murders. Steve had more experience at keeping witnesses alive, so they brought him in. He supervised cleaning out my apartment and everything. Believe me, he's damn good at his job or Chad and I wouldn't be here."

"How many more attempts on your life were there?"

"Enough. See, you have to understand that guys like Frankie Costenzo and Duke Donner are basically sociopaths. They think they're smarter than everyone else, they have no compassion, and they really believe they're above the law. To them, I was just a broad, you know? A little nobody schoolteacher they could intimidate into silence."

One side of John's mouth curved up in a wry grin. "They'd never tangled with a Montana gal before."

"That's what Steve kept telling me," she said. "I guess he was right. It was like a psychological war. We were constantly on the run, paranoid, off balance. They just kept coming after me and coming after me, but the harder those bastards pushed, the more determined I was to put them away."

"And you finally did it."

Anne nodded with grim satisfaction. "It took four years, but they both ended up in maximum security at the federal penitentiary in Marion, Illinois. That's where they put the really bad guys."

Scowling, John said, "I guess you're pretty proud of yourself."

"Shouldn't I be?" she asked, not liking the note of disapproval in his voice one damn bit.

"What you did took a lot of guts." He rose from the sofa, facing her with an intense, challenging stare. "But you paid one hell of a price, Annie. Was it worth it?"

"Between their drug dealing and outright murder, those creeps destroyed thousands of lives. If you were the only person who could stop them, would you have been able to refuse and still face yourself in the mirror every morning?" she demanded. "I don't think so, John."

"Maybe you're right."

"Dammit, there's no *maybe* about it. I *am* right. And I was right to keep you and the girls out of it, *wasn't* I?"

Chapter Twelve

Furious, John curled his hands into fists. "Oh, you'd really love for me to admit that, wouldn't you?"

Annie raised her chin another notch. "Yes. I would. Surely you can see that it was no place for kids."

"You kept Chad with you."

"I already explained that." Tossing her hands up beside her head in a gesture of frustration, Annie turned her back on him. Her shoulders slumped and the bitter note of defeat in her voice cut through his fury like a hot spoon through ice cream.

"Why didn't I keep my big mouth shut?" she muttered. "I knew you'd just get mad at me again if I told you."

"I'm not mad *at* you, Annie. I'm mad *for* you. For all the suffering you went through. And I'm mad at myself for not being there when you needed me."

She cast a wary look over her shoulder. "That wasn't your fault, John."

"Sure it was. When you filed the divorce papers, you said you couldn't count on me anymore, and you were right. I was gone all the time, and for what?" He shook his head in disgust. "A chance to prove to my dad that I was a man even though I didn't want to be a rancher? That I could make it on my own?"

Annie crossed the room and stood directly in front of him. "You *did* make it on your own, and I was proud of you, John. You just didn't know when to quit, that's all. It didn't make you a bad person. And we both know Mike would have run our whole lives if you hadn't stood up to him."

John couldn't bear to see the entreaty in her eyes. He looked away, taking a deep, shuddering breath. "Dammit, Annie, stop defending me. And for God's sake, stop protecting me. I feel emasculated enough as it is."

"Emasculated?" she demanded with a disbelieving snort of laughter. "You?"

Looking back at her, he snarled, "Yeah. Me! I feel like a damned gelding."

She rolled her eyes. "Do you know what you're doing? You're wallowing in misplaced guilt. You didn't have a thing to do with what happened to me. I was a crime victim. Nobody can control something like that. It just *happens.*"

"Yeah, I'll bet you really told yourself that when you were lying in the hospital, hurt, and you didn't even feel like you could call out for me."

"I called out for you plenty! I wanted you with me so bad—" She stopped, swallowed, sighed. "But when the federal agents told me what it would be like in the program, I just couldn't drag you and the kids into it."

"Because *you* had to protect *me,*" John snapped, thumping her chest, then his own. "It still comes right back to that, and *that's* why I feel emasculated. You didn't think I could handle it."

"No, dammit!" Her face contorted with anguish, and suddenly she became a wild thing. She grabbed the front of his shirt and shook him with astonishing strength, shouting at him, "Will you *listen* to me for once? I knew *you* could handle it. If I'd only had *you* to worry about, I'd have

screamed my head off to get you there. It was watching
Donner shoot those *children,* John!''

''Annie, honey, calm down,'' John begged, horrified to
see tears literally gushing from her eyes.

''No! You *have* to understand me this time,'' she insisted, shaking him again, her words coming faster and faster. ''Those little kids were just *babies* and he *murdered*
them! He shot them like they were just *rats.* And I knew
they would hire somebody just like him to do the same thing
to Rachel and Holly without one shred of remorse. The girls
needed one of us, and it had to be *you,* because *I* couldn't
be there for them.''

''God, sweetheart,'' John whispered. ''I'm so sorry.''

''I don't *want* you to be sorry,'' she wailed. ''I want you
to understand, once and for all, that I *did* count on you! I
counted on you to take care of my babies. Every time those
bastards tried to kill me, I thanked God that I'd married a
man who was strong enough to be a good father. A man I
could *trust* to put his children's well-being at the top of his
priority list. That was the most important thing you could
have done for me and you did it. I'll always be grateful to
you for that.''

Releasing her grip on his shirt, she sagged against him as
if she'd used up her last scrap of strength. John wrapped his
arms around her and held her close, stroking her hair and
murmuring reassurance. If he wasn't the biggest damn fool
this side of the Mississippi... aw, hell.

He should have understood from the minute she mentioned children in the other car. And dammit, she *had* been
right to keep Rachel and Holly away from that mess. Given
the same set of circumstances, he would have done the same
thing. He just had to convince his damned ego of that.

Annie began to talk again, her voice a raw whisper. ''I
mourned when I thought Chad would never know you. I
wasn't just trying to make him feel good when I told him his
daddy was the most wonderful man in the world. If he
grows up to be half the man you are, he'll do fine.''

John lowered himself to the sofa and pulled Annie onto his lap. She snuggled into his embrace like an exhausted child. He wiped the tears from her cheeks, swallowed at the lump of concrete lodged in his throat when she rubbed her cheek against his chest and silently thanked God that this gallant little woman had survived and come back to him.

He had no idea how long they sat there together. It must have been a long time, but it didn't matter. Nothing mattered but having her in his arms at this moment.

Finally she pulled back a little and gave him an abashed smile. "I'm sorry I screamed at you."

"I'm not. I'm sorry I was so thickheaded you had to go through that."

"Do you forgive me?"

He had to clear his throat twice before he could speak. "There's nothing to forgive. You did what you had to do, and I'm so damned proud of you I don't know what to say."

"Don't say anything," she whispered, tracing his lips with an unsteady fingertip. "Just hush up and kiss me."

He probably should have argued with her. He knew it wouldn't end with a kiss, and he knew she was too vulnerable to make a rational decision. But he could no more refuse her request than he could refuse to draw his next breath.

Angling himself more comfortably into the corner of the sofa, he tilted her head back against his arm and reverently covered her mouth with his own. Kissing her had always excited him beyond reason, but this time, it was like walking off the end of a mile-high diving board and plunging into a deep, warm pool of pleasure.

The barriers that had stood between them were finally down. They'd stripped themselves emotionally naked and found a deep, abiding connection, a faith and trust in each other he'd feared was dead. But like the hardy seeds that sprouted after a forest fire, it had survived. He needed to celebrate that survival—just as he needed to celebrate Annie's survival—with an affirmation of life.

Turning more fully toward him, she buried her hands in his hair, patted his cheeks, stroked and caressed his neck and shoulders as if assuring herself that he was real, not some phantom lover who would vanish into a lonely dream. As if she'd reached for him in her sleep, wanted him, needed him for a thousand nights and more. As if he were the only man on earth who could give her what she craved.

The thought humbled him and filled his chest with a sweet ache unlike anything he'd ever known. At the same time, it pumped such a violent surge of arousal into his system, he felt dizzy—an exultant, strange, falling-down-drunk kind of dizzy that owed nothing to alcohol and everything to loving one special woman to the depths of his soul. And knowing she loved him back. Oh, God, *please,* let her love him back.

Fearing her touches would drive him into losing control of himself, he captured her hands in one of his and gently pushed them down to her lap.

"Easy, sweetheart," he whispered. "I'm right here and we've got all the time in the world."

He kissed her again, taking it deeper this time, absorbing her eager response the way parched ground soaks up raindrops. He stroked the side of her neck, smiling to himself when her delicate shiver assured him that making love to Annie really was like riding a bike; he hadn't forgotten the locations of all her most sensitive spots. He intended to revisit every one of them with his hands, his lips, his tongue, to shower her with all the tenderness and passion he possessed.

Her head lolled back against his arm, inviting him to explore further. He trailed a string of warm, wet kisses from her mouth to her jaw, down her neck to the sweet hollow created by her collarbones. Lord, but she had soft skin. Her little cries of delight made the most erotic music he'd ever heard.

While his lips were occupied at the V of her blouse, he put his fingers to work on the fabric-covered buttons down the front. When he slipped the second one free, she stiffened, her eyes flew open and she grabbed his wrist.

"What's the matter, sweetheart?" he whispered.

"Turn out the lights, John," she whispered back.

"Don't be shy with me, Annie." Nuzzling at the lapels of her blouse, he inhaled the rich fragrance of her perfume, the warm, womanly scent emanating from her cleavage. "I've always loved looking at you."

"You'll think I'm . . . ugly now."

Her grip on his wrist tightened. Hearing a note of panic in her voice, he pulled back and found her biting her lower lip so hard it was white.

"I've seen scars before. I've got a few of my own."

"Not like this—"

He silenced her with a kiss, then gazed deeply into her worried eyes. "I don't just make love to your body, babe. I make love to *you*. I may be a little shocked when I see this thing, but it won't turn me off, no matter how bad it is. I'll guarantee that."

"But, John—"

He cut her off again in exactly the same way, then rested his forehead against hers. "No way. I don't intend to make love in the dark for the rest of my life. We can get past this in about thirty seconds if you'll trust me the way you trusted me with the girls."

She hesitated long enough to make him realize he was holding his breath. Then she slowly released his wrist and gave him the most reluctant nod he'd ever seen. Steeling himself to control his reaction, he finished unbuttoning her blouse and smoothed back the fabric.

Her scar was shaped like a horizontal figure eight, indicating that the bullets must have struck her shoulder side by side. Though nobody would ever call the scar unnoticeable, it was hardly the disfigurement Annie obviously thought.

So it wasn't the white, puckered ridges of flesh that tore a choked, anguished gasp from his throat.

But unfortunately she didn't know that. She looked at his face, yanked the edges of her blouse together and started to get up. John pushed her back against the arm he'd been cradling her with and forced her hands into her lap again.

"It's not that bad, honey."

"Oh, *right*. That's why you looked so horrified."

"Yeah, I'm horrified. But not about this old scar. Hell, that's nothing."

Ignoring her mutinous glare, he opened her blouse again and laid his palm over her chest. He could feel her heart thumping furiously beneath her sternum. Well, tough. It was one thing to hear her talk about someone trying to kill her; it was something else entirely to see direct evidence that the son of a bitch had come damn close to succeeding.

"I'm horrified because of where it is," he said, struggling to soften his voice. "From what Chad told me, I thought it was higher up in your shoulder. Another inch lower and a hair to the left and you'd have been dead."

After searching his eyes for a long moment, she raised one hand to the side of his face. "I told you I was lucky."

He kissed her palm, then slid his free arm under her knees. Holding her against his chest, he got up and carried her to her bedroom. Closing the door with the heel of his loafer, he flipped the light switch with an elbow. A lamp sporting a frilly white shade came on, illuminating the way to the bed. He turned back the covers and deposited her in the middle of the mattress.

Sitting beside her, he reached out and slowly traced her scar, then leaned down and kissed it. He felt her hand caress the back of his neck, felt her lips brush the top of his head. It was a moment of acceptance and healing and mutual comforting. Then he raised his mouth to meet hers.

"Chad sleeps like a rock," she murmured after a long, drugging kiss, "but it wouldn't hurt to lock the door."

Retracing his steps, he punched the lock. Then he stripped off his tie as he returned to the bed. She rolled onto her side and propped her head on her hand, watching him through half-closed eyelids.

Her skirt had ridden up, revealing an enticing stretch of slender thighs, a darker strip of material at the top of her stockings. Lord have mercy, was that a garter peeking at him from under the hem of her skirt? Allowing his gaze to travel up her body, he noticed that her blouse had fallen away from her torso, exposing half of a lacy black bra.

The temperature in the room climbed ten degrees. He sensed a subtle shift in the atmosphere, a mixture of longing, tension and anticipation. It was as if the act of locking the door had shut out the horrors of the past, freeing them to be nothing more than a man and a woman, meeting at this time, in this private place, to share the most intimate of pleasures.

He paused beside the bed, fighting the sudden, fierce need clawing at his insides. She looked tousled enough to touch, wanton enough to romp with and inviting enough to make his shaft strain eagerly against his fly. Dropping his tie to the floor, he slipped off his shoes and stretched out on his side facing her.

They silently studied each other for a heartbeat. Then another. And another. Vivid, lusty visions of the last night they had spent together pulsed through his mind, and somehow, looking into her eyes, he knew she was sharing those memories with him.

Her sultry smile raised the temperature in the room ten more degrees. He traced her lips with one finger. She licked his fingertip, sending a jolt of excitement straight to his groin. He reached for her.

The years of separation fell away with each article of clothing removed, each lingering kiss and caress, each shiver of arousal and groan of approval. Loving her was wonderfully familiar, but this time, there was a new depth of emotion he'd never felt before.

What if he'd never again been able to taste her luscious breasts? What if he'd never been able to hear her voice go all husky when he coaxed her into telling him what she wanted? Feel her legs wrap around his waist, her fingernails digging into his shoulders, her shudders of delight when he entered her, those wonderful, inner contractions when he brought her to climax? See her neck arch until the tendons stood out in bold relief, her head thrash back and forth on the pillow, her eyes turning smoky and sleepy with satisfaction?

The idea of how close he'd come to never again experiencing any of those things with Annie drove him on and on, sharpening his senses with stunning intensity. Every murmur and sigh, groan and whimper, texture and flavor and scent took on new meaning, as if the world had shrunk to this bed, this moment, this woman who wept with joy as they clung together in the aftermath.

He had shared more than one chuckle with his dad over how skinny and exhausted their Hereford bulls looked at the end of the breeding season. Now he empathized with their desperate need to mate again and again. He felt exactly the same way, but he didn't want a herd of women to choose from. He wanted only Annie.

Her uninhibited response to his lovemaking wakened an undeniable life force in his loins, in his head, in his heart. As corny as it sounded, she brought out the best in him. With her, he could do anything, create anything, be anything. She made him feel like a hero.

He wanted to be *her* hero. To be there in the night and hold her when she had those bad dreams Chad had told him about. To help her feel safe again. To give her soaring heights of passion and quiet moments of understanding. To make up for all the times he'd failed her, grow old with her and watch their children become happy, productive adults.

Most of all, he wanted to become the man she deserved. The man she loved. The man she needed.

In a fever of excitement, she clutched at his hips, urging him deeper and harder and faster. He gritted his teeth and tilted his head way back, hoping that if he couldn't see the ecstasy on her face, he'd be able to prolong the incredible sensations.

Her inner muscles tightened around him, demanding all he had to give, and there was no denying the inevitable. Arching into his thrusts, she shrieked with delight. The sound tumbled him headlong into a violent release that left him gasping and sweating and utterly, gloriously drained.

Exhaling a gusty sigh of satisfaction, Anne looked up into John's face and ran her hands down his heaving sides. She'd thought she remembered everything about what it was like to make love with him, but her most vivid memories had been a paltry substitute for the real thing.

Nothing could possibly replace the feel of his hot, smooth skin and the strong, fluid muscles beneath. The wonderful weight of his hard body pressing her into the soft mattress. The raw power in his thrusting, driving hips. The unique sensation of being filled and connected in the most intimate way possible.

He shook his head as if trying to clear it, braced himself on his elbows and gazed down at her. A wicked, infinitely smug grin spread from his mouth to his eyes. And no wonder, she thought, since he'd just demonstrated the stamina of a twenty-year-old.

"You still love me, Annie?" he said.

"Yes, John, I do."

A chuckle rumbled out of his chest at her blunt reply. He lowered his head and kissed her nose, her cheekbones and eyelids. "Then marry me again. Let's put our family back together and get on with our lives."

Had anyone ever spoken words she wanted to hear more? Not in this lifetime. A resounding yes danced on the tip of her tongue. She had to bite down hard to hold it back. Finally she gently shook her head.

"I don't think Rachel's ready for that yet, John."

His eyebrows swooped into a scowling V. Sliding his hands under her shoulders, he rolled onto his side, bringing her along with him to share the same pillow.

"She'll come around, Annie."

"I think she will, too, eventually. But I don't want to rush her. Give me a little more time with her."

"How much more time?"

"I can't give you an exact date. She came closer tonight, but I wouldn't be surprised to see her back off again tomorrow. It seems to be kind of a two-steps-forward-one-step-back process.''

He heaved a disgruntled sigh, reached up and wrapped one of her curls around his index finger. ''I suppose you're right, but we could speed things up if you and Chad moved out to the ranch. It'll be harder for her to avoid you if you're living right under her nose.''

Anne considered his suggestion for a moment. He had a point about Rachel's avoiding her. Still, she couldn't quite bring herself to consent. ''I don't think that's the kind of example we want to set for the kids. They know we're not married, and it won't be long before the girls start dating.''

''So? We'll sleep in separate bedrooms.''

She raised an eyebrow at that, then laughed out loud and pinched his bare tush. ''Uh-huh. *Sure* we will. Pardon my grammar, but you ain't no gelding, honey.''

The observation earned her a hug and an enthusiastic kiss. But when the kiss ended, John flopped his head onto the pillow and heaved another disgruntled sigh.

''Okay, you're right about that, too,'' he grumbled, his expression reminding her of Chad when he intended to do some serious sulking. ''But hell, Annie, I want to be with you, and I'm too old to enjoy sneaking around. Especially when I have to sneak around my own kids.''

''I agree. How about an alternative suggestion?''

''I'm listening.''

''Why don't we hitch your dad's camper to my van, pile everybody in and go on a vacation together? You and Chad could sleep in the van or we could bring a tent along.''

John smiled at that. ''That just might work. We could go to Yellowstone or over around Ennis and Virginia City. The kids would get a kick out of that.''

''Exactly. It doesn't have to be a big trip. We just want to build in lots of family time.''

John wrapped his free arm around her waist and pulled her closer. ''When did you get to be so smart?''

''I was always this smart,'' Anne told him, tweaking a tuft of his chest hair. ''You were just too busy to notice.''

"Well, I'm not too busy now. I've noticed a lot of things about you lately."

He rolled onto his back and pulled her on top of him. Straddling his hips, she braced her hands on either side of his head. "Oh, yeah? What have you noticed?"

Spanning her midriff with both hands, he walked his fingers up her ribs. "You've gotten pretty dang skinny."

"You liked me better chubby?"

"I never thought you were chubby." He scraped his thumbs up over her nipples, grinning when she gasped at the swift, sharp bolt of desire his action ignited. "If you were any sexier, I'd probably have a stroke."

She lifted one knee as if she intended to climb off him. Laughing, he grabbed her elbows, slid his palms down her forearms and linked their fingers together. Then he flipped her onto her back and rolled on top of her.

"And just where did you think you were going?"

Feigning a sad expression, she said, "I wouldn't want to risk giving you a stroke, you poor old man."

He stretched her arms over her head and rubbed his whiskery chin into the crook of her neck in punishment. "Oh, you're gonna pay for that one, sweetheart. I'll show you who's an old man."

She giggled at his outraged expression and hunched her shoulder, trying to push his chin away from her neck without much success. "Now, John, I didn't even get to harass you on your fortieth birthday."

"Trust me, the girls took care of it. Rachel baked me a black cake and Holly bought me a cane. I'll be sure to pass it on to you when your turn comes."

"I'm not going to turn forty. When I hit thirty-nine next year, that's it. No more birthdays."

"Good luck pulling that one off." He leaned down and teased her lips with his teeth. "Being forty's not really so bad. Especially if all of your parts still work."

She raised her hips, brushing them against his swollen flesh. "Yours seem to be working fine."

"Mmm." Still holding her hands above her head, he settled his weight between her legs. "Maybe we'd better test 'em out again, just to make sure."

That delicious, floaty feeling spread through her limbs as his mouth roamed over her, nibbling, nipping, licking. His voice became raspy, his breathing choppy, but his hands were sure and delightfully clever. Her heart pounded, her blood raced, her nerve endings rejoiced at his touch.

By the time he released her hands, she was frantic to touch him back, to lavish his body with the same sweet torment, to stroke and fondle and seduce him into fulfilling the naughty suggestions he had whispered in her ear. They rolled over and over across the bed, tossing pillows onto the floor, tangling in the sheets.

It was glorious and fun, erotic and sensuous, exciting and piercingly sweet, leaving no doubt in either of their minds that his parts were in perfect working order. When they had shared another mind-shattering climax, he held her in a tender embrace while they drifted off to sleep. She awoke two hours later when the warm hard shoulder she'd been using for a pillow moved.

"What's the matter?" she murmured.

"Nothing, honey." He kissed her cheek. "It's almost dawn, and I've got to get out of here before Chad gets up. Go on back to sleep if you want."

She yawned and stretched. "I'll have to let you out and reset the alarm."

He pulled on his pants while she slipped into her robe. "Is that really necessary? This is Bozeman. And this is such a nice neighborhood you shouldn't have any trouble."

"It's not Bozeman people who worry me."

Pausing in the middle of buttoning his shirt, he said, "I thought you were out of danger. That all of the bad guys were dead. What's going on?"

"Nothing, really."

He crossed to her side and gripped her shoulders in his hands. "Come on, Annie, tell me. It has something to do with Anderson's phone call last night, doesn't it?"

Biting her lower lip, she nodded, then quickly recounted what Steve had told her about Manny Costenzo. "So, you see, it's probably nothing, but I'll never ignore Steve's instincts. He can smell danger five miles off."

John released her. A suspicious glint darkened his eyes and a hard edge entered his voice. "Were you going to tell me? Or just disappear again if you thought it was necessary?"

"That's not fair, John."

"Isn't it? Dammit, Annie, you've got to start trusting me more than this."

"Hey, I told you, all right? Besides, I'm through with running from creeps."

"Well, good. I'm glad to hear that. But this puts a different light on things as far as I'm concerned."

"What do you mean?"

"I don't want you and Chad to be here alone. I really think you should move out to the ranch. If your safety's at stake, I'll stay out of your bed."

"That's silly, John. If anything happens with Manny Costenzo, Steve will give me plenty of warning, and I'm perfectly capable of defending myself and Chad."

"Annie—"

"No. Let's go on our vacation and forget this mess."

He opened his mouth to protest again, but she raised one hand to hold him off. "Hush. You've got to start trusting *me*. I promise I'll tell you if there are any new developments."

His eyes narrowed and his lips compressed into a tight, grim line. She held her breath, praying that he wouldn't fight her.

"All right, Annie, you win," he said with obvious reluctance. "But we're in this together now. You'd better keep that promise."

She put her arms around his neck and gave him a loud, smacking kiss. "I will, John. Now get out of here, will you? Our son will be up any minute."

When he'd finished dressing, she walked him to the door and watched him drive away. Feeling let down by the way their wonderful night together had ended, she went into the kitchen and started a pot of coffee. Darn it all—why did everything have to be so complicated?

Why couldn't this nightmare with drug dealers and hit men be over? Why couldn't Rachel accept her without going through all these adolescent gyrations? Why couldn't she and John marry and, as he'd said, get on with their lives?

Better yet, why hadn't John said he loved her? She knew darn well he did. She'd seen it in his eyes and felt it in every aspect of his lovemaking. But he hadn't said the words, not even when he'd heard them from her.

"It's the same thing that's going on with Rachel," she muttered, watching the last drops of water hiss and sputter into the filter basket. "Two steps forward, one step back. Give it time, Annie, old girl. Just give it time."

She was really starting to hate the sound of those words. Dammit, how much longer did she have to wait?

Chapter Thirteen

"Aren't we there yet?" Holly whined.

"I've gotta go to the bathroom," Chad announced for what had to be the tenth time since breakfast.

"Jeez, Dad, this is *so-o-o* boring. Let's go back to Virginia City. At least there's something to do there," Rachel added.

Holly batted her eyelashes at Rachel. "You mean *boys*."

Rachel reached over the back of the middle seat and thumped Holly on the head. "Shut up, you little snot."

"Dad, she hit me," Holly yelled.

"Did not."

"Did, too."

Taking one hand off the steering wheel, John rubbed the back of his neck. "Knock it off, kids. One more cross word and I'll play my Dolly Parton tape again."

As if on cue, all three kids poked fingers into their mouths and made retching noises. Torn between laughter and a fierce urge to shriek in frustration, Anne massaged her aching temples.

It had been hot and dusty forever, and she could cheerfully go at least ten years without seeing another gravel road. It seemed as if they'd been on this one for days. For the life of her, she couldn't remember what was supposed to be so great about family outings.

Casting a wary glance over her shoulder at the renegades in the rear of the minivan, she sighed and shook her head. Holly and Chad shared the middle bench seat along with an unbelievable clutter of books, crayons and toys. Rachel had claimed the back seat as her personal territory, venturing out of her regal isolation only when she felt like tormenting her younger siblings.

Fulfilling Anne's prediction that she would probably want to back off again, Rachel had fiercely resisted the idea of this vacation from the start. While she did unbend enough to enjoy herself in occasional ten-minute spurts, she inevitably found a new reason to gripe. If teenagers took classes in sulking, Rachel would easily earn an A-plus.

After six days and nights of sharing close quarters in the van and the camper, her surly attitude was starting to grate on everyone. Add the fact that they were all tired and hungry, and the atmosphere in the vehicle was more tense than an IRS office filled with people facing an audit. The van rounded a sharp curve, and at long last, Anne saw a sign announcing the entrance to Beaverhead National Forest.

"Thank God for small favors," John muttered.

Anne shot him a sympathetic look before turning her attention to the scenery. Aspen and pines lined the road on either side, and the majestic peaks of the Tobacco Root Mountains loomed ahead. The August heat had parched the grass to a pale gold and made the wildflowers droop.

The weight of the camper strained the van's engine as the road became steeper, forcing John to turn off the air-conditioning. Holly and Chad groaned. Rachel's griping took on an all-too-familiar theme—blaming Anne for everything that went wrong.

"The Suburban's got more power. I don't know why we had to bring this stupid van."

"Give it a rest, Rachel," John warned. "We'll be there in ten minutes."

Uh-oh, Anne thought after a quick look at him. The man deserved a trophy for the patience he'd demonstrated with Rachel over the past six days. But the kid had finally pushed him to the edge. His knuckles stood up like miniature white mountains along the top curve of the steering wheel. A muscle twitched at the side of his jaw, and if he clenched his teeth any harder, they'd probably crack and fall out in pieces.

Mercifully, the campground appeared around the next bend. John backed the trailer into a shady parking spot and everyone piled out of the van like prisoners escaping from jail. While the kids ran off to explore, Anne climbed into the trailer and carried the makings for sandwiches to the picnic table.

The pine-scented air eased her headache. She set out paper plates, plastic knives, bread and packets of sliced ham, turkey and cheese, along with chips, dip and a tray of condiments. Craving a few minutes of peace, she decided to let the kids run around for a while longer. She sat on one of the benches, braced her elbows on the table behind her and stretched her legs out in front of her. Then she closed her eyes and tipped her face toward the sky.

She heard John come out of the camper. The table wobbled when he set the cooler at one end. A moment later a warm, firm mouth touched the base of her throat.

"Go away," she said, struggling to keep a straight face. "I'm communing with nature."

The mouth slid up her neck and brushed the underside of her chin. "Don't mind me," John murmured. "I'm just a friendly forest elf."

She opened one eye, shook her head and closed the eye again. "Elves are supposed to be shorter."

"What can I say?" He kissed the tip of her chin, then smooched along her jawline to her left ear. "I'm a mutant elf who has an obsession for pretty ladies named Annie."

Anne hooked one arm around the back of his neck and turned her head, aligning her nose with his. "What you are," she whispered, "is a lech."

His lips closed over hers in a hot, breath-stealing kiss. His tongue skated along the edges of her teeth and plunged into the deepest recesses of her mouth. He pulled her T-shirt out of the waistband of her shorts and slipped his hand inside to caress her back.

The irritations of the day floated off on the breeze murmuring through the weeds. Her heart raced, and there was roaring in her ears that blocked out all other sounds until Chad yelled from less than ten feet away.

"Oh, *gross!* They're kissing again!"

With a muffled groan, John straightened to his full height and offered Anne a hand up. Feeling a tide of heat flowing into her face, she tugged the hem of her T-shirt down over her hips and accepted his help. All three kids approached from the opposite side of the table. Holly and Chad broke into fits of giggles. Rachel rolled her eyes.

"If there was any traffic out here, I'd tell them all to go play in it," John whispered.

Anne elbowed him in the ribs and gestured toward the table with her other hand. "Everything's ready, so I guess we might as well eat. Grab a plate and help yourselves."

The girls didn't need any more encouragement, but Chad sidled up to Holly and gave her his most winsome smile.

"Will you make me a ham sandwich, Holly?"

"Sure, Ditto. Do you want mustard or mayo?"

Before Chad could answer, Anne handed him a plate. "None of that, buster. You know how to make a sandwich."

"Aw, Mom, Holly makes 'em better and I'm starvin'."

"Then you'd better get to work, hadn't you? Holly's hungry, too, and she's done enough waiting on you."

"He's just a little boy," Rachel said, her voice bordering on insolence. "If Holly doesn't mind helping him, I don't see why you should object."

Clamping her hands on her hips, Anne silently counted to ten while she met and held Rachel's challenging stare. "Look at it this way," Anne said when she had a firm grip on her temper. "Chad won't always be a little boy. Someday he'll be an adult, and I don't think his wife will appreciate it if he's a big, helpless lug who expects her to wait on him all the time."

"I'm never gonna have a wife," Chad protested. "Especially if you have to kiss girls to get one."

Anne ruffled his hair. "Then you'd really better learn to take care of yourself. Get busy now. You can do it."

Though Rachel subsided, the withering look she gave Anne indicated she didn't think much of her mother's explanation. She slapped a sandwich together, grabbed a handful of chips and a can of soda and carried her lunch to a big rock about five yards from the table. Anne's headache returned with a vengeance, stealing her appetite and weighing her down with depression.

As she saw the problem, Rachel had become used to being the oldest female in the family, and she wasn't about to give up that position without a fight. Since the trip had begun, she'd taken a this-family's-not-big-enough-for-both-of-us stance. Though Anne couldn't point to any specific incident that would have triggered such an attitude in the girl, she suspected it had something to do with the return of affection between John and herself.

Every time he kissed her in front of the kids, held her hand or even put an arm around her, Rachel displayed her displeasure, usually by starting an argument with Holly or Chad. It was as if the girl feared that if her father spared any love and attention for the interlopers who had invaded her family, he wouldn't have enough left for her.

She continually found ways to challenge Anne's parental authority over Chad, as she had with the sandwich business. In doing so, she was sending an obvious message that she didn't plan to accept any correction from her mother. Anne could understand that. No self-respecting teenager wanted any more authority figures breathing down her neck.

But on the other hand, she *was* Rachel's mother. If she married John again and moved into the ranch house, there would inevitably be times when he wasn't around to act as a buffer. Anne would be the adult in charge, and at some point, Rachel would have to accept that.

Unfortunately Anne had to admit that at the rate she was going, she might never get through to Rachel. And if she couldn't . . . well, there was no way she could subject the entire family to years of power struggles.

Darn that kid. Sure, she was scared and confused. But she wasn't the only one involved in this situation. What about Holly and Chad? What about herself and John? Didn't their needs and desires matter? And yet, seeing Rachel sitting alone on that damned rock, her shoulders slumped with dejection while Holly and Chad laughed and talked with John, tore into Anne's heart like steel claws.

As if he guessed the direction of her thoughts, John grasped her hand under the table and gave it an encouraging squeeze. She looked up at him and tried to smile, but simply couldn't force her mouth to cooperate. She wanted to be with him so much she ached, but she couldn't—not if it meant Rachel would end up being alienated from the rest of the family the way she was now.

Come on, baby, Anne thought, looking back at Rachel. *Just meet me halfway. We can work this out if you'll give me a chance.*

When everyone had finished eating, John got out a couple of folding lawn chairs and offered one to Anne. Chad and Holly sat nearby on the grass playing crazy eights. Rachel sprawled belly-down on a blanket, lazily flipping through a stack of fashion magazines.

"I want to go fishin'," Chad announced after Holly had beaten him for the third time.

"The fish won't be hungry now. We'll probably have better luck after supper, or maybe early tomorrow morning," John replied. "How about a hike, instead?"

Chad gave John the charming smile that always worked on the girls. "It's too hot. The thing is, I've only been fishin' once, and I thought maybe you'd help me practice. There's a creek right over there we could try."

John glanced in the direction Chad had indicated, then gave Anne a where-does-he-come-up-with-this-stuff? look. She grinned and shrugged.

"Please, Dad?" Chad insisted. "Pretty please?"

John pushed himself out of the chair. "All right. You can help me dig out the rods and the tackle box." Turning back to Anne, he said, "I don't suppose you want to come along and supervise."

She wrinkled her nose at him. She'd always hated fishing, and he knew it. "And spoil your male bonding? I wouldn't dream of it. If you run across my book in the camper, toss it this way."

Ten minutes later, the guys emerged with their gear. John pitched Anne's novel to her and accompanied Chad to the stream. She shifted her chair to a spot where she could watch them without being too obvious about it.

In moments the two most important men in her life were into a deep discussion of such fascinating items as sinkers, bobbers, lures and hooks. John patiently answered Chad's endless questions and demonstrated the proper techniques in a way that warmed Anne's heart. No wonder he enjoyed teaching so much.

Now, this was more like it, she thought, stretching her legs out and opening her book with a contented sigh. A good read, a warm, lazy afternoon and a peaceful setting were what vacations were supposed to be about. Unfortunately, as John continued to work with Chad, Rachel began to fidget.

She shoved her magazines aside and sat up, her gaze trained on the action by the creek. Holly invited her to play cards, but Rachel refused. She fiddled with her long hair, stacked and restacked the magazines, crossed and uncrossed her legs, pulled her knees up to her chest and wrapped her arms around them.

"What's wrong, Rachel?" Anne finally asked.

The girl shot her a disgruntled glance before looking back at John and Chad. "This is boring. How long are they gonna mess with that stuff?"

"Does it matter? All we had planned was a relaxing afternoon. If you and Holly want to go on a hike..."

"We don't hike without Dad."

Holly looked up from her game of solitaire. "Leave Dad alone, Rachel. Ditto got to him first. Can't you see how much fun they're having together?"

"Yeah, I see what's going on, all right," she grumbled. Then her mouth twisted into a bitter smile. "If you weren't so dang dumb, you would, too."

"What are you talking about?"

Rachel waved one hand toward the creek. "*Look,* will you? Dad always wanted to be with us before he found out he had a *son.* Can't you see when you're being replaced?"

"That's not true, Rachel," Anne said quietly. "Naturally your father has wanted to spend extra time with Chad this summer, but that doesn't mean he loves Chad more than you girls. Nobody could ever replace either of—"

"Oh, *right.* All he talks about anymore is Chad, and to hear Grandpa talk, Chad's the only one who could possibly take over the ranch when he retires. He used to want me to do that."

Anne visualized wrapping her hands around Mike's neck and squeezing hard. "Your grandpa has some old-fashioned ideas about men and women, and he's full of hot air. Everything at the ranch is exciting for Chad right now, but he may not want to be a rancher when he grows up any more than your dad did. I think you're worrying about something that might never be a problem."

Sniffing in disbelief, Rachel tossed her hair back over her shoulder. "That's not what it sounds like to me."

"Think about it logically. Your grandpa probably won't want to run the ranch too much longer, and you're a lot older than Chad. If you take over when you finish college, you'll have been running the ranch for five years by the time he's eighteen. By the time he finishes college, you'll have been in charge for nine years. It seems to me that should give you a pretty good head start."

"Yeah," Holly said. "And besides, you'll probably get married and move away, so it won't matter to you if Ditto takes over someday. What's the big deal?"

"Or maybe you and Chad could work together," Anne suggested. "Heaven knows, the Flying M keeps you and your dad *and* your grandpa busy. There are lots of ways to work these things out."

Rachel rested her chin on her knees and thought that over for a moment. Then she sighed and leaned back on her elbows. "Maybe you're right. It just feels . . ."

"A little scary?" Anne asked.

"A little."

"You're not the only one who feels that way, honey," Anne said. "We've all got a lot of adjustments to make, and that's always uncomfortable. We need to talk to each other more so things don't get blown out of proportion."

"Hey, Rachel," John called at that moment. "Would you bring that can of night crawlers we bought in Sheridan over here? I think I stuck it under the camper."

"Sure, Dad." She scrambled to her feet and went to carry out John's request without another word to Anne.

Still, Anne felt heartened by their conversation. If she could get Rachel to discuss her feelings, instead of hoarding them inside and building resentment, maybe there was hope, after all. The first thing she planned to do when they returned to Bozeman was have a talk with Mike.

"Do you think Dad would mind if we went over there to watch?" Holly asked.

"Why don't we go find out?"

Anne pushed herself to her feet. Holly skipped along beside her, swinging their clasped hands. When they arrived at the creek, John, Chad and Rachel were squatting in a circle, studying a tangled pile of night crawlers on the ground.

John separated a long one from the heap. "Okay, Chad, hand me your hook, and I'll show you how to put the bait on."

Chad shook his head. "I already know how. See?"

Gripping the hook tied to the end of his fishing line, Chad straightened out the wiggling worm and quickly proceeded to stab the poor creature in five different places. A choked sputter of laughter came out of John's throat. Rachel wasn't half as polite.

She rocked back on her heels and hooted in Chad's face. "What dipstick taught you to do it *that* way?"

Chad's face turned red and his chin came up. Ignoring what Anne knew to be a serious danger signal, Rachel continued. "That's the dumbest thing I've ever seen."

"Rachel," John said, his voice laced with warning.

"Well, *really,* Dad, he doesn't know anything."

"I do so!" Chad shouted at her. "It works, doesn't it? And ya don't even hafta touch the slimy old worm."

"That's for sissies. Only an idiot would bait a hook that way."

"Don't you call my mom an idiot!"

Moving so fast he was practically a blur, Chad lunged at Rachel, knocking her onto her behind. He slammed one fist into her abdomen. Before he could use the other, she shoved him away with such force he landed flat on his back. He howled with pain and started flailing his left arm.

"Mommy, Mommy! The hook's stuck in me!"

Horrified to see that he was right, Anne rushed forward and grabbed his thrashing arm before he could do any more damage to himself. A combination of protective instincts and devastating disappointment at having her fragile hopes so quickly dashed engaged Anne's mouth before her brain could catch up with it.

Turning on her older daughter, she said, "Rachel, how *could* you? Go to the camper and stay there."

"Wait a minute, Annie," John protested, helping Rachel to her feet. "Chad hit her first."

"She taunted him into it," Anne said. "And she's twice his size. She didn't have to push him so hard."

"I didn't mean to hurt him," Rachel said. "If he'd stop screaming like a big baby—"

The hook still embedded in his arm, Chad jerked out of Anne's grasp and went after his sister again. John grabbed him by the back of his shirt and plunked him smack on his bottom.

"Knock it off, Chad," he roared. "You don't hit girls. Ever." Then he focused on Rachel. "And *you* be quiet. I don't want to hear one more word out of you."

Her chin rose in defiance, but a single tear slid down her face. "Oh, thanks, Dad. I knew *she'd* take his side, but I thought you'd at least try to be fair."

"I'm not taking anyone's side," John said. "You were both wrong."

"I didn't do anything," Rachel insisted.

"You most certainly did!" Anne shouted. "And I've had just about enough out of you for one day."

"Calm down, Annie," John said.

"Calm *down!* Have you looked at Chad's arm? For God's sake, the hook's poked right through his skin and the worm's still on it!"

Trembling with fury, Holly let out a piercing shriek that brought the argument to an abrupt halt. "Stop it! All of you just stop it! Why can't we all just get along and be a family? That's all I've ever wanted."

"We *are* a family, honey," John said quietly.

"Well, nobody's acting like we are," she wailed. Tears poured from her eyes, and she inhaled a shaky breath before she went on. "I thought this vacation would be so much fun, but it's all wrecked now, 'cause you're all screamin' at each other. And I want you to quit!"

With that, she ran back toward camp, her sobs trailing behind her. Anne and John exchanged guilty looks. Rachel knelt beside Chad.

"Hey, little bro, I'm sorry," she said softly. "Let me see your arm. Maybe I can get the hook out."

Chad eyed her warily for a moment before holding up his injury for her inspection.

"Yeow," she said, wrinkling her nose at him. "That's major disgusting. Does it still hurt pretty bad?"

He raised one shoulder in a shrug. "Nah. It sure is yucky, though. And I ain't no baby, Rachel."

She grinned and ruffled his hair. "Of course not. The oldest kid always says that kinda stuff to bug the younger ones. Dad's got a pair of wire cutters in the camper. I think we can chop off the barbed end of that hook and just slide the other part right out. Will you be okay if I go get the cutters and the first-aid kit?"

"Yeah, but hurry. I don't like lookin' at it."

"Then don't look at it, silly. I'll be right back."

Climbing to her feet, she turned away, pausing to look over her shoulder when Chad called out to her.

"Hey, Rachel? I'm sorry, too. I won't hit you anymore."

She made a thumbs-up and hurried off, giving both parents a wide berth. Wishing she had kept her mouth shut from the beginning of the squabble, Anne watched until Rachel was out of sight. Then she sat cross-legged beside Chad, trying not to show how much the sight of that wormy hook revolted her.

John examined Chad's injury and patted his shoulder. "I think you'll live, pal. While you're getting patched up, I'll check on Holly."

"Will you come back and show me the real way to bait a hook, Dad?"

John shook his head. "Ask Rachel. She's the best hook baiter in the family."

Rachel returned in a few moments with the promised items in hand. She set about removing the hook and disinfecting the wound with a calm efficiency Anne admired. Chad bore the inevitable pain with a stoicism beyond his years, at least partly, Anne suspected, because he didn't want to lose stature in his big sister's eyes.

When the operation was completed, Anne sent Chad to check on John and Holly, then helped Rachel pack up the first-aid supplies.

"You did a wonderful job with Chad," Anne said. "Thank you."

Rachel shrugged. "He's really a pretty neat little guy. He just surprised me, you know. I really didn't mean to hurt him."

"I know you didn't," Anne said. "And I didn't mean to lose my temper with you. It's just an instinctive reaction for me to protect him. I was more upset by the way you were putting him down earlier, Rachel. He's liable to get a worse scar from that than he will from the fish hook."

"Did you ever defend me like that when I was little?"

Anne smiled. "Do you remember the boy who lived a couple of houses down the block from us in Chicago? The redhead with the big ears?"

"You mean Barry Bishop?"

"That's the one. I went to meet you at the bus stop one day when you were just a kindergartner. He'd taken your umbrella and was holding it over your head, just out of your reach. You were crying and begging him to give it back."

Rachel nodded. "I remember that a little bit. What did you do?"

"I took it away from him and gave him a lecture that just about blistered his ears. His face turned redder than his hair. And I'd do my best to protect you again if anyone tried to hurt you. It doesn't matter how grown up you are, you'll always be my little girl, Rachel. Holly, too."

"Aw, Mom. You don't have to get all mushy."

"It's my job to get mushy," Anne said. "I want you to know I love you every bit as much as I do Chad."

"Except when I'm acting like a pain in the butt, right?"

"No, it's harder to show it then, but the love never goes away. Someday when you're a mother, I think you'll understand that better."

A reluctant grin tugged at the corners of Rachel's mouth. "Are you done being mushy yet?"

"For now," Anne said, returning that grin. "Do you think we could try a little harder to get along, though? We've still got a few more days before we go home. I'd rather not spend them making each other miserable."

"I'll try if you will."

A lump grew in Anne's throat as she watched Rachel walk away again. Would she ever understand the young woman her daughter was so rapidly becoming? Would Rachel ever understand her? Were they making any real, lasting progress? Or would they just continue to find new issues to fight over?

"Two steps forward, one step back," she reminded herself in a hoarse whisper. "Just hang on and you'll get there. Eventually."

After Annie and the kids had gone to bed that night, John sat on the bank of the creek, smoking his daily cigarette and tossing pebbles into the water. A full moon rose overhead, casting shimmering lights into the stream, and a cool breeze whispered through the pines. He loved the quiet and the isolation from the bustle of the outside world, but the peace of mind he'd come out here to find eluded him.

On the surface, everyone had settled down after the argument that afternoon, but he knew they had a long way to go before they'd ever be a real family. He felt as if he was continually being caught in a cross fire. Too bad he didn't have any idea how to go about fixing the situation.

He loved being with Annie and Chad, but Rachel resented every scrap of attention he gave them. The funny thing was, he wasn't sure if she was more afraid that her mother would abandon her again or that she would stay and displace her. He didn't think Rachel could answer that, either, which probably explained her Jekyll-and-Hyde behavior. What more could he do to reassure that kid?

And what could he do to reassure Annie, who was suffering as much as, if not more than, Rachel? Man, she'd looked so discouraged today he wouldn't have been surprised if she'd demanded they forget the rest of the vacation and go home. As rough as Rachel had been on her, he wouldn't blame her if she did just that.

Then there was Holly to consider, God love her. Until today, she'd handled Annie's return so well he hadn't worried much about her. After their talk in the camper, however, he was painfully aware that the conflict between Rachel and Annie was tearing Holly apart inside. And he didn't know what he could do to reassure her, either.

He took a long, hard drag on his cigarette, blew out the smoke and muttered at the moon, "Women. There's no living with any of them."

Of course, in his own way, Chad wasn't any easier to deal with. He'd been raised as an adored only child. He wasn't used to sharing his mother's attention with anyone else, any more than Rachel was used to sharing John's, and he did his fair share of provoking Rachel.

Before they'd left on the trip, John had been convinced that moving Annie and Chad to the ranch would be the best way to reintegrate their family. Now he wasn't at all sure that Rachel could handle the pressure of living under the same roof with her mother. Or that Holly could handle the conflicts Rachel and Annie were bound to have. Or that he and Annie could work together and present a united parental front. If they couldn't, all three of their kids would eventually resort to divide-and-conquer tactics that would rip their family apart in no time.

Cursing under his breath, he stubbed out his cigarette and stuck the butt into his shirt pocket for later disposal in a trash can. Then he closed his eyes and rubbed both hands down his face. Hell, the only thing he was sure of anymore was how much he wanted Annie.

Being this close to her every day without being able to make love to her was killing him. He wished they could have left the kids with Mike and gone off somewhere by themselves for a couple of weeks. They could have all the long, heartfelt talks in the world, but that wouldn't reassure him of her love and commitment half as much as having her share his bed every night.

He'd thought he'd learned a lot about patience over the past six years. All he could do now was hope and pray that he'd learned enough to get through the next few months. Surely by then he'd have a better idea of whether or not he and Annie could put their marriage and family back together.

His throat tightened and his chest ached when he realized that he'd admitted things might not work out for them. No, dammit. Failing was not an option. He couldn't give Annie up again—not for Rachel or Holly or Chad. He just couldn't.

Chapter Fourteen

Anne glanced over her shoulder at the kids as John turned into her subdivision, faced forward again and smiled to herself. Everyone was tired and grubby from camping, but the last two days of their vacation had gone better than she'd expected. Though she didn't dare predict that this harmony would last, at least she now knew it was possible.

When John turned onto her street, however, an uneasy feeling prickled the hairs at the back of her neck. She'd never seen the blue Chevy parked in front of the white house before. Or the gray Ford across the street. Or the beige van parked two doors down.

"Don't turn in at my house, John," she said quietly. "Something's wrong."

He shot her a startled look, then focused his attention back on the road. "What are you talking about?"

"Just keep driving like we're cruising through the neighborhood."

She looked back at the kids, reassuring herself that they were still slouched down in their seats. Turning back around, she pushed her sunglasses up the bridge of her nose and studied her house as John drove past it. Oh, hell. She'd left the living-room curtains closed. Now they were half open.

"Dad, you just missed Mom's house," Rachel called from the rear seat.

"It's all right, Rachel," Anne said. "I want all of you kids to keep your seat belts fastened and your heads below the windows."

"Are the bad guys back, Mom?" Chad asked.

"I don't know, honey. But somebody's been in our house, so we're not going to stop until we know what's going on. Everybody stay calm."

Using her extra set of keys, Anne unlocked the glove compartment and pulled out her automatic pistol.

"Good Lord," John muttered when he saw it. "You brought that thing with us?"

"It's like my American Express card." She reached for the ammunition. "I never leave home without it. Turn right at the corner and head for the police station."

The car phone buzzed before he made the turn. Anne grabbed the receiver, exhaling a sigh of relief when Steve's voice came over the line.

"Glad to see you were paying attention," he said. "But you can come on home. Nobody here but us good guys."

"Dammit, Anderson, you scared the devil out of me," she said. "We'll be there in a minute. The street's not wide enough for a U-turn with the camper, so we'll have to go around the block."

"How did you know?" John asked when she'd hung up.

Anne shoved her gun into her purse and told him about the unfamiliar vehicles and the open draperies. "I'm used to watching for details."

"How did Anderson know we were out here?"

"There's probably an agent with a radio in that beige van." She turned and spoke to the kids. "Don't take anything with you when we get to the house. Keep your heads down, go directly inside, and stay away from the windows.''

"Aw, come on," Rachel said. "That sounds paranoid."

"Don't argue with me this time, Rachel," Anne replied, her tone intentionally sharp. "Steve wouldn't be here if there wasn't any danger. Please, just do as you're told."

Steve was waiting on her front porch when they arrived. Anne sent Holly and Chad to play in the family room. Everyone else gathered around the dining-room table. His face more grim than Anne had seen it in years, Steve delivered the bad news.

"Manny Costenzo escaped when the DEA raided his operation last week. Nobody's seen him since."

"You think he's coming after Annie?" John asked.

"That's my prediction," Steve said. "One of the men they arrested has been talking to get himself a better deal with the prosecutors. According to him, Frankie Costenzo knew all about you folks here in Montana."

"Then why didn't he come after us?" John asked.

"Because he also knew that Anne wasn't in touch with you. If she didn't know you were being threatened, it wouldn't stop her from testifying. Besides, I think he had a personal grudge against Anne for sending him to prison. She was the one he really wanted."

"How did he find out about John and the girls?" Anne demanded.

"A DEA agent was killed in the raid. Our source claims he was on Frankie's payroll, and he told Frankie everything he could find out about you. Unfortunately he was one of the guys who helped clean out your apartment, so he knew you had kids and a whole lot more. When Frankie went to prison, this guy apparently went to work for Manny."

"Wait a minute, I know the basic story of what happened to Mom, but I'm getting confused," Rachel said. "Why would Frankie Costenzo's brother want to hurt her after all this time? Why wouldn't he leave the country?"

Steve shrugged. "He might do that, Rachel, but I don't think he will. We know Manny and Frankie were extremely close. Our source says that Frankie knew he wouldn't last long in prison, and he made Manny promise to get your mother if she ever surfaced from the Witness Security Program. If that's true, I'd bet my retirement Manny's had all of you under surveillance from the minute Duke Donner died."

"You don't know any of this for sure, though," Rachel said. "You're just following a hunch?"

"That's right. But until Manny's behind bars, we're not taking any chances. I don't think he's rational, and he's just as vicious as his brother was. If he's got a personal vendetta cooking in his head, he won't give up until he's caught or your mother's dead."

"What do you think we should do, Steve?" Anne asked.

"I know you're not going to like it much, but I want to put all of you, including Mike, into protective custody."

"You're right. I don't like it. What if I left?" Anne suggested. "I could go back into WITSEC by myself."

John slammed his palm onto the table. "No way in hell, Annie."

"You don't know how awful protective custody is," she argued. "It's like being under house arrest. You can't go anywhere, you can't do anything, not even talk on the phone. As long as I'm around, none of you will be safe."

"I'm not sure they'll be safe even if you leave, Anne," Steve said quietly. "For one thing, I don't know how reliable this source is. And for another, Manny's finished in this country. If he hasn't already left the U.S., he also knows he doesn't have a snowball's chance in hades of getting out. That doesn't leave him with much to lose. I wouldn't put it past him to try to take out your whole family as a tribute to Frankie."

"In other words, it wouldn't do the rest of us any good if you left, Annie," John said. "We'll all have to be in protective custody, anyway."

"That's the way I see it," Steve agreed.

"Will we have to leave Bozeman?" John asked.

Steve shook his head. "I don't think so. We have an advantage here. Because it's such a small town, the cops will be able to spot anyone who seems out of place. A female agent who looks like Anne will live in this house, and I'll take the rest of you out to the ranch. With luck, Manny will strike here first and we'll get him before he figures out we've made a switch."

"How long will this take?" Rachel asked.

"Who knows?" Steve replied. "A few weeks—"

"Or maybe months," Anne interrupted, tossing her hands up in frustration. "Or maybe forever."

"Don't stop trusting my instincts now, Anne," Steve said. "We'll get him, and then this nightmare will be over for good."

"What about my dad's stock?" John asked.

"I'll have three other guys working with me. We'll take care of everything outside. You'll all stay in the house for the duration."

"No way!" Rachel protested. "I'll go nuts if I have to stay in the house for weeks."

"Then you'll damn well have to go nuts," John told her. "I mean it, Rachel. This isn't TV or a movie. You'll follow the rules like everyone else."

"There's no way we can patrol the whole ranch, Rachel. It covers too much territory and there are too many places for a man to hide," Steve added. "But as long as you stay in the house, you'll be safe."

Anne's heart plummeted at the mutinous glare Rachel leveled at Steve. Dammit, this nightmare was supposed to have been over months ago. Was it never going to end? John reached for her hand. "Don't start, Annie."

"Start what?"

"Looking all guilty. This isn't your fault."

"How do you figure that? If I'd stayed in Denver, none of this would be happening."

"And I never would have known about Chad, and the girls would have gone on believing you abandoned them. We can handle it."

Grateful for his support, she squeezed his hand. "I hope so, John. But, God, I wish I could have spared all of you this kind of learning experience."

Three weeks later, John sat at the desk in his den. He was finally beginning to understand what Annie had meant that day at her dining-room table. As far as he was concerned, protective custody was even worse than what she'd tried to describe for him.

It hadn't been so bad at first, because Annie had kept them all busy cleaning out closets and cupboards, waxing furniture and floors, scrubbing walls and woodwork. This old house hadn't been so spotless since his mother had died. When she couldn't find anything else to clean, Annie dug out his mother's cookbooks and they all experimented with any exotic recipe that looked promising. They'd filled the freezer with enough pies, cakes and cookies to last until Christmas.

The only problem with eating so well was that everyone but Annie started gaining weight because they weren't getting any exercise. She shoved all the furniture in the family room to the walls, and they now worked out with the fitness programs on TV. They played board games and card games and taught the kids to dance. The marshals rented movies for them and brought in bags full of books.

Even when they were having fun together, however, they were all painfully aware that they were prisoners. Granted, it was a nice, comfortable prison. But it was still a prison.

How Annie had tolerated living like this for more than six years, in far less comfortable circumstances and with a baby to take care of, John would never understand. His admiration for her inner resources grew stronger every day. He had come to admire and respect Steve Anderson, as well. The other marshals were nice enough guys, but Steve was obviously a cut above the norm.

He was professional in his dealings with the family. His hearing was so acute there were times when John expected to see antennae sprouting out of the guy's head. Though he couldn't be getting more than four or five hours of sleep at night, he always appeared to be alert and looking for ways to improve their security.

At the same time, he had all the natural friendliness of a native Montanan. Before the first week had passed, he'd managed to blend into the group until he seemed more like a member of the family than an armed guard. While there wasn't a doubt in anyone's mind that he was in charge, he didn't come across like a dictator.

Still, despite Steve's and Annie's efforts to boost morale, they were all starting to show signs of cabin fever. Tempers flared over little things. Complaints increased. The real world seemed farther and farther away, and it was becoming increasingly difficult to feel interested in anything but getting out of the house.

It was also becoming increasingly difficult to maintain a healthy sense of fear. Manny Costenzo hadn't surfaced. John frequently found himself wondering if they were all enduring this torture for nothing. He had visions of that creep lounging on a South American beach, sipping rum drinks paid for out of a fat Swiss bank account. God, how he'd love to get his hands on Costenzo for five minutes.

He heard Annie's voice outside in the hallway for a second. As it faded away, John propped his elbows on the desk and swore under his breath. He might live through this whole mess if he could get his libido under control. Every time he saw her, he wanted her, which doubled whatever tension he was already feeling. And there wasn't a blessed thing he could do about it.

Space in the house was at a premium, and since they wanted to set a good example for the kids, he'd wound up with Chad for a roommate, instead of Annie. They could hardly find the privacy for a decent kiss. On the rare occasions they did have a moment alone, all she seemed to want from him was a hug.

Though she remained cheerful on the outside, John suspected she was beating herself up on the inside. At times he wanted to yell at her to stop feeling guilty. As uncomfortable as this situation was, he was damned glad she wasn't going through it alone.

Hell, he'd love it if she would turn to him for comfort and support. But she hadn't, and he didn't believe she was going to, either. Since their initial meeting with Steve, she had surrounded herself with an invisible barrier of self-sufficiency he hadn't been able to penetrate.

A knock startled him out of his reverie. Steve entered the room and shut the door behind him. Then he settled into the wing chair on the other side of the desk without waiting for an invitation.

"We've got a problem," he said, tossing a dog-eared file folder onto the end table beside him. "It's Rachel."

"What about her?" John asked.

"She's coming unglued on us."

Too restless to sit still, John got up and walked over to the bookcase. "Hey, I know she's been restless, but what do you expect? School's going to start next week and she misses her friends."

"I'm not criticizing her, John. I've seen all kinds of people go through this, and your family's done a great job of hanging tough. But Rachel's not coping anymore." He paused, rubbed his chin for a moment, then looked John right in the eye. "I just caught her trying to sneak out of the house. Anne sent her to her room, but I know she'll try it again unless we do something."

"Well, what the hell _can_ we do?" John demanded. "Beat her? Starve her? Lock her in a closet?"

Chuckling, Steve shook his head. "Come on, you know we don't work like that. The problem is she's not afraid anymore. In fact, I don't think she's ever really believed there was a serious threat here. It's just too far beyond her realm of experience."

John paced back to his chair and sat down again. "I'm starting to feel the same way. It's been three damned weeks and nothing's happened. What makes you so sure Costenzo hasn't already taken a powder?"

Steve's jaw hardened. His eyes narrowed. He leaned forward and clamped both hands onto the chair's armrests.

"Because I can smell that bastard," he said with such intense conviction John couldn't doubt that he believed every word.

"What you just said is exactly the kind of thinking that's going to get somebody killed," Steve continued. "This is a psychological war we're fighting. Manny knows what it's like to have to lay low. He knows how antsy you're getting, and he's counting on one of you losing it."

"What if you're wrong, Steve? What if he's been killed in some kind of weird accident and his body's never identified? How long do we stay in protective custody?"

Steve shifted in his chair, leaning back in a more relaxed posture. "Look, we've got every law-enforcement agency in the country watching for him. There's so much heat on him now, none of his crooked pals will touch him with a barge pole. He doesn't have any family left, and he can't use his credit cards or tap into his bank accounts without us knowing about it. If he's still in the U.S., he can't hold out much longer."

"I thought drug dealers always had a lot of cash available."

"But it probably wouldn't be in large bills," Steve said. "And money's bulky. How much could he carry around with him?"

"How should I know?" John shouted. He sucked in a couple of deep breaths, sighed and shook his head. "I'm sorry. I know you're trying to help us. It's just so damn frustrating having to sit here day after day."

"Of course it is. But let's get back to Rachel. I have an idea, but I know Anne will never give me permission to try it."

"Then why are you asking me?"

"Because you're more in touch with Rachel's feelings. Anne's been through this waiting game so many times she's a pro. She doesn't realize how twitchy Rachel's getting."

"What do you want to do?" John asked.

Steve picked up the file folder and pulled out a stack of photographs held together with a rubber band. "These are from the original crime scene Anne witnessed. They're gruesome as hell, but I think if Rachel could see them, she'd have a better idea of what we're dealing with."

"Is it Rachel you want to see them? Or is it me, Anderson? Are you afraid I'm flipping out, too?"

"Nope," Steve said with a slight grin. "You seem to have a pretty good head on your shoulders." Then he glanced at the top photograph and frowned. "Teenagers are the ones who have the worst time coping because they think they're indestructible. These pictures will do more to convince Rachel she's not than any lecture any of us could give her. But as I said, they're gruesome. They're bound to upset her."

Steve handed the photographs across the desk. John hesitated for a moment, picked up the stack and slowly flipped through it. Gruesome didn't begin to describe what he saw. Each image was more horrifying than the last. Bile rose in his throat and his chest ached with pity for the victims. Rage replaced the pity when he recognized the bloodstained front seat of Annie's car in the last picture.

"My God," he whispered. "How could anyone do something like this?"

"To a guy like Donner, it was just business," Steve said. "Manny's done more than his share of that stuff, too. It took the Costenzo brothers a few years before they could afford to hire guys like Donner to do their dirty work."

John set the pictures down and gulped. "You want to show those to *Rachel?*"

"What else can we do? If you've got any other ideas, I'm ready to listen, but we can't watch her twenty-four hours a day. Wouldn't you rather have her upset than dead?"

Annie would never forgive him for allowing this, but as far as John was concerned, there was only one answer to Steve's question. He pushed back his chair and crossed the room. After resting his forehead against the door for a moment, he said, "I'll go get her and bring her back here."

Moving quietly to prevent attracting anyone's attention—especially Annie's—John hurried upstairs to Rachel's room. She didn't answer his knock, which didn't
surprise him. If she thought it was her mother at this point,
the kid would never answer. He turned the doorknob and
poked his head inside. The bed looked rumpled, but Rachel wasn't there.

An uneasy tingle skated up his spine, but he told himself
that Annie might have let Rachel come out by now, or the
kid might have snuck up to the attic. He moved quickly
down the hallway, checking each room he passed and finding all of them empty. An icy sweat broke out under his
arms when he reached the attic and discovered that it, too,
was deserted.

His heart pounding with fear, he thundered down both
flights of stairs, shouting Rachel's name at the top of his
lungs. Steve ran out of the den. Holly, Mike and Chad came
out of the living room. Annie rushed out of the kitchen.

"What's the matter, John?" she asked.

"Has anyone seen Rachel?"

"Not since Annie sent her upstairs," Mike said.

"I've looked everywhere up there," John said. "You guys
search this floor. I'll check the basement."

He took off at a dead run with Steve half a step behind
him. They didn't find Rachel, but they found a wooden
chair shoved against the wall behind the furnace, directly
under a window. The window was cracked open an inch.
Cursing, John kicked the chair hard enough to break it.

"Don't panic," Steve said, already turning toward the
stairs. "She can't have gone far. We'll find her."

The others converged on the hallway when John and
Steve came out of the basement. Four worried sets of eyes
searched John's face. Since his throat had slammed shut on
him, he shook his head. Steve took over.

"Everybody stay calm. I'm going to alert my men. I want
all of you to search the house again in case she's just hiding
from us. Take your time and let us look for her outside,

okay? We'll find her faster if we don't have to worry about the rest of you.''

"We'll be fine, Steve," Annie said. "Just get going."

John's stomach roiled the entire time they spent searching the house again. After seeing that chair, he wasn't at all surprised when they didn't find Rachel. Everyone gathered in the living room, watching the grandfather clock's pendulum tick off each agonizing minute.

Holly and Chad huddled on either side of Mike on the sofa. John paced, rhythmically slamming his left fist into the palm of his right hand. Her arms wrapped around her middle, Annie stood to one side of the picture window, gazing out at God only knew what.

As if drawn by the gut-wrenching tension, Chad's puppy, Rex, wandered into the room, sat on his haunches in front of the sofa and cocked his head to one side. After studying the humans with a quizzical expression for a moment, he jumped into Chad's lap and curled up for a nap. Though the dog wasn't supposed to be on the furniture, none of the adults said a word.

Dammit, Rachel, where are you? John thought over and over again. She'd been gone for at least an hour. The marshals should have found her by now.

He looked at Annie. She hadn't moved so much as a hair. He wanted to go to her, put his arms around her, cling to her, but her rigid body language warned him off.

Another hour passed. Steve checked in once on the walkie-talkie, but he didn't have any good news to report. He told them where the marshals had searched and where they were heading next, then warned John again to keep everyone in the house.

"That kid knows every inch of this ranch," Mike said when Steve signed off. "They'll never find her unless she wants 'em to. Maybe we oughtta go out there and give those boys a hand whether they want us to or not."

Annie turned away from the window at his suggestion. "I was just thinking the same thing. Steve stored some extra bulletproof vests on the back porch."

Chad shoved Rex off his lap, ran across the room and threw his arms around Annie's waist. "No, Mom! We're s'posed to do what Steve says. You'll get killed if you go out there!"

Gently stroking his hair, she went down on one knee in front of him. "It's different this time, honey. I can't hide in the house while Rachel's in danger."

"But I'm scared, Mom. Really, really scared."

"I know, sweetie. Your grandpa will stay with you and Holly."

Mike lunged to his feet. "I sure as hell won't. John and I'll do this. You've got no business even thinkin' about goin' out there, Annie. We know the ranch better than you do."

"Calm down, Dad," John ordered. "We can't start fighting each other."

"That's right," Annie said, straightening to her full height. "And get this straight, Mike. I've been practicing at a target range for years. I'm probably a better shot than the two of you put together. Rachel's *my* daughter, and I'm going out there to find her."

"Daddy?" Holly said, her voice quavering on the edge of hysteria. "I think maybe I know where Rachel went."

John crossed the room in three long strides. "Where, Holly? Tell me where right now."

"There's a wide spot in the creek behind the old barn."

"The one with the big willow tree?"

Biting her lower lip, Holly nodded. "Sometimes she goes out there to write in her diary and stuff. If she wanted to be alone for a while, I think she'd go there."

"Dammit, those marshals just took off in every direction but that one," Mike said.

John grabbed the walkie-talkie, but couldn't raise anyone. "They're all out of range." Passing the device to Mike, he said, "Keep trying, Dad. When they check in again, tell 'em where we are."

Mike opened his mouth as if he intended to argue, but Annie gave him a fierce look that shut him up. She kissed both children goodbye, then hurried upstairs. Assuming she was getting her gun, John rushed into the den, unlocked the gun cabinet and pulled out Mike's favorite hunting rifle. Though John didn't hunt for sport, he'd blasted enough tin cans and empty beer bottles to be a reasonably good shot.

By the time he found the ammunition and met Annie on the back porch, she had already strapped on her vest. Her face a picture of barely controlled rage, she helped John put on his and stuck her pistol into the waistband of her jeans at the small of her back. John tried to talk to her while they put their shirts on over the vests.

"We're just going to go see if she's out there, right? We'll let Steve do the cowboy stuff?"

"It depends on what we find," she said. "I'll do whatever it takes to protect Rachel."

He grabbed her elbow as she turned to leave, hauling her back around to face him. "Dammit, Annie, we're supposed to be in this together. Promise you won't do anything stupid out there, or we won't go at all."

She leveled a stare at him that damn near froze his blood. "You're wasting time, John. This is something I have to do. Let go of me and stay the hell out of my way."

With that, she jerked her arm out of his grasp and slipped out the back door. Muttering a savage curse, he picked up the rifle, shoved the box of shells into his hip pocket and followed her.

Chapter Fifteen

From the moment she decided to leave the house, Anne felt the tension and guilt that had been eating at her insides for weeks lifting. The conviction she was on the right course grew with every step she took, leaving no room for doubt, fear or hesitation.

She'd played by Steve's cautious rules long enough. It was time to take control of her own destiny and that of her family's. By God, it was time to act.

She was vaguely aware of John's brooding presence beside her, but she was in too much of a hurry and too intent on her purpose to spare any breath on conversation. She prayed that Manny Costenzo hadn't found Rachel, but Anne hoped like hell that *she* would find *him*.

Using trees, bushes and grazing cattle for cover, they cut a wide path around the old barn. They discovered Rachel's diary under the tree Holly had mentioned. Anne had to bite her lip to keep from crying out when they found a fresh set of parallel grooves dug into the soft dirt. Her heart climbed into her throat when she knelt beside them and traced one with her finger.

"Heel marks from her tennis shoes?" she whispered, looking up at John.

John gulped, then nodded grimly. "And see the way the grass is all torn up there? Looks like she put up one hell of a fight."

"Let's check out the barn."

Crouching, they crept closer to the dilapidated building and squatted behind a stand of bushes ten yards from the barn's double doors. Her senses honed to a scalpel's sharpness, Anne felt the hot summer breeze, heard the rustling of the weeds, saw the fluffy dandelion heads bobbing gently in the clearing ahead.

At first inspection, the barn appeared to be deserted. The doors and windows were closed. There was no sign of a vehicle. It was what she *didn't* hear and see, however, that convinced Anne they'd found their quarry. There should be insects buzzing around, birds darting after them, chipmunks running around the pile of rotting logs beside the building.

It felt as if nature's small creatures were hiding, holding their breaths along with Anne and John, waiting for something to happen. And then she heard it. A scuffling sound. A yelp of pain. More scuffling.

A masculine voice snarled, "Bite me again, you little brat, and I'll blow your head off."

"Let me go, you big jerk," Rachel snarled back, her voice breathless with exertion.

Anne pulled out her pistol and slid the clip into the grip until she heard it click into position. Then she looked over at John and murmured, "Lock and load."

Nodding, John inserted the magazine and jacked a round into the rifle's chamber. "Sounds like she's holding her own so far," he whispered. "Let's wait for Steve. He should be here any minute."

They heard a muffled grunt, then a series of crashes that sounded as if Rachel were shoving the mover's boxes Anne hadn't gotten around to unpacking at Costenzo.

"Ever shot anyone before?" John asked.

"Only on paper." She gave him a grim smile. "But I'm damn good on paper."

The door opened an inch. Rachel screamed for help, then cried out. The pain in her daughter's voice propelled Anne to her feet. John grabbed the back of her shirt and yanked her back down.

"Dammit, Annie, what the hell do you think you're gonna do? Rush him?"

"If that's what it takes. He could kill her any—"

"Yeah, and you'll get yourself killed, too. I don't want to lose both of you."

"This is *my* decision, John. Now, let me go."

"I'll go," he insisted. "You can cover me."

"You've got the better distance weapon. It makes more sense for you to cover *me*. I can talk to him. Keep him busy until Steve gets here."

"All right," he said after what seemed to Anne like an agonizingly long hesitation. Slowly releasing her shirt, he added, "But be careful."

The barn door banged open. Rachel charged out, but only made it two steps before the man was on her. Wrapping one arm around her neck from behind, he jerked her back against him and whipped the barrel of a handgun up to the side of her head.

"Damn you, you little—"

Holding the automatic pistol in front of her with both hands, Anne jumped to her feet. "Hold it right there."

Her eyes rolling with fear, Rachel clawed at the arm around her neck. "No, Mom! Get back! It's my own fault—"

"It's all right, Rachel. I'm not going anywhere."

The man jammed his gun harder into Rachel's temple and turned toward Anne, shielding himself with the girl's body. He had black, wavy hair and a swarthy, acne-scarred complexion. His feral smile reminded Anne so vividly of Frankie Costenzo's, bile rose in her throat.

"Well, if it ain't the lady I've been waiting to meet," he said. "Drop the gun."

"Not until you let her go, Manny."

"Oh, so you know who I am?"

"Yeah. You're just as ugly as your brother. And if you don't let her go, you'll be just as dead."

"You think I'm afraid of that little peashooter you got there?" He let out a harsh bark of laughter and tightened his grip on Rachel's neck. "I'll bet you couldn't hit that old barn with it."

Anne adjusted her aim a foot to the left, fired a round into the barn wall, then trained her sights on Manny's head again. "I've still got twelve rounds. Let her go."

"No, I don't think so," Manny said, tapping Rachel's temple with the barrel of his gun. "I think maybe I'll kill this kid, instead of you."

Anne snorted in derision. "Yeah, you're a lot like Frankie was. He didn't mind killing children, either. Only he was too much of a coward to do it himself."

"Frankie was no coward."

"Sure, he was. And he was a dumb son of a bitch, too."

"Don't you talk about my brother that way!"

"What's the matter, Manny? Can't stand to hear the truth? Frankie was nothing but a parasite who lived off other people's misery. When he got caught, he wasn't even man enough to accept responsibility for his own actions."

Manny's face flushed a dull red, and his gun wavered toward Anne for a moment. John scooted to his left, aiming the rifle through a gap in the bushes. Pretending not to notice, Anne continued relentlessly.

"You know what else your brother was? A weenie. I enjoyed hearing him whimper like a baby when they led him out of the courtroom. You'll probably do the same thing, won't you, Manny?"

Manny's voice rose half an octave, and his gun wavered again. "Shut up! Frankie wasn't a weenie. He had a sweet deal going and you killed him. I promised him you'd pay."

"Fine. I'll pay. But Rachel's not going to. Let her go, and I'll come out so you can take your best shot at me."

He jammed the gun against Rachel's head again. "Forget it, lady. Drop the gun, dammit."

"Hey, Manny, *I'm* the one you want," Anne said, trying to inject a coaxing, reasonable note into her voice. "And you don't have time to drag your little game out. This ranch is crawling with feds, and they'll be here any second now. Your one chance to avenge Frankie is to let Rachel go and kill me before one of them picks you off."

Manny's head whipped from side to side, as if he was expecting to see the agents closing in on him. Anne stepped out from behind the bushes. Ignoring John's quiet curse of protest, she dropped her left hand and held the gun loosely in her right.

"Come on, Manny. What are you waiting for? Afraid you'll miss?" she taunted. "Maybe you're the one who can't hit the broad side of a barn, huh? Is that the problem? As soon as Rachel's out of the way, I'll move a little closer. The feds are coming for you."

Sweat trickled down the side of Manny's forehead. His eyes darted back and forth. The arm he held at Rachel's neck loosened, and as if drawn by a magnet, the barrel of his gun veered toward Anne. Never one to miss an opportunity, Rachel sank her teeth into his wrist, stomped the heel of her left foot onto his toes and lunged away.

Releasing her with a startled screech, he tightened his finger on the trigger, spraying four bullets in Anne's direction. She barely heard the report of John's rifle before something incredibly heavy hit her square in the chest, knocking her off her feet. The back of her head smashed into the ground, dimming the blue sky overhead like a movie scene fading out. The last thing she heard before it turned completely black was Rachel screaming, "No, Mom! No-o-o!"

* * *

Barely able to believe what had just happened, John crashed through the bushes. Costenzo lay on the ground, clutching his bleeding thigh with both hands, his gun in the dirt near his shoulder. He reached for it as John approached.

Levering a fresh round into the rifle's chamber, John shoved the barrel into Costenzo's face. The man turned a sickly shade of gray. "Don't kill me," he begged, slowly raising his hand beside his head. "Please, don't kill me."

"Give me one good reason not to, you sorry son of a bitch," John snapped.

He kicked Costenzo's pistol far out of his reach, then grabbed the back of his collar and dragged him closer to Annie. His heart lurched when he saw her spread-eagled on her back, her eyes closed. Rachel knelt beside her, pleading with her to wake up.

John silenced Costenzo's shrieks of pain with one look and crouched on Annie's other side, feeling for a pulse at the base of her neck. His heart lurched again when he couldn't find it.

"She's dead," Rachel wailed. "She's dead, and it's all my fault!"

"Be quiet," John said sharply, searching for Annie's pulse again. "Oh, thank God," he muttered when he found it at last. It didn't feel very strong to him, but at least it was there. He hadn't felt enough pulses to know how to judge them, anyway. She was breathing, too, in shallow little gasps, he noted gratefully.

"Hey! What about me?" Manny shouted. "Shouldn't you be calling an ambulance? I'm bleeding to death here."

Ignoring him, John squeezed Rachel's shoulder. "She's not dead, honey, but I need your help. Are you okay now?"

Swiping at her eyes with the backs of her hands, Rachel gulped and nodded. "Yeah. What should I do?"

"Come over here and take the rifle. You remember how to use it, don't you?"

Rachel nodded again and scrambled to her feet. "You want me to blow his brains out?" she asked loudly, jerking her head toward Costenzo.

"Only if he moves," John answered in an equally loud voice, giving her a reassuring wink as he handed her the weapon. "I'll check your mother out."

"Don't let that kid near me with a gun," Costenzo shouted. "She'll kill me!"

"No, I won't," Rachel said, jacking another round into the chamber as she strolled toward him. "At least not right away. I'll probably just shoot off all your favorite body parts one at a time."

Steve Anderson and one of the other marshals trotted out of the trees to John's left. "I wouldn't blame her if she did, Manny, old boy," Steve called. "You wrecked her summer vacation."

"Get her away from me," Manny begged.

The other marshal grinned at Rachel. "Go for his knee-caps first, honey. From what I hear, he's done it to plenty of other people."

"You're a little late, Anderson," John snarled. "Get over here and help me get this damned vest off Annie. She's not comin' around like she should."

"Probably got the wind knocked out of her," Steve said, kneeling in the spot Rachel had previously occupied. "It's a damn good thing she wore that vest, but she's still gonna feel like a horse tap-danced on her chest."

John's hands suddenly started to shake, making his fingers fumble at the buttons on Annie's shirt. Sweat poured into his eyes. He sat on his heels and wiped his forehead with the back of his arm.

Steve glanced up at him, then took over with Annie's buttons. "That was a pretty good shot you made, Miller."

John snorted in disgust. "I was aiming for his chest."

"Hey, the leg shot brought him down. That's good enough for me. Hunt much?"

John shook his head. "A coyote now and then during calving season."

"Try to think of Manny as a big, two-legged coyote. Although, come to think of it, that's probably an insult to the coyotes."

Steve yanked on the Velcro straps that held the vest together, spread it open and cursed under his breath. John leaned over to see what had upset him and muttered the same four-letter word at the red stain spreading slowly across Annie's left hip. The waist-length vest hadn't come low enough to protect her from one of Manny's bullets.

"Take it easy," Steve said. "It's too close to her hipbone to have hit any vital organs."

Nevertheless, he pulled out his walkie-talkie and told whoever was on the end to get two ambulances out there pronto and tell them to be ready for gunshot wounds. The next hour passed in a blur for John. He couldn't take his eyes off the blood leaking through the makeshift bandage Steve held against Annie's side.

It seemed as if one minute the marshal was talking to him in a calm, quiet voice. The next minute the clearing was swarming with law-enforcement people and paramedics. The ambulance ride into Bozeman lasted forever. John had so much trouble focusing his mind on the questions the emergency-room receptionist kept trying to ask him, Steve finally took over and made him sit in the waiting room.

It helped a little when Mike and the kids arrived. But then they wheeled Annie into surgery. All he could do was sit and wait and feel as helpless as he'd felt when Annie had been standing there, bold as brass, inviting that maniac to shoot her. If she survived the operation, John wasn't too sure he wouldn't strangle her with his bare hands as soon as she got well.

After half an hour, Holly took Chad outside for a walk. Rachel came over, sat beside John and slipped her hand into his. "I'm sorry, Daddy," she said, her voice wavering.

"Well, you damn sure oughtta be," Mike said from the other side of the small room. "If you were my kid, you wouldn't sit down for a week."

John scowled at his father. "Leave her alone, Dad. Rachel made a big mistake, but she handled herself like a champ out there."

No one spoke for a moment. Then Rachel squeezed John's hand. "Do you think Mom will ever forgive me?"

Raising his free hand, he gently brushed the backs of his knuckles over her dusty, tearstained cheek. "Aw, honey, you saw your mother put her life on the line for you out there. If she loves you that much, she'll forgive you for anything."

"Yeah. If she lives," Rachel whispered.

"She'll make it," Steve assured her. "Your mom's fought too hard for too long to come back to all of you. She won't give up now."

"What did she mean when she said that stuff about killing children out there?" Rachel asked.

Steve looked at John, his eyebrows raised as if asking permission to answer. John nodded, and Steve described the crime Annie had witnessed in vivid detail. At the end of his explanation, he softened his voice.

"Don't ever doubt that she loved you and Holly, Rachel. She mourned every year on your birthdays and at Christmas, wanting to be with you. And everywhere we went, she'd watch kids who were about your ages, and I could see her just...hurt."

"Oh, God, Daddy, she has to be all right," Rachel murmured, nearly crushing his fingers with her desperate grip on his hand. "She just *has* to be."

John pried his fingers loose and wrapped his arm around Rachel's shoulders. A strained silence filled the room. Leaning his head back against the wall, he shut his eyes and tried not to think about that nightmarish scene at the barn. Of course he failed miserably, because deep down in his gut, he felt that he'd failed Annie out there, too.

What had possessed her to take such a risk? Yeah, he'd been scared to death for Rachel, but didn't Annie know how much *she* meant to him? Hell, no, she didn't. He hadn't told her he loved her since she'd come back.

Not when they'd made love. Not when she'd said those words to him. Not even when they'd walked out the back door this afternoon, knowing they were probably walking into a life-and-death situation.

Why hadn't he told her? If he tried hard enough, he could come up with plenty of excuses—not enough time together, not enough privacy, too much tension and stress. The truth was, he'd been afraid to say those words to her.

He'd been doing exactly what she'd accused him of doing once before—wallowing in guilt over the past. He hadn't known what to make of the *new* Annie, either, which didn't make a whole lot of sense when he thought about it. He wasn't a die-hard chauvinist.

He'd worked with hundreds of assertive, independent women, both in the business world and at the university. He'd respected them and enjoyed the mental stimulation they had given him. He'd done everything he could to encourage Rachel and Holly to be the same way.

But Annie's fierce desire for independence had thrown him for the proverbial loop. He hadn't accepted her for who and what she was now. He'd wanted her to go back to being *his* Annie, his sweet, adoring, accommodating little wife, who had always put his needs and desires ahead of her own—until the divorce, anyway. Hadn't he learned a damn thing from all that pain? Apparently not.

Annie had been magnificent out there today. She'd been foolhardy and reckless, too, but she'd done what she had to do. She'd gone out there like a lioness, determined to protect her cub at any cost, the danger be damned.

And what had *he* done? He'd been so afraid of screwing up and making things worse, he'd cowered in those bushes, unable to force himself to stand up and distract that son of a bitch so Annie could get a clear shot at him. There wasn't a doubt in John's mind that *she* wouldn't have missed Costenzo's chest. No, she would have saved the taxpayers the expense of a trial.

She'd counted on him, and wound up taking a bullet because he hadn't been willing to trust that she knew what she was doing. Yeah, that was the real truth. He'd hesitated because he'd expected the marshals would get there in time. He'd needlessly risked Annie's and Rachel's lives because he hadn't wanted to shoot a man who wasn't fit to clean their muddy boots.

The realization shamed him as nothing had ever shamed him before. He'd wanted to be her hero. Hah! He was such a damned sorry excuse for a man he might as well give that notion up right now. *She* was the hero. He wasn't what she needed and he never would be.

"Mr. John Miller?"

Starting at the sound of his name, John looked up and saw a uniformed nurse standing in the doorway. "Annie?" he asked, his voice raspier than he'd ever heard it.

"She's in recovery, but we'll be taking her to her room soon. If you'll come with me, you can wait for her there."

Something was wrong, Anne thought, fighting to open her eyes. It shouldn't be so hard to do that, should it? And why did her head feel so heavy? Well, she'd figure that one out in a minute. There were other parts of her body demanding attention.

Her chest. Lord, it ached every time she drew a breath. And what was that wretched stinging in her hip? Had she been in a car wreck or what? No. The pain in her hip was familiar somehow. She had a distinct impression that it was going to hurt like hell if she tried to move.

With fierce concentration, as fierce as she could manage with a brain that felt as if someone had taken an eggbeater to it, anyway, she forced one eye open. Mmm. She'd better see an optometrist. Everything looked...fuzzy. The other eye opened more easily, and a moment later, the foot of a hospital bed swam into focus.

That's good, she thought. Forget the optometrist. Cautiously turning her head to the side, she caught sight of a man sleeping in a chair. Poor guy was gonna have an awful crick in his neck.

Wait a minute. What was she doing in a hospital bed? And that wasn't just some guy. It was John. Impatient with her sluggish thought processes, she shook her head and immediately paid for the action with a jolt of pain that traveled all the way down to her toes.

"Oh-h-h," she groaned, clutching her head with both hands, one of which had an IV needle sticking out of it.

John bolted upright, scrambled to his feet and leaned over her with such a worried expression she figured she must be in terrible shape.

"Hi, honey," he said softly. "Where do you hurt?"

"Where don't I hurt?" She reached out to touch his cheek. The whiskery texture scraping her palm made her smile, for no reason she could name. "What happened? Did I get run over by a train?"

"You've had surgery. Costenzo shot you. Remember?"

Unfortunately she did. It all came rushing back to her in vivid detail, right up to the point where she'd heard Rachel screaming. After that, there was nothing.

"Rachel okay?" she croaked. Dammit, her mouth was drier than dust and it tasted the way the inside of Chad's dirty sneakers smelled.

"She's fine," John said. "Worried as hell about you, but she's making plans to take care of you when you get out of here."

"Tha's nice. Water?"

He poured a glass from a plastic pitcher on the nightstand. Sliding his arm beneath her shoulders, he helped her sit up enough to sip. Even that small motion hurt like the devil, and she lay back, gasping from the effort.

"I'd better get the nurse in here," he said, reaching for the call button.

"Not yet," Anne protested. "They'll just knock me out again. Are you all right?"

He pressed the button, anyway. "I'm fine."

Anne thought his tone sounded a little abrupt, but her head was still so muzzy she wasn't sure. There was one more question she needed to ask. What the heck was it? Oh, yeah. "Manny? Did you have to...kill him?"

John gazed off toward the window before answering. "God knows I should have, but I didn't. I'm sorry, Annie."

The nurse bustled in at that moment. She checked Anne's vital signs and despite her protests, administered more pain medication. Though Anne knew there was something vitally important she still needed to discuss with John, the nurse stayed in the room too long. By the time the woman left, the potent drug in the IV line was already pulling Anne farther and farther into a dreamy, cottony world.

She felt John's lips brush her forehead. Heard him promise to see her in the morning. And then she was gone, or he was gone, she wasn't sure which. She was just too tired and dopey to care.

Chapter Sixteen

Two days later Anne lay against the upraised head of her hospital bed, gazing out the window. Though her room was filled with flowers, helium balloons and funny cards, and the staff couldn't have been nicer, the only thing she could think about was going home. Her kids had been allowed a brief visit yesterday, mainly to reassure them she was going to be okay.

She'd still felt too miserable to talk much, but today would be a different story. A good night's sleep and a shower had gone a long way toward making her feel human again. She could hardly wait to see everyone, especially John and Rachel.

Anne intended to find out why they had both acted so subdued yesterday. She was anxious to get this wretched experience behind them and get on with living a normal life. The thought of being Mrs. John Miller again and being able to mother her children in peace made her almost giddy with excitement.

She'd start driving in car pools, attend school programs, steal romantic weekends alone with John. Oh, life was going to be fantastic! Maybe she'd get her teaching certificate renewed. Or write a book about her experiences in the WITSEC program. Or just wallow in domestic bliss. The possibilities suddenly seemed infinite.

At a soft knock on her open door, she turned her head and smiled as Chad, Holly and Mike entered her room. Though her chest was still abominably sore and bruised from the bullets smashing into the vest she had worn, she gathered both children into the best hug she could manage.

"Where are John and Rachel?" she asked, accepting a peck on the cheek from Mike.

"They'll come in when we're done," Mike assured her. "We don't want to wear you out with a crowd."

Swallowing her disappointment at not being able to surround herself with all her loved ones at once, Anne spent the next twenty minutes chatting and catching up. When Chad started showing the first signs of restlessness, Mike firmly ushered the children out of the room.

Anne lowered the head of her bed, closed her eyes and rested while she waited for John and Rachel to come. Heavens, she must be getting old if such a short visit could make her feel this tired. Then she heard another soft knock, and her heart contracted at the sight of John and Rachel hovering tentatively in the doorway.

"Hi," Anne said. "Come on in."

"We can come back if you're tired," John said.

"Don't you dare." Anne smiled and pushed the button that raised the head of her bed again. "I've been anxious to see you two."

Rachel cautiously crossed the threshold. "We've been anxious to see you, too, Mom."

John remained in the doorway, looking distinctly uncomfortable. "I think you and Rachel need some time alone," he said. "I'll be back later."

Before Anne could protest, he left, shutting the door behind him. Wondering what the heck that was all about,

Anne turned to her daughter. Anxiously twining her fingers together, Rachel stood in the middle of the room as if her shoes had been nailed to the floor. She gazed at Anne for a moment. Then her eyes suddenly filled with tears.

"I'm sorry, Mom," she said. "I'm so sorry."

Anne scooted over and patted the mattress beside her. "Come here, honey."

After a moment's hesitation, Rachel slowly approached. Facing Anne, she gingerly perched on the side of the bed. She looked down at her hands, as if she felt too ashamed to meet her mother's eyes. "I didn't mean for you to get hurt," she whispered.

"I know you didn't, Rachel." Desperately needing to touch Rachel, but fearing the girl would bolt if she hugged her, Anne gently brushed a lock of hair behind her right ear. "It's over, so don't worry about it anymore. Everything's going to be all right now. Sweetie, please look at me."

Rachel obeyed with obvious reluctance. Tears poured from her eyes and her chin wobbled. She wiped her cheeks with trembling fingertips. "H-how...how can you be so nice to me after the way I've treated you?"

"You're my daughter, Rachel. I've always loved you and I always will." Anne's throat constricted, and her own eyes misted over. "I'm just so glad you're safe."

Sobbing, Rachel threw herself into Anne's arms. Anne practically bit a chunk out of her lower lip to stifle a cry of pain at the impact, but it felt so wonderful to hold this child again she gladly accepted the discomfort. She stroked Rachel's hair and rocked her back and forth, fervently thanking God for this moment.

"Go ahead, sweetie," she crooned, "cry it all out."

And cry Rachel did, soaking the front of Anne's hospital gown while the hurt and confusion of the past six years poured out of her.

"I missed you so much, Mom," she wailed, clutching at Anne's shoulders. "I n-needed you and you were n-never th-there."

"I know, baby, I know," Anne whispered.

"I tried not to believe it when I heard Daddy tell Grandma and Grandpa you'd run off with some guy. I u-used to tell myself that you had to be d-dead, or y-you'd come home. And th-then when you did come home and you weren't dead, after all, I was so mad at you. I guess that sounds pretty awful."

"No, it doesn't. You were just a little girl when I disappeared. You had every right to feel angry with me for not being there when you needed me. I'm *glad* you were angry at me."

"Y-you are?"

"Sure I am. It showed me you still cared enough about me to *be* angry in the first place. I understand, honey. And I'm so proud of you."

Rachel straightened, staring at Anne from swollen, bloodshot eyes. "Proud of me? For what? I've been nothing but a pain in the rear end since you came back."

"You've had your moments," Anne agreed, wiping her own streaming eyes with the back of one hand. Then she chuckled and pointed toward the box of tissues on the nightstand. "Hand me one of those before I drown."

Rachel managed a wobbly grin. She grabbed a tissue for herself and handed the box to Anne. "It looks like we've both sprung a leak."

"It feels good, though, doesn't it?" Anne said. "I always used to hate the way I cried so easily, but I found out it's worse when you need to and can't."

"So, uh, why did you say you were proud of me?" Rachel asked.

"Because you've grown up into a beautiful, intelligent young woman who's got backbone and courage—"

"Oh, jeez, Mom. You were the one with the guts out there. I was so scared...."

"You think I wasn't?" Anne demanded incredulously. "Honey, my knees were shaking so hard I could barely stand up. Of *course,* you were scared. But you fought back like a little hellcat, and I can't begin to tell you how proud I was of you for that."

A blush climbing her cheeks, Rachel ducked her head. When she finally looked up again, she said quietly, "Steve told me what you, uh, went through in Chicago."

"Darn him," Anne muttered under her breath.

"No, Mom, *you* should have told me what happened. Maybe I wouldn't have acted like such a jerk. Why didn't you want me to know?"

"It was too ugly," Anne said, barely repressing a shudder. "I didn't want any of that mess to touch you or Holly, Rachel. Not ever."

"We're tougher than you think." Suddenly businesslike, Rachel pushed herself to her feet, leaned down and dropped a quick, bashful kiss on Anne's cheek. "I'd better get out of here. I promised Dad I wouldn't stay too long."

"Are you all right now?" Anne asked.

"Yeah. Maybe we can talk more when you get home."

"Count on it. We'll have lots of nice long talks."

Rachel walked to the door, turned back to Anne and opened her mouth as if she would say something else. She hesitated for an instant, then closed her mouth again.

"What is it?" Anne asked.

"I was just wondering if you were planning to marry Dad again. If you are, I wanted you to know I'd like that. I'll even help Grandpa baby-sit the monsters when you go on your honeymoon."

Anne wanted to hug the kid all over again. "Thank you, Rachel. I guess that's something your dad and I will have to talk about. Why don't you go find him and send him in?"

"All right. Catch ya later, Mom."

Anne pinched herself to make sure she hadn't dreamed the past half hour. While she would undoubtedly have conflicts with Rachel in the future, she sensed that they had finally put the past to rest. Now their battles would be the normal ones all mothers had with teenage daughters. After what they'd been through, Anne figured clothes, curfews and boys were bound to be a piece of cake.

She settled back for a moment, then got her brush out of the nightstand and fluffed out her hair. Why didn't John come? Her heart started pounding when she heard footsteps in the hall, but it was Steve who entered her room next.

Trying to hide her disappointment, she forced a smile onto her face. She should have known better than to try to fool Steve, however. He took one look at her and gave her a knowing grin.

"Relax. John went home with the rest of the gang for a while, but he said to tell you he'll be back tonight."

"Am I that transparent?" Anne asked with a rueful chuckle.

"Yup." Steve pulled up one of the blue vinyl chairs provided by the hospital and lowered himself into it. Then he leaned forward and took her right hand between his palms. "You showed a hell of a lot more guts than brains out there. Are you well enough for me to yell at you yet?"

"Don't bother. We did what we had to do, and you know it. What's going on with Manny?"

Releasing her hand, he sat back in a deceptively relaxed pose. "Tell you what. I won't yell at you if you don't yell at me."

"Why would I do that?"

"Because you're not going to like what I have to tell you."

Reading the truth in his eyes, Anne shook her head in denial. "No. Don't you *dare* tell me they're going to let that creep make a plea bargain."

Steve lifted one shoulder in a helpless shrug. "Just on some of the drug charges. He won't get off completely, but he knows an awful lot the prosecutors are dying to use. He's already on a plane to Chicago."

"What about the crimes he committed here, Steve? What about kidnapping and attempted murder?"

"He'll stand trial for those, all right, if he lives that long." Steve's voice took on a note of grim satisfaction. "Once the word gets out that he's cooperating, he'll be in one big pile of trouble."

Anne crossed her arms over her midriff. "Don't tell me. Let me guess. Manny's going to learn all about the joys of protective custody."

"You've got it. I figure he'll go stir-crazy in about a week. I'm just grateful I didn't get assigned to his case. Man, I've never heard anybody whine like him."

"How long will it be before we'll have to testify against him?"

"Months. Probably years. You don't have to worry about him anymore, though, Anne. The DEA's seized all his assets, and he's going to be too busy trying to save his own worthless hide to give you any trouble. You're safe."

"That's what you said the last time, Anderson."

Steve grimaced. "True, but if you'd waited another six months to come back..."

"Don't remind me. But I just couldn't stand anymore to think about how fast the girls were growing up. It could have been years before the DEA was ready to arrest Manny."

"That's true enough," Steve said with a wry smile. "Anyway, it's all water under the bridge now. Manny's helpless, and there's nobody else left who'd profit from killing you. I want you to relax and heal up and enjoy being with your family."

"That's exactly what I intend to do," she said. "What about you? When will you go back to Denver?"

"My flight's in the morning." Steve scooted his chair closer to the bed and clasped her hand again. His voice softened when he spoke. "I feel a lot better about leaving you here this time. John's a good man."

"Yes, he is," Anne agreed. "I think we can make it work this time."

"Then I'm glad you're back together. Much as I hate to admit it, you really do belong with him."

Anne squeezed his fingers in protest. "That sounds like a goodbye."

"I guess it is. I'll miss you, Anne."

"Hey, don't make it sound like I'll never see you again. You *are* planning to stay in touch, aren't you?"

Giving her a crooked grin, he shook his head. "I need a little time to myself. But one of these days, you'll hear from me. I've got a big investment in that kid of yours."

"You certainly do." Aw nuts, she'd sprung another leak. "You've done so much for us...."

Steve cupped her face with his hands and used his thumbs to wipe away her tears. "None of that, now. I'm the one who should be thanking you. You've taught me a lot."

"Oh, yeah, I'm sure—"

"You have," he insisted. "The most important thing I learned is that if you really love somebody, sometimes you have to put their well-being first. You made the ultimate sacrifice for your family by letting them go. Now it's my turn to do the same thing for you. I want you to be happy."

"I will be." Determined not to ruin this moment with uncontrollable bawling, she sniffled and blinked rapidly. "I just wish..."

"That I could be happy, too." He lowered his hands and shook a finger at her. "Well, it's not your job to worry about that. Who knows? Maybe I'll finally find the woman who can give me earthquakes and fireworks."

"You'd better, Anderson. It would be a sin to waste your parenting skills."

He grinned at that. Then he stood and gazed down at her as if memorizing her face.

"There's one more thing I want to say to you, lady, and I want you to listen. You've had to be tough for a long time," he said slowly, as if carefully choosing each word. "And I know you've needed to feel independent again since you left WITSEC."

"But..." she said, coaxing him to go on when he hesitated.

"But, your family doesn't need you to protect them now. And you don't have to be so tough and independent anymore."

"I'm not sure I understand what you're driving at."

"You're gonna have to learn to lean on your family again, Anne," he said earnestly. "They're finally beginning to understand why you left them. Now they need to understand why you came back to them."

"They know I love them," she said. "Isn't that enough?"

"There's more to love than giving and sacrificing. Sometimes you've got to be able to receive, too."

Still wondering what had prompted him to give her this advice, Anne shook her head in confusion. "You're not making much sense, pal."

Chuckling, he leaned down and kissed her cheek. Then he walked to the door and turned to face her. "Just think about it. Get some rest and be good to John, will you? You've put that poor guy through sheer hell lately."

Anne puzzled over Steve's parting remarks for hours after he left. He'd seemed so concerned. What did he know about her family that he hadn't told her? There was a clue in his last reference to John, she knew that much.

She'd hardly seen John since that day at the barn, but she'd assumed he'd simply been giving her time to start feeling better. Steve's words suggested a deeper problem at work, but what? The danger was over. Rachel had accepted her. What could possibly stand in the way of their happiness now? Nothing that Anne could see, unless...

Gulping, she forced herself to complete the thought. Unless she'd misread John's feelings for her. He had never said he loved her since she'd come home.

Maybe that was the real reason he hadn't spent any time alone with her since the shooting. Maybe watching her with Manny Costenzo had forced him to see she was never going to be his sweet little Annie again. Maybe he couldn't love the tough, independent woman she had become. Was that what Steve had been trying to tell her?

John parked in front of the hospital later that day and sat in the Suburban. He wanted to see Annie again, but he didn't want to be alone with her. She'd want to talk about the shooting, and he wasn't ready to do that.

When he'd stalled as long as he could, he climbed out of the vehicle, marched up the steps and went to her room. Her bed was empty. Good Lord, was she having problems? Had they taken her back to surgery? Poking his head back into the hallway, he looked both ways.

"Yo, John," she called from the end of the corridor, waving her free hand at him. Her other hand clutching the wheeled IV stand, she hobbled toward him, favoring her left leg with every step.

"What are you doing out of bed?" he demanded, rushing to meet her.

She tipped her head toward the IV pole and grinned at him. "My friend and I decided to go for a walk. I'm supposed to get some exercise, so I don't turn into a lazy, shiftless blob."

Feeling foolish for acting like a worried hen with a missing chick, John walked beside her. "Does it hurt much?"

She lifted one shoulder in a careless shrug. "It's a little stiff and the stitches pull, but the farther I go, the more it loosens up. I'll be fine in a few days."

"How much farther do you plan to go?"

"This is my last lap."

She turned into her room, dragged the pole over to her bed and gingerly lowered herself to the mattress. John helped her swing her legs up, gritting his teeth as he watched her face contort with pain while she settled herself into a more comfortable position.

"Look, uh, you're probably tired after your walk," he said. "Why don't I go home and let you get some rest?"

"No way," she said, scowling at him. "I haven't really talked with you for days. Haul that chair over here and tell me how Rachel's doing."

Reluctantly obeying her order, John stretched his legs out in front of him and linked his fingers together over his stomach. "She's a lot better since she saw you this afternoon. Whatever you said to her really eased her mind."

"I'm glad," Annie said, smiling at the memory. "I think we healed a lot of old wounds."

John nodded. "Yeah. She's planning to be your nurse until school starts next week."

"Oh, that's sweet of her."

"You might not think so by the time she's done with you," John said with a grin. "She can be bossy as hell."

"That sounds like the voice of experience talking."

"When I had the flu last year, that kid practically drove me insane. I got well out of self-defense."

Annie uttered a delighted laugh. "Gripe all you want, but I can't wait to get home."

"Yeah, your house will seem nice and quiet after this place."

Her smile fading, Annie sat up straighter and stared at him for a moment. "I meant the ranch, John."

Oh, jeez, here it comes, he thought. Dammit, he didn't want to fight with her, but the determined look in her eyes told him there was no help for it. "That's not a good idea. You'll get more rest in your own home. Chad can stay at the ranch and Rachel can move in with you for a while."

"Define 'a while,' " she said, her voice taking on a frosty edge.

"Just until you're back on your feet. I think it'll help Rachel to get over feeling guilty if you'll let her help you out now."

Annie studied him intently, remaining so silent his nerves started to shred. Then she asked, "What about us?"

John lowered his gaze to his hands. "We'll have plenty of time to sort that out when you're well."

"Will we?" She raised a skeptical eyebrow. "Or will you suddenly find a lot of reasons to avoid me?"

"I haven't been avoiding—"

Her chin came up and her eyes flashed with impatience. "Oh, *please.* If you're having second thoughts about marrying me again, just say so. I can handle it."

And that, John thought, was the crux of the problem. She *could* handle it if he didn't want to marry her again. She could handle anything without him.

"All right," he said, looking her straight in the eye. "I'm having second thoughts."

"Why? For God's sake, we just made it through a harrowing experience together."

"No, *we* didn't, Annie. *You* did."

"Right. I did a great job of getting myself shot. You're the one who brought Manny down. If you hadn't—"

"Cut it out, Annie. I made a hash out of everything, and you know it. I should have stood up there with you, or distracted that son of a bitch or done *some*thing."

"You don't know that. If you'd stood up, he might have panicked and murdered Rachel on the spot. It doesn't make a damn bit of difference who did what. We all survived, John. Nothing else matters."

"Oh, yeah? I'll remind you of that when you have to get back up on a witness stand and testify again. I'm sure you'll be real grateful for that, Annie."

"That's no big deal," she said. "At least this time, I won't be the only witness. The defense attorneys will have a rough time trying to discredit all three of us."

John snorted in disgust. "Well, I still think I should have finished that bastard off. It's the least I could have done for you."

"You're really impossible sometimes, you know that?" she demanded. "I'm not sorry you didn't kill Manny Costenzo. When the DEA squeezes enough information out of him, they'll get all his suppliers. You probably saved hundreds of lives by *not* killing him."

After mulling that over for a moment, John had to admit her argument made a certain amount of sense. Maybe in time he'd be able to see the outcome of their battle with Costenzo in a different light. That didn't mean he believed that he and Annie should get married again, however.

"You may have a point there," he conceded grudgingly.

"Thank you." She crossed her arms over her chest and leaned back. "So, what's really the problem, John? What else is worrying you?"

Unable to sit still while she stared holes in him with that cool, utterly composed expression, John got up and paced to the window.

"I guess I'm just not sure we're right for each other anymore, Annie."

"Why not?"

"I... well, it has more to do with me than it does with you," he said, knowing damn well that this conversation was rapidly getting out of hand. But he couldn't stop now, could he? "It's something I've struggled with since you came back, but I'm not making any progress with it."

"Would you mind telling me what *it* is?"

He shot her an irritated glance, then turned to face her. "I'm trying, okay? I have this feeling that you've grown beyond me. You used to ask for my advice about things. We used to make important decisions together."

"No, we didn't," she said. "We talked things over, and then *you* made our decisions."

"Maybe that's true," he conceded, feeling more defensive by the second. "But at least we talked them over. We don't even do that now, because you make them all by yourself. You don't... need me anymore."

Her mouth fell open as she stared at him. "I what?"

"You heard me. You don't need me anymore."

"That's ridiculous."

"Is it? Hell, you buy your own car and your own house, and why shouldn't you? You've got more money than you can ever spend. You face criminals down without turning a hair, and you've won Rachel over. What do you need me for?"

"You're going to throw away everything we could have together because of *that?*"

"Don't make it sound petty." He rammed the fingers of his right hand through his hair, searching for a way to make her understand how he felt. "Dammit, the second you found out Costenzo was coming here, you were ready to leave by yourself again. And you risked your life without giving me a second thought—"

"To save our daughter!"

"You could have told me what you were planning. But you didn't think I had anything to offer, did you? You just did what you wanted to do and expected me to blindly follow your lead."

"I was better equipped to deal with Costenzo because I had training and experience you didn't have. So what?"

"So, maybe I don't want to spend the rest of my life waiting for the next time you'll decide what's best for everyone. Maybe I don't want you protecting me anymore. Maybe I'm tired of feeling guilty and inadequate next to my heroic ex-wife."

"Oh, *now* I get it." Rolling her eyes, she huffed in exasperation. "It would have been fine and dandy if *you'd* been the one standing there inviting a bullet, and I was the one down there in the bushes."

"Damn right. That's the way it's supposed to be."

"Says who? Where is it written that a mother can't protect her child? That a wife can't protect her husband?"

"It's not *what* you did," he snapped. "It was the *way* you did it."

"Of all the outdated, chauvinistic—"

John raised his voice to interrupt the coming tirade. "That's right. And this time, *you're* the chauvinist. I know I dominated you sometimes when we were married, and it didn't work. It won't work any better if you're always trying to dominate me."

"I'm not trying to dominate you!" she shouted.

"Hah! Whenever we need to work out a problem, you wave your independence in my face. It's like a buzzword that automatically forces me to back off. That's not an equal partnership. I can't feel close to you anymore because you won't let me. And I've let you down so many times I can't even blame you for that."

"What on earth is going on in here?" a uniformed nurse demanded from the doorway. "Mr. Miller, I'm afraid I'll have to ask you to leave. Ms. Martin is in no condition—"

"I was just on my way out," John said, striding across the room. He paused in front of the nurse and looked back at Annie. "I'll be here tomorrow to drive you home."

Annie drew herself up proudly and sent him a look that made him feel about an inch tall.

"Don't bother. I don't need you, remember? Why don't you and your guilt and your wounded ego just...go home? I'm sure you'll all be very happy together."

Chapter Seventeen

Fueled by righteous indignation, Anne went home in a taxi the next morning. So, John didn't like her independence, huh? Tough beans. But he was right about one thing. She didn't need him or any other man who couldn't accept her the way she was now.

She finally had her freedom back. She had her kids back. She had a beautiful new home and plenty of money, and by God, she would enjoy her new life. If John didn't want to share it with her, it was his loss, not hers.

The cabdriver carried her suitcase to the door for her. She watched him drive away, stepped inside and felt the first crack in the wall of anger she'd built around herself. Suddenly her beautiful new home seemed like nothing more than a big empty house.

Assuring herself that this lonely feeling would pass, she marched into the bedroom and unpacked. If she kept busy until Rachel arrived, everything would be fine. The only problem was she didn't have the energy to stay busy. The doctor had said she would tire easily for a few months. She was not amused to discover he hadn't been kidding.

The bed mocked her with memories of the night she'd spent making love in it. With John. Feeling another crack in her wall of anger, she fled to the living room as fast as her darn stiff hip would allow.

Of course, the living room offered zero comfort. This was where she'd finally told John about the most traumatic event of her life, which had led to the episode that had just driven her from the bedroom. She fled again, but the kitchen was no help, either. This was where John had given her such generous support the night of Rachel's birthday party and suggested they start dating again.

Wasn't there anywhere in this damn house that wouldn't haunt her with memories of him? Exhausted, she perched on a stool at the breakfast bar and caught sight of the phone. Steve should be home now. He would let her cry on his shoulder. He'd tried to warn her, after all, even if he hadn't been very clear about it at the time.

No, she couldn't call him. He'd done enough for her, and he'd said he needed some time to get over her. Besides, after what he'd said yesterday, he probably agreed with every indictment John had made against her.

Propping her elbows on the countertop, Anne covered her face with both hands. Despite her best efforts to maintain it, the wall was crumbling fast now.

You can run, but you can't hide, a taunting little voice in her head told her. *Steve was your only friend. Maybe he's right about you. If he's right, John is, too.*

"I wasn't trying to dominate him," Anne protested. "He made me sound like a weird control freak."

Everything in your life has been out of your control for years. It must have felt great to get some control back. Isn't it possible you went a little too far with this independence thing? Think about it.

Looking at her watch, she realized she wasn't going to have much choice. Rachel wouldn't be here for hours, because Anne had checked herself out of the hospital earlier than her family had expected.

Because you wanted to wave your independence in John's face again if he tried to drive you home, the voice reminded her. *Very mature behavior, Anne. John will definitely appreciate it.*

"Leave me alone," Anne grumbled. "Just get off my back and leave me alone."

Gladly, the voice replied. *And if you keep acting like such an idiot, so will everyone else.*

Groaning, Anne dragged herself off the stool, took a can of soda from the fridge and carried it out to the deck. If she was going to torment herself, she might as well do it outside. She hadn't had any time alone for weeks. Maybe the fresh air and sunshine would clear the dust out of her brain and allow her to think more objectively.

She settled into one of the padded swivel rockers that had come with the umbrella table, kicked off her shoes and curled her toes on the edge of the wooden deck railing. The automatic sprinkler system came on, and she watched a fat robin enjoy a shower. Good thing Rex was still at the ranch. Along with her heart and everything else that meant a blessed thing to her.

Was John right about her? Had she been holding him at arm's length, refusing to let him get close to her again? Was she obsessed with being tough and independent and in control?

"Hell, yes," she muttered, shaking her head in disgust at her own stupidity.

Well, maybe not stupidity exactly. John was carrying around enough guilt and self-recrimination for both of them. She could afford to be kinder to herself. She'd been conditioned by some darned scary circumstances to trust only Steve and herself. To depend only on Steve and herself.

Among all the other adjustments she'd been trying to make, what with moving and dealing with Rachel, sharing Chad with the family and trying to learn how to feel safe, maybe she hadn't concentrated on opening herself up to John again. Was that such a crime? How much change could any one person tolerate at a time?

That rationalization made her feel a little better about herself. But not enough better that she could forget how wonderful John had been to her all summer. Oh, he'd pitched a fit or two, especially at first. But he'd been going through some heavy-duty changes, too. She really had put the poor guy through sheer hell lately.

And when the chips had been down, when she'd really needed his support and understanding, he'd come through for her like a champ. He'd held her while she wept for her parents. He'd helped her with all the kids. He'd even endured protective custody with more patience than she ever would have dreamed possible. What more had she expected him to give, for pity's sake?

So, he had macho pride and a male ego that couldn't handle playing second banana to a woman sometimes. Given his background, that wasn't surprising. If she'd reacted with a sense of humor, instead of with her own wounded pride and ego, he would have come around. Eventually.

"Well, what are you gonna do about this mess?" Anne asked herself. "Are you gonna sit here and wallow in guilt and depression? Or get off your duff and go apologize?"

While she was tempted to do the latter, she forced herself to stop and think it over. For one thing, she wasn't supposed to drive until her stitches came out. For another, John had been so angry last night he probably wouldn't be ready to listen to an apology just yet.

It wouldn't hurt to give him a few days to cool off. It wouldn't hurt to plan a strategy to approach him, either. A male ego was a delicate thing, after all, and she'd stomped on John's pretty hard. What she needed was a gesture. Something that would show him she didn't blame him for anything, that she wanted an equal partnership with him, and that she needed him.

Linking her fingers behind her head, she tipped her face to the sun and closed her eyes. After a moment, she slowly started to smile.

Late on a Thursday afternoon three weeks later, John sat at the desk in his office at the university, the telephone receiver clamped to his right ear. "What the hell were you doing way out there?" he demanded.

"I just needed to get out of the house," Annie said tartly. "Look, if it's too much trouble, don't bother. I'll call a wrecker. Would you mind looking up the number for me? I don't have a phone book in the car."

"Forget it. I'll be there in half an hour."

He slammed down the receiver, shoved his lecture notes into his briefcase and stormed out to the parking lot. After reviewing the directions she'd given him, he climbed into the Suburban and headed for Manhattan. Dammit, he should have let her call a wrecker.

It wasn't as if he didn't know what Annie was up to. He'd been receiving oh-John-I-need-some-help calls from her for days. She'd already broken every major appliance in her new house. He'd wondered how long it would take her to do in her minivan. Just how dumb did she think he was?

Well, it wasn't going to work. If she wanted to talk to him, she could damn well come right out and say so. He'd swallowed enough of his pride. It was Annie's turn to swallow a chunk of hers.

She wasn't going to get to him with sex, either. Every time he'd gone into town to fix her latest sabotage victim, the little wretch had been flitting around in a pair of indecently short shorts, her blouse unbuttoned halfway to her navel. The woman had flaunted more cheeks and cleavage in his face than an issue of *Playboy* magazine.

If he wasn't so damn mad at her, it would be funny, he thought, spotting the dirt road he was supposed to take up ahead. Why he'd put up with this nonsense for so long he didn't know. Well, okay, so maybe he did.

The truth was, Annie's dumb phone calls gave him a legitimate excuse to see her. And mad or not, he did want to see her. Despite the cold showers her behavior was forcing him to endure, he enjoyed seeing her cheeks and cleavage. But the most important reason was he liked knowing she cared enough to pursue him. He was also curious to find out how far she'd go with this little game of hers.

He rounded a curve, and there was the van, pulled off to the side of the road. He parked behind it, plastered his impatient scowl back onto his face and stepped out onto the hard-packed dirt. He looked around for Annie, but didn't see her or anyone else.

In fact, if this wasn't the most desolate spot in Gallatin County, it had to be in the top five. There was nothing out here but grass and fences and sky. Something told him that wasn't an accident. But where was Annie?

Then he heard a soft click. A sensuous country ballad drifted to him on the breeze. A latch gave, and the van's side door rolled open. Feeling his pulse picking up speed, he braced himself to resist whatever crazy plot the woman had cooked up for him this time.

"All right, Annie," he said gruffly, walking around the back end of the vehicle. "What seems to be the prob—"

Oh, man. The woman wasn't just crazy, she was seriously demented. She'd taken out the rear seats, put a mattress—with purple satin sheets, no less—in the empty space, and if that wasn't a bottle of champagne sticking out of that ice bucket, he'd eat his boots. A man would have to be dead for six months to ignore the woman stretched out on her side in there.

Talk about cleavage and cheeks! She had on some kind of black frilly little number that barely covered her nipples on one end and left even less to his imagination on the other. She had one leg bent, knee pointed toward the roof, showing off a sheer silk stocking attached to a garter, which was attached to the frilly little number. If he tugged on that garter, he'd bet ten bucks her breasts would just tumble right out.

His mouth went dry, his palms itched and a certain part of his anatomy was suddenly harder than the fence posts lining the road.

This woman had never been a wife and mother. Uh-uh. This woman was every horny teenager's fantasies come to life. The smiling pout on her red lips and the come-hither look in her eyes said she damned well knew it, too.

"Hi there, cowboy," she drawled in a soft, sultry voice that made his knees feel weak. "Want to go for a ride in my car?"

It took every ounce of willpower John possessed, but he curled his hands into fists and stood his ground.

Crooking a finger, she beckoned him closer. "Come on in, handsome. Don't be shy. I won't bite you—not very hard, anyway."

"Dammit, Annie," he said, fearing he was going to pop a blood vessel any second. "You don't fight fair."

Propping herself on one elbow, she slid her free hand up her bent leg to her knee, drawing his gaze over each delectable inch of thigh. "John, honey, I didn't call you out here to have a fight. I know you've had a long hard day. Come on over here and I'll make you feel better."

Anne saw John's shoulders begin to shake, and she heaved a silent sigh of relief. She hadn't been too sure she could pull this off in the first place, and the wretched man had held out so long she'd been trying to work up the courage to start stripping. It would be the ultimate desperate measure, but then, she was a desperate woman.

His laughter booming out over the parched hills, he staggered to the doorway and plunked his behind onto the narrow strip of carpet between the door and the mattress. She crawled over behind him, draping a leg on either side of his hips. Reaching her arms around, she loosened his tie and went to work on his shirt buttons.

It wasn't an easy task when he was laughing so hard. For heaven's sake, did he have to stomp his foot like that? She hadn't been *that* funny, had she? Oh, great, now he was repeating lines of her come-on dialogue *and* slapping his knee while he stomped his big foot.

"Hi there, cowboy." Laugh, laugh, slap, stomp, slap, stomp, laugh, laugh. "Wanna go for a ride in my car?" Laugh, laugh, stomp, stomp. "Come on in, handsome. I won't bite very hard."

She was *never* going to live this down, she thought, tugging his shirttails out of his slacks. Well, he sounded as if he needed it, and at least he wasn't resisting her anymore. She peeled his shirt down his arms and tossed it aside. Now for the belt buckle.

Every time he started hooting again, his abdominal muscles tightened and bounced, making it impossible to get a decent grip. She finally gave up, scooted back onto the mattress and locked her hands together in front of his chest. With a judicious yank at the right moment, she wrestled him into the vehicle.

He flopped onto his back, chuckling and gasping for air like a beached trout. Anne closed and locked the door, climbed up beside him and with brisk, efficient motions stripped off the rest of his clothes. Then she straddled his hips, leaned down and kissed the last of his laughter into a breathless groan of need.

When she pulled back, he raised one hand to the side of her face and gave her a crooked smile. "Maybe we should talk first."

"I'm afraid to," she whispered. "It seems like every time we do, we end up in a stupid argument. And I went to so much trouble to lure you out here I'd hate to wreck an opportunity to jump your bones."

"My bones aren't going anywhere. So why did you lure me out here, honey?"

"Because I miss you."

"And?"

"And I love you."

"And?"

"And I'm sorry. I didn't mean to wave my independence in your face. It was just so wonderful to finally have some, and it's been so long since I could trust anybody but Steve, and everything was so screwed up when I came back, I guess I forgot how to be your partner. But I can learn again, and I really *do* want to—''

''Apology accepted.'' He pulled her down for another kiss. ''There now, that wasn't so bad, was it?'' he said when he let her up for air.

''If I apologize some more, will you do that again?'' she asked, tracing his eyebrows with her index fingers.

''God, you're a flirt, woman.''

''Only with you.''

''That's good,'' he said, pulling her down to lie beside him. ''Because I have something to say to you that I should have said a long time ago.''

He turned to face her. She cuddled as close as she could, laying her palm over his heart. He covered her hand with his and gazed deeply into her eyes.

''What's that?'' she asked.

''I love you, Annie. I always have, and I always will. That's why I was so angry at you for baiting Costenzo the way you did.''

''I don't understand.''

''I didn't understand it myself until after we had that last fight and I thought I'd really lost you for good this time. After we got you to the hospital that day, all I could think about was how close that bastard had come to killing you. I didn't want you to risk your life—not even for Rachel. I feel like an awful father to say that, but it's the truth.''

''Oh, John, we've been over that enough.''

He silenced her with a kiss. ''It's okay, honey. I'm not angry now. I just need to explain one more thing.''

''Okay. I'm listening.''

''I knew, logically, that you did the right thing, but I just couldn't tolerate the thought of you being dead, Annie. Especially when I hadn't told you I loved you again. It was just like when you disappeared, you know? I thought you knew I was coming back to work things out, but I hadn't said so.

I hadn't even told you I loved you more than my damned job that time."

"I knew. That's why I went shopping for scanties."

He smiled. "You'll never know how relieved I was when you told me about it. I've felt so guilty about that sometimes, I've wanted to die. And when I saw you lying in the dirt, bleeding—"

"Hush, love. We've both made mistakes, and guilt is nothing but a waste. Please, don't torture yourself anymore." She rested her forehead against his and sighed. "This hasn't been an easy transition, has it?"

"God, no," he said with a choked laugh. "It seems like ever since you came back, there's been too much to take in. Every time I'd start to find my balance, you'd drop another bombshell on me or Steve would intrude or Rachel would act up, and I'd be completely confused again. And I've been scared to death all along."

"Of what?"

"That you'd leave me. That's why your acting independent freaked me out so much. It's not the actual idea of it. I'm glad you can take care of yourself."

"You are?"

"Sure. I want the girls to know how to buy their own cars and houses and handle their finances. Women need to know that stuff. But with you . . . well, I was afraid you wouldn't choose to stay with me if you didn't need me. I guess I've never gotten over your going through with the divorce. How's that for digging up ancient history?"

She smiled in sympathy. "We've had an awful lot to resolve, John. And maybe we've both had some unrealistic expectations of each other. Can we just wipe the slate clean here and now and start over again?"

He eyed her doubtfully. "From scratch? Gee, I don't know if I can stand going back to the dating stage now that I've seen you in your little outfit. Where in the world did you get that thing?"

Laughing, she sat up and thrust out her chest to give him the full benefit of the underwired bra. "Frederick's of Hollywood. Special credit-card phone order. I bought one just like it seven years ago. Think it would have saved our marriage?''

He nuzzled her cleavage and said fervently, "If it hadn't, the marriage deserved to die. Lord, you look naughty."

Grasping his chin, she raised his head until his nose had cleared the edge of her bodice, what there was of it, anyway. Then she pushed him flat on his back and put her elbow in the middle of his chest to hold him there.

"And I'll be naughty with you as soon as we finish talking," she said, using the same tone she'd once used on a classroom of third graders. "About starting over again. I didn't mean we had to go clear back to the dating stage."

He eyed her cleavage with a wistful expression and slid his hand up her arm to her bare shoulder. She dug her elbow into his sternum in warning.

"Okay, I'm listening," he said. "What did you mean?"

"I think we need to remember why we got married in the first place. If you'll think about it, you'll see I have plenty of reasons to need you."

"Such as?"

"Such as, you were my very best friend in the whole world for over a decade."

"I thought your pal, Anderson, filled that job."

"It wasn't the same thing at all, you silly man. Steve and I became friends through necessity. But you *chose* me. Out of a whole campus of other girls, you thought I was hot stuff, Miller. Don't you know how special that makes you?"

"Yeah." He gave her the slow, cocky grin that had dazzled her the first time she'd met him. "I hear what you're saying. Go on."

"Well, you gave me three gorgeous, wonderful children. Nobody else could ever love my kids as much as you do. That's a pretty strong bond all by itself."

"That's true. What else do you need me for?"

"You're the only one who always gets my jokes. You've always got a hanky when I need it. I've always felt sexy with you. Even when I was fat and pregnant, and when you saw my scar, you still wanted me. Maybe it's just all that history we built up together, but somehow, I know you're always on my side."

"You lost me with that last one, honey," he said. "How can you say that when I neglected you to the point you had to divorce me to get my attention?"

"I never said you were perfect, John. Sometimes you act like such a jerk I want to ring your fool neck. But even then I still love you, because I know you're not intentionally trying to hurt me. That's why I've always had a hard time staying angry with you for very long, which was probably why you never took my threats to divorce you very seriously. Am I right?"

His eyes glinted with laughter. "If I followed all of that correctly, I'd say you're absolutely right. And I feel the same way about you, Annie. It all kind of got lost there in the hubbub, though, didn't it?"

"That's the way I see it. So what do you think? Are we ready to trust each other again? Be best friends again?"

"Be married again?" John asked. "That's the only way I'll ever really feel secure about you, Annie."

"Don't move," she ordered, pointing her finger at his nose. "I've got something to show you."

Then she reached behind the ice bucket and brought out the velvet pouch she'd carried with her for so long. She tipped the little bag upside down over her palm and picked up the diamond-studded set of rings he'd given her in a Billings church seventeen years ago.

"I had these in my purse that day at the mall. I couldn't wear them later because of my cover story, but I took them out every night and tried them on. In my heart and mind, sweetheart, we've always been married."

He took the rings from her and carefully slid them onto the appropriate finger. Cupping her face in his big, callused hands, he kissed her as solemnly as he had at their wedding. Then his arms closed around her back, and he pulled her down beside him again, and it was eminently clear he was done talking.

He had her out of her "little outfit" in about five seconds. The glowing wonder in his eyes as he gazed at her was enough to make her feel sexy and beautiful and cherished. Then he began to kiss his way down her body, searching out her pleasure points with unerring accuracy, arousing her beyond anything she'd ever felt before. Giving herself up to his passion seemed as familiar and natural as breathing.

She felt his love in each lingering touch, each long, sensuous kiss. She heard it in his husky whispers of approval, his guttural moans of pleasure when she managed to sneak in a caress of her own. She saw it in his captivated expression as he watched his hands gliding from her breasts to her belly to her thighs and calves, then slowly retracing the route.

By the time he brought his mouth back to hers, she couldn't touch him enough, taste him enough, get close enough or hold him tightly enough. Nothing would ever be enough to fill the aching void inside her. Nothing but his love, his passion, his body. Nothing but him.

The world suddenly flipped over and she was straddling his waist. He reached between her thighs and touched her, giving her a moment's relief from the escalating need threatening to overwhelm her. She let her head drop back and moved against his fingers.

And then he was there, deep inside her, filling her completely. Gasping at the joy of it, she raised her head and looked down into his eyes. Oh, yes, he felt the same jolt of sensation, the connection that went beyond any physical joining. In that moment, she knew that despite violence, years of fear and separation, her own insecurity and stubbornness, and John's and even Rachel's, they had won the ultimate victory. They had finally found their way back to each other.

She didn't doubt that they would argue and bicker in the future, but nothing would ever destroy their love for each other. They had forged a bond with their hearts and bodies and their children that was as ageless and enduring as life itself.

Leaning down, she kissed him with all the depth and wealth of emotion she felt. He plunged his fingers into her hair and returned the kiss, hot and wet and deep. Then his hips began to move in a sure, steady rhythm, driving her up and up. They were climbing together, struggling together, reaching for a bright, elusive something they had only glimpsed from a distance until now.

She heard his harsh breaths tearing from his lungs. Her own high, keening whimpers. Sweat dampened their skin. Her thighs trembled with the effort to meet and keep up with his wild, demanding thrusts. And then they were there, bathed in the awesome, wonderful power of a simultaneous release that went on and on and on.

His arms were there to catch her as she collapsed on top of him, just as she'd known they would be. She rubbed her cheek against the hair on his chest, then kissed his right nipple and closed her eyes in the most delightful exhaustion she had ever known. He stroked her back from shoulders to buttocks before letting his arm fall heavily across her waist.

"I hope you don't want to breathe anytime soon," she murmured, kissing his nipple again.

"No problem. I'll have to get my heart started again first."

They stroked and petted and planned their wedding and sipped from the same glass of champagne, giggling like newlyweds. Then the sun dropped behind the mountains and a cool evening breeze forced them reluctantly back into their clothing. John eyed the sweatshirt, jeans and sneakers Anne dug out from under the front seat and a chuckle rumbled out of his chest.

"What's so funny?" she asked.

"You really planned this whole thing out, didn't you?"

Grinning wickedly, she held up the scrap of lingerie, which had done its job so well, between her thumb and forefinger. "Did you think I drove out here in this?"

"Lord, I hope not."

He climbed out of the sliding door, turned and looked inside again. Then his shoulders started to shake and his laughter echoed off the hills, startling a deer out of the ditch. For some demented reason, that only tickled John more. He sagged against the side of the van and went into his foot-stomping, knee-slapping routine.

Anne tolerated it until he started quoting her come-on dialogue again. Quietly dipping her hand into the ice bucket, she retrieved five soggy cubes, leaned out and dumped them down the back of his shirt. He yelped, yanked his shirttails out of his pants and hopped around until the ice fell out. Then he reached into the vehicle, grabbed her wrist and hauled her outside.

"I'm sorry," he said, lacing his fingers together at the back of her waist. "I didn't mean to laugh. It was just such a surprise to find you out here like that."

"I haven't had much practice at seducing men," she said. "But it seemed to work on you."

"Oh, honey, did it ever. And you can practice on me all you want. In fact, you'd better practice on me a lot."

"Like this?" She slid her arms around his neck and kissed him until there should have been steam pouring out his ears.

"Yeah," he said when she finally released him. "Just like that. Damn, but it's good to have you back again, Annie. Welcome home."

She looked up at him, grinned and said in her best drawl, "Well, it's about damn time you said that, Miller."

* * * * *

A SPECIAL NEW LOOK

Silhouette are pleased to present a new look for the
Special Editions you know and love. We will continue to
bring you six realistic, emotional stories by favourite
Silhouette authors every month, and hope you'll agree
that the new design really does make the novels look
even more special!

From: July 1994   Price: £1.95

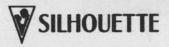

▼ SILHOUETTE

⟩ SPECIAL EDITION ⟨

THREE STEAMING HOT LOVE STORIES FOR SUMMER FROM SILHOUETTE

When the entire South-East of the United States is suddenly without power, passions ignite as the temperature soars.

Available from July 1994   Price: £3.99

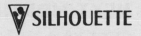

SILHOUETTE

SPECIAL EDITION

COMING NEXT MONTH

SALLY JANE GOT MARRIED Celeste Hamilton

That Special Woman!

Sally Jane Haskins was the local scarlet woman. So what did the town's most eligible newcomer see in her? Maybe he didn't believe the local gossip. Maybe he *did*...

HE'S MY SOLDIER BOY Lisa Jackson

Mavericks

Dark, sexy and dangerous, Ben Powell had left Carlie Surrett with shattered dreams because he blamed her for the tragedy that followed their passion. Now he was back and his time in the army had not softened his attitude!

WHEN STARS COLLIDE Patricia Coughlin

Rachel Curtis had given up everything to protect her niece, but state prosecutor Mitch Dalton inadvertently threatened their safety. How did Rachel get rid of him when she really wanted him to stay?

MARRY ME KATE Tracy Sinclair

Hunter Warburton's son was running circles round his busy dad and Kate Merriweather found herself falling hard for both of them. But could she marry a man who didn't love her?

WITH BABY IN MIND Arlene James

How did a bad-boy bachelor transform himself into a family man? Parker persuaded his friend Kendra to marry him so that he would retain custody of his baby niece; but could he seduce his wife?

DENVER'S LADY Jennifer Mikels

Kelly Shelton was her own woman—until she met Denver Casey rodeo champion. Could she risk everything for a bittersweet spell as Denver's lady?

COMING NEXT MONTH FROM

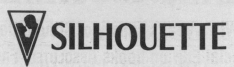 SILHOUETTE

Intrigue

Danger, deception and desire—
new from Silhouette...

NIGHT MOVES Nora Roberts
TIGER'S DEN Andrea Davidson
WHISTLEBLOWER Tess Gerritsen
MURDER BY THE BOOK Margaret St George

Desire

Provocative, sensual love stories for the
woman of today

WILD INNOCENCE Ann Major
YESTERDAY'S OUTLAW Raye Morgan
SEVEN YEAR ITCH Peggy Moreland
TWILIGHT MAN Karen Leabo
RICH GIRL, BAD BOY Audra Adams
BLACK LACE AND LINEN Susan Carroll

Sensation

A thrilling mix of passion, adventure,
and drama

MACKENZIE'S MISSION Linda Howard
EXILE'S END Rachel Lee
THE HELL-RAISER Dallas Schulze
THE LOVE OF DUGAN MAGEE Linda Turner

HEART  HEART

Win a year's supply of Silhouette Special Edition books ABSOLUTELY FREE?

Yes, you can win one whole year's supply of Silhouette Special Edition books. It's easy! Find a path through the maze, starting at the top left square and finishing at the bottom right. The symbols must follow the sequence above. You can move up, down, left, right and diagonally.

START

FINISH

Please turn over for entry details

HEART ⊕ HEART

SEND YOUR ENTRY NOW!

The first five correct entries picked out of the bag after the closing date will each win one year's supply of Silhouette Special Edition books (six books every month for twelve months - worth over £85). What could be easier?

Don't forget to enter your name and address in the space below then put this page in an envelope and post it today (you don't need a stamp). Competition closes 31st December 1994.

HEART TO HEART Competition
FREEPOST
P.O. Box 236
Croydon
Surrey CR9 9EL

Are you a Reader Service subscriber?   Yes ☐   No ☐

Ms/Mrs/Miss/Mr _____ COMSE

Address _____

_____

_____

Postcode

Signature _____